Praise for

CAUGHT STEALING

by **CHARLIE HUSTON**

CAUGHT STEALING

BALLANTINE BOOKS   New York

CAUGHT
STEALING

CHARLIE HUSTON

A Ballantine Book
Published by The Random House Publishing Group

Copyright © 2004 by Charles Huston
Excerpt from *Six Bad Things*, copyright © 2005 by Charles Huston.

All rights reserved under International and Pan-American Copyright Conventions. Published in the United States by Ballantine Books, an imprint of The Random House Publishing Group, a division of Random House, Inc., New York, and simultaneously in Canada by Random House of Canada Limited, Toronto.

Grateful acknowledgment is made to WARNER BROS. PUBLICATIONS U.S. INC. for permission to reprint excerpts from the lyrics of "Keep On Keeping On" by Curtis Mayfield on page 213. © 1971 (renewed) Warner-Tamerlane Publishing Corp., Warner Bros. Publications U.S. Inc., Miami, Florida 33014. All rights reserved. Used by permission.

Ballantine and colophon are registered trademarks of Random House, Inc.

www.ballantinebooks.com

This book contains an excerpt from the forthcoming book *Six Bad Things* by Charlie Huston. This excerpt has been set for this edition only and may not reflect the final content of the forthcoming edition.

Library of Congress Control Number: 2004097462

ISBN 0-345-46478-8

9 8 7 6 5 4 3 2 1

Manufactured in the United States of America

First Edition: May 2004
First Trade Paperback Edition: June 2005

For Scotty
A toughguy who loved his mom and dad

ACKNOWLEDGMENTS

Thanks to Maura Teitelbaum at Abrams Artists for believing in this book and hustling it to anyone and everyone. To Simon Lipskar of Writers House and Mark Tavani, my editor at Ballantine, for making the deal to get me published and, more importantly, for their hard work and support as the book was knocked into shape. Thanks also to Robyn Starr and Simone Elliot for the key roles they played in getting this book published. This book would not have been published without all of these people, but my greatest thanks are reserved for my friend, Johnny Lancaster, without whom none of them would ever have seen it. Thanks, J., you're a good friend.

Above all, thank you Mom and Dad for a life of unconditional love and support. I love you more than I can ever say.

And thank you, Virginia. Wife, I am nothing without you.

CAUGHT STEALING

PART ONE

Eight Regular Season
Games Remaining

My feet hurt. The nightmare still in my head, I walk across the cold wood floor, shuffling my feet in the light grit. I'm half-drunk and I have to pee. I'm not sure which woke me, the piss or the nightmare.

My john is just a bit smaller than the average port-o-potty. I sit on the pot and rest my forehead against the opposite wall. I have a pee hard-on and if I try to take a leak standing up, I'll end up hosing the whole can. I know this from experience. Plus my feet still hurt.

It takes a while. By the time I finish I'm just about asleep again. I get up, flush, and shuffle back to bed. On the way, a last bit of piss dribbles onto my thigh. I pick up a dirty sock from the floor, wipe the urine off and toss the sock in a corner.

I crawl back under the covers and twist around a bit until I'm arranged. I start to drift back asleep and the nightmare begins to rise up again in my mind. I force myself fully awake to keep it from getting back in. I think happy thoughts. I think about a dog I used to have. I think about Yvonne. I think about baseball: long, lazy games of baseball, plastic cups of cold beer between my thighs, peanut shells crunching beneath my sneakers. Fly balls soaring over loping outfielders. The beautiful ease of the long pop fly out . . . No! Wrong! Baseball is a mistake and the nightmare is rushing back in. I think about home. Home does the trick and I start to ease back asleep. And only then as I finally fall asleep do I register the blood I saw on the sock when I wiped my leg, the blood from my piss. I sleep.

* * *

These things are not related: my aching feet, the nightmare, the blood. My feet have hurt for years because of the job. The nightmare has been going on for half my life. The blood in my piss is brand new, but I know exactly where I got that too.

I got the bloody piss from the beating I took from a couple of guys last night. By last night I mean a few long hours before the nightmare woke me up. And when I say I took a beating from these guys, I really mean they gave it to me. Free. I got lucky; they both had small hands. Go figure, two big guys with small hands. It happens. They didn't want to bust up those little hands working on my face, so they gave it to my body. It didn't take long. They put some good ones in my gut and ribs and I dropped. Then I took a couple boot shots in the kidneys. That's where the blood is coming from.

The alarm goes off at 8:00 A.M. Now that the booze has worn off I hurt everywhere, but my feet are what's really killing me. I go to the can, sure enough: more blood. I brush my teeth and hop in the shower. Bruises are starting to well up all over my torso and the hot water feels good. I leave the shower running and walk dripping to the fridge, grab a cold beer and take it back to the shower. The water feels good, but the beer is better. It takes the edge off my hangover, kicks up the dust of last night's drunk and gives it life. I take the washcloth from the shower caddie and gently scrub my feet.

Out of the shower now, I finish the last of the beer while trimming my toenails. I clip them very short and even and make sure there is no grit hiding at the edges. I find a clean pair of socks with no holes and get dressed. I head out the front door. There's time for breakfast.

At the diner I have bacon and eggs and another beer. The first beer was good, but the second is even better. I'm heading into the third week of a pretty good binge and the first couple drinks of the day are always the best. I have to ease into it with beer because my job starts late. If I hit it too early I'll be drooling by the time the shift begins. I sip the beer, eat my chow, and look over the sports pages.

As a rule, the *Daily News* consists of equal parts violent sensationalism, feel-good human interest, celebrity gossip and advertising. I read it every day and feel dirty all over. But it's New York, and everybody gets dirty sooner or later. Today it's all election coverage and stories about yet more dotcoms biting the dust. I flip past the photos of the interchangeable candidates and get to the important stuff. See, the reason I started buying this rag in the first place is because it's the only way to get West Coast scores in the morning. Unless you have cable. I can't afford cable.

Back in California, the Giants are suffering their usual late season collapse. A week ago they were in striking distance of first place. But after a seven-game skid, they've been eliminated from contention for the division and are trailing the Mets for the wild card by four games with eight games left in the season. Meanwhile the Dodgers are red hot and have the division clinched after winning twelve of their last fourteen.

I look at my watch and it's time to go see the doctor.

I hate the Dodgers.

I've had this appointment for a week. I'm not here about the blood, I'm here about my feet. I've tried every kind of shoe and insert I can find and my feet are still killing me. So now, after years of bitching, I'm finally seeing a doctor. I could ask about the blood while I'm here, but what the hell is he gonna tell me? He's gonna tell me to go to an emergency room and they're gonna tell me that it's not life-threatening. They're gonna charge me a few thou I don't have to tell me to rest a bit and not to drink alcohol or caffeine. I don't drink caffeine. It makes me jittery. I sit in the waiting room and think about that second beer and how good it was.

I'm not worried about the kidney. If the kidney was serious, I'd be unconscious by now. It's contused: my kidney is scraped and it's bleeding a bit. Dr. Bob comes out of his office and calls my name.

Dr. Bob is a great guy. He's an Ivy League med school graduate who came to the Lower East Side and opened a community practice. He'll take anybody as a patient insurance or no insurance, his rates are as low as they get, and you pay your bills whenever you can. All of which suits my situation. He told me once he didn't want to make people healthy just to make them poor. Like I said, a great guy.

I told him about the feet a week ago and he sent me out for some X rays. Now, in his tiny office, he turns from where the X rays are clipped to one of those light things on the wall and sits on the stool in front of me. He starts to look at my feet. He really takes his time, inspecting them. He holds each foot, first one and then the other, and kneads a bit, searching for some imperfection. All the while, he directs his eyes upward, as if they might interfere with the examination: a safecracker with his eyes shut.

—Doc?

—Shhh.

He squeezes my feet a few more times, then stands up. He's talking now, but I'm having trouble hearing what he's saying. He's gesturing from my feet to the X rays. I'm thinking about getting out of here and drinking my next beer. I'm thinking how I wish I were lying down right now because I feel a little strange. He is looking at me oddly.

The roaring in my ears is not the hangover. I cannot hear over it and it occurs to me that something must be wrong. The examining table spins out from underneath me and I thump to the floor. I try to lift myself up, but I can't. I feel a warm wetness spreading over my lap and down my legs. I can see the tops of my feet. I can see the tips of my three-hundred-dollar sneakers that are supposed to be the most comfortable things that money can buy but are not. And I can see the bloody urine trickling out the cuffs of my jeans. Something is very wrong. I sleep.

This is how life changes.

You're born in California and raised as an only child in a pleasant suburb a ways east of San Francisco. You have a nice childhood with parents who love you. You play baseball. You are tremendously gifted at the game and you love it. By the time you are seventeen you have a room full of trophies. You have played on two teams that have competed for the Little League World Series and are the star player on your high school's varsity squad. You're a four-tool player: bat, glove, arm, and legs. You play center field. You lead the team in homers, ERA, RBI, stolen bases, and have no errors. Pro scouts have been coming to see you play all year and when you graduate, everyone expects you will skip college to be signed for development by a Major League club. At every game you look into the stands and your parents are always there.

In the regional championship game you are caught stealing third. You slide hard into the bag as the third baseman leaps to snare a high throw from the plate. Your cleats dig into the bottom of the base and as you pop up out of your slide, the third baseman is coming down with the ball. He lands on the ankle of your caught foot and, as you continue up, he falls down with his full weight on your lower leg.

The bone sticks straight out from your calf, and you just stare at it.

The pins they stick in your fibula restrict growth in the bone. It will not heal properly and for the rest of your life you have a hard knot of scar and bundled muscle tissue that aches in cold, wet weather. No one even pretends you will play again.

You stay away from the games and don't see much of your old friends. You have new friends, and you get in a little trouble. You work after school and buy a Mustang and fix it up with your dad, the mechanic. You drive everywhere and drag all the local motor-heads. You always win. When there's no one around to race, you drive fast on the back roads outside of town and get a rush from the speed. It's not baseball, but it's something.

Out by the cattle ranches, after midnight, a calf wanders into the road through a split in the fence. You swerve and pound down on the brake pedal. The wheel crazes out of your hand and the car heels down on the front right tire. The tire explodes. The wheel rim bites into the tarmac and the car flips up and begins to sail end over end. You are suspended in the car, held tight to the seat by the four-point harness your dad insisted you install. The car tumbles through the air and passes harmlessly over the calf. The Ford completes a full revolution, lands on its bottom, careens across the road and slams its front end into an oak.

Your friend Rich does not have his seat belt on. When you first saw the calf and slammed the brakes, Rich was kneeling on his seat, turned around and rummaging in the back for a sweatshirt.

During the flip you are for a moment suspended upside down. Rich bounces around the interior of the car and falls to the roof, sprawled on his back. He is looking at you, into your eyes, his face less than a foot away, inches away. The car flips with sudden violence, Rich disappears from your vision, and as you plow into the tree he appears to leap at the front windshield from somewhere behind you. He launches through the glass and flies the short distance to where the oak catches him brutally.

Lots of people show up at the funeral and cry and hug you. You have a bruised sternum and a cut on your cheek, and you look no one in the eye. Afterward your parents take you home.

In the spring you graduate and in the fall go to college in Northern California. You think about being a physical therapist or an EMT. You think about teaching like your mom. You won't go to work in your dad's garage. You don't want to work on cars anymore. You don't even drive.

You never graduate. You go to college for six years and study a bit of everything and do well at all of it, but you never graduate. You're not sure what to do and then you meet a girl. She's an actress.

You show up in New York with your girl and the two of you stay on the couch at her friend's place. Two weeks after you get to the city, she gets a job on the road and leaves. The friend tells you that you have to move out.

New York has great public transportation. You never have to drive. You decide to stay. You find an apartment the size of your folks' kitchen. You get a job tending bar. For the first time in your life you start drinking. You're good at it.

You live in New York, but you always act like a guy from a small town in California. You help winos out of the gutter, you call an ambulance when you see someone hurt, you loan money to friends who need it and don't ask for it back, you let folks flop at your pad and you help the blind across the street. One night you go to break up a fight in the bar and get knocked around pretty good, so the next day you start taking boxing classes. You drink too much, but your parents don't know that.

You're a good guy, you're tough and you have a reputation in your neighborhood for helping people out. It's nice. It's not the life you expected, but it's nice enough for you. You feel useful, you have friends and your parents love you. Ten years pass.

One day the guy who lives across the hall from you knocks on your door. He needs a big favor. That's when life really changes.

When I wake up, the first thing I think about is the fucking cat. I'm looking after this guy's cat for a couple weeks. God knows how long I've been out and if the thing is even alive. Fuck! I knew this would happen. I told the guy I wasn't good with animals, that I can barely take care of myself, but he was really up against it, so I took the damn cat. Then I see I'm in the hospital and figure out I may have more important things to worry about.

A joke: Guy is born with three testicles and spends his whole life feeling like a freak. Boys make fun of him in gym class, girls laugh at him. Finally, he can't take it and goes to have one of them lopped off. The doctor takes one look and tells the guy no way, it's too dangerous, might kill him or something, but he sends him to a shrink who might help out. This counselor or whatever he is tells the guy to take it easy, he should be proud of this third ball, he's special. I mean, how many guys have three testicles, right? So the guy feels great after that. He leaves the doc's office, walks into the street, goes up to the first man he sees and says, "Did you know, between you and me we've got five balls?" This dude looks at him funny and says, "You mean you only have one?"

First guy I see when I walk out of the hospital I go up to and start talking.

—Did you know, between you and me we only have three kidneys?

He doesn't say anything, just walks around me like I'm not there.
New York, baby, New York.

I've been in the hospital for six days: one unconscious and five con-
scious. The doctors removed the kidney, which had been nearly rup-
tured by the two big guys with four small hands and further damaged
by my negligence and massive consumption of diuretic liquids. Booze.
The kidney was at "four plus" when they took it out. At "five," they
simply explode and kill you. I have been told that I should never again
consume alcohol in any amount for the rest of my life on pain of
death. Likewise no smoking or caffeine. I don't smoke and, like I said,
caffeine makes me jittery.

  After I blacked out, Dr. Bob called the EMTs and had them take
me to Beth Israel. He rode with me in the ambulance and when we
arrived he got me past all the emergency room crap and directly into
an operating room. He saved my life. One of the doctors told me all of
this and when Bob showed up I tried to thank him, but he waved it off
in a just-doing-my-job kind of way. Then we get to my feet.

—So, your condition is chronic and brought on by the amount of time
you spend on your feet at work.

  I'm a bartender. I work a ten-hour shift five nights a week. Sometimes six or seven nights.

—You could buy a lifetime supply of Dr. Scholl's and get your feet
massaged every night and it would not help. If you want the pain to go
away, you are going to have to get off your feet.

—What if I?—

—Off your feet. You're like a computer worker with carpal tunnel: if
you want it to go away, you are going to have to change your work
habits forever.

—Wow.

—Yes, wow. Furthermore, the pain in your feet has been exacerbated
by poor circulation, which I would say is related to excessive alcohol
consumption.

—Wow.

—Yes. So stop drinking. Period.

—Yeah, sounds good.

And that was that. He told me good luck and was on his way out when I asked about the bill.

—When you get a new job and you've paid off your bill here, we'll talk about money.

A great guy.

Booze and my kidney. Booze and my feet. A pattern emerging.

I called the bar and talked to Edwin, the guy who owns the place. I apologized for the lack of notice, but Edwin was cool and just told me not to be a stranger.

Would I have quit if it was just the booze and the kidney? If someone said, "Get away from the booze and the drinking life or you're gonna die," would I have quit? I don't know, but my feet are killing me and that tears it.

I called my folks, made sure they knew I was OK and told them not to come out or expect me to come home to be nursed. Mom cried a little, but I made her laugh in the end, telling her the testicle joke. Dad asked if I needed money and I said no. We talked about Christmas a bit and how long I'd stay when I come out and then I told them I love them and they told me they love me and we hung up and I just fucking stared at the ceiling for a while.

I called one of the other bartenders from work. Her name is Yvonne, we used to see each other quite a bit, still do from time to time. So she's a girl I see from time to time. She's more than that. She's my best friend. But I also see her from time to time. She has a key to my place, so I told her about the cat and she promised to check on it until I got home. She offered to come by the hospital, but I said no. I want to be alone. I need to figure out what the hell I'm gonna do.

So now I'm out. I walk up to the stiff on the street and tell my kidney joke, and then I'm taking a cab home. They wanted me to stay for ten days so they could keep an eye on me and take out my staples before I left, but my lack of a) cash and b) insurance encouraged them to let me go. I'll have the staples out in a few days and just take it easy until then. I have one kidney, I'm being forced to go cold turkey, I have a hospital bill that makes the ten grand I carry in credit card debt look like a bad joke, and I have no job. On the other hand, I pick up a paper and the Giants are on a four-game winning streak and have picked up two on the Mets, who split a four-game stand against the Phillies. I lean back into the cab seat and feel a sharp stab in my former kidney and wonder what the hell was eating those guys who beat the crap out of me.

This is how I got the cat.

The guy's name is Russ and he has this cat. Russ lives in the apartment across the hall from mine and hangs out a bit at Paul's, the place I tend bar. I know him OK and I like him. He's never any trouble and the few times I've had to float him, he's paid his tab right away. He brings me sandwiches at work sometimes. Now, one night, a couple weeks or so back, he's outside my door holding one of those pet carriers and I can smell what's coming. I take my eye away from the peephole and lean my forehead against the door. Russ knocks again. I take another look and he's still there, bouncing up and down on his toes like he has to go. I let the peep snap shut and unlock the door.

Russ has a problem. Russ has a problem and he wouldn't even ask, but he really needs a big favor. Russ's dad is sick. This is true. I know it's true because Russ has mentioned before in the bar that his dad has been sick for a while. The thing is, Russ's dad is dying now and Russ needs to take off for Rochester right away and he can't find anyone to watch the cat and he knows this is a pain, but he really needs help. Can I take the cat for a few days, a week or two at the most?

I'm already half in the bag and I tell him I'm gonna be drunk for a bit and I'm worried about the cat. Russ assures me the cat will be fine. He'll bring me the cat's special feeder that you can fill once every couple days and its litter box and all that. The cat will take care of itself. I say yes. What are you supposed to do? The guy's dad is dying.

Russ hands me the carry box with the cat inside and goes across the hall to get the rest of the gear. I get a beer from the fridge and stare at the box. I had a cat when I was a little kid. I had it for years and one day my mom brought home a stray puppy and a few days later the cat split. Nobody's fault, my mom felt terrible, but I never blamed her. I blamed the fucking cat, first sign of competition and the cat splits. Fickle, cats are fickle. I like dogs.

Russ brings back the feeder, the litter box, the shit scooper, the litter, the food, and a couple cat toys. He offers me money, but I refuse. He thanks me a couple more times and I tell him to take care of his dad and call if he needs anything and he takes off. The carry box is sitting on top of the crate that passes for my coffee table. I'm sitting there on the couch with my beer and I realize that Russ didn't tell me the cat's name. I lean down and look through the thin bars of the carry to get a look at the cat. It's a house cat, a mutt cat. Gray-striped back and head with a white belly and face. Looks to be a boy. He's wearing a collar with a little tag. I put down the beer, unlatch the door and reach in. He comes right out, no fuss. I turn him around so he's facing me and he looks me right in the eye. The tag on the collar is flipped around and I turn it so I can read the name. Bud. I pick up my cold can of Bud while Bud the cat gets comfortable in my lap and flops down and starts to purr.

The days roll by and I don't hear from Russ. And to tell the truth, I just don't mind that much at all.

At home I have a lot of booze to deal with. I could give it to one of my neighbors, but I figure it will be good for me to actually dispose of it. In the fridge I have eighteen cans of Bud, a few bottles of white wine, and a Silver Bullet. In the freezer I find a liter of Beefeater, half-full, and a pint of some Polish buffalo grass vodka, untouched. The cabinet under the sink is the real danger zone. There are bottles of Cutty Sark,

Wild Turkey, Cuervo, Myers's, a variety of mixers in various states of undress, and full backups of the bourbon and Scotch. I also have three bottles of a killer Chianti and a tiny bottle of sake someone gave me on my birthday a few years back. I pile everything on the kitchen counter. I start with the beer, pouring it in the sink, but the smell backs up in there and my mouth starts watering, so I change my plan. I take the whole load into the bathroom and start pouring it all into the toilet. It works great and I feel very efficient: instead of drinking all this and pissing it back out, I've cut out the middleman. Bud comes in, props his paws on the toilet seat and takes a look at what I'm doing. He gets splashed with a little rum, shakes it off his snout, and wanders back into the other room. Smart cat.

When I'm done, I throw all the bottles and cans into a blue plastic recycling bag and take it down two flights and out to the curb, where it will sit for God knows how many days before it's picked up. It's a fantastic day at the very beginning of fall. The air is clear, with the slightest chill. I go back in and get the piled-up mail from my box. I go upstairs and sort through all the bills, the advertising and credit card and calling card and insurance card offers, which leaves me with a letter from my mom and a jury duty notice. I empty the cat box. Yvonne filled Bud's food thing and made sure he had plenty of water, but she left the crap for me. That's all right. I take the bag with the kitty litter and junk mail out to the curb and put it next to the blue bag full of empty booze bottles. I wonder if I missed something, if maybe there's still a full can of beer in there or the dregs of that sake. The air is just as cool as it was before, but I break a little sweat. This could be harder than I thought. I go back up, grab the phone, call my dealer and tell him I need some grass. He says he'll be right over.

The days I spent in the hospital got me through the worst of the shakes and nausea of coming off a binge, but I had a little help from the morphine they gave me. Before I checked out, the doctor set me up with a bottle of Vicodin, but I don't like pills, they make me feel stupid. The bag Tim is bringing over should bridge the gap.

Tim is a regular from Paul's. He's a forty-four-year-old jazz head and boozer who got lucky. A few years ago, Tim was a junkie living off welfare and the aluminum cans he picked out of other people's trash. Then he fell into a great job and got himself off junk. The job: delivery-man for a dealer. Every morning, Tim goes to his boss's office, where he and the other delivery guys pick up a list of clients and the product. They handle pot, hash, mushrooms, acid, and coke, and they will deliver to your home or office for no additional fee. Tim wanders all over the city, receiving a per-delivery commission and carefully saving his taxi receipts so he can get reimbursed at the end of the day. He carries a little extra grass so he can make impromptu deals on the side. He will also, in the course of the day, consume at least a fifth of Irish whiskey and some beer. Let's face it, you don't kick junk without filling that hole with something else. Everyone has to figure out a way to get through the day and booze is a very popular strategy. Tim is what we call a functioning alcoholic.

I let him into the apartment and he flops on the couch. Tim was at the bar when I got worked over. He holds his backpack in his lap and looks me over.

—Hey, man, how you feel?

I tell him I feel OK. We chat about folks from the bar while I slip *Kind of Blue* into the CD player and Tim rolls a joint. We light up. Tim is a professional and informs me in detail about the weed we are smoking: it is a Virginian crossbreed of a classic skunk and a very potent Thai stick.

—Most importantly, this shit was raised in the wild, not in a hydroponics tank by some mad scientist. Hold the smoke. Hold the smoke, man, you can taste the mountain air.

I cannot, in fact, taste the mountain air, but I am getting high and, as I do, I start to think less about having a drink.

—Hey, you got anything to drink around here?

So much for that.

Tim takes off a short while later. He's a true boozer; if he doesn't have a belt soon, his hands will start to shake. On his way out, I give him some cash for the bag and he waves as he goes down the hall, then stops for a moment.

—Hey, did you ever find out what was up with those assholes, why they had it in for you?

I tell him it beats me and he says so did they and gives a lame laugh, realizing it's a bad joke. Then he leaves. It *is* a bad joke, but it's a great question, and as soon as I can think straight, I'll deal with it.

You can only smoke so much pot. I have smoked a great deal already and it's time for a break. I really just want to have it around to smooth out the edges for the next week or so. I figure after that I should be in good shape. This is not the first time I've stopped drinking. I've hopped on the wagon a couple of times to see how it would go and, the fact is, with the kind of motivation I have, I don't expect to have much trouble. Just as soon as I get the system all flushed out. But right now I'm just sitting here alone in my apartment with someone else's cat in my lap, listening to the Clash's *Combat Rock*, being unemployed and in debt and thinking about beer. I decide to do the laundry.

Tasks are good when you're trying to give up something. They keep you occupied and make your life seem useful. I stuff my dirty clothes in a sack. I grab a handful of quarters from my change jar, but on the way to the door, I stop. Bud has a little blanket in his carry box and I decide to wash that too. Russ should be back in a day or two and it would be nice if Bud has a clean blanket. This is the way I think. It's my mom's fault. I grab the blanket and pull and it snags on something in the box. I tug harder and hear the blanket rip a little. I put the laundry sack down, get on my hands and knees, and reach into the box to unsnag the blanket.

* * *

Paul's Bar closes at 4:00 A.M. On a Thursday it's usually all regulars by 2:00 A.M. So when I'm working, that's when I start my serious drinking. Last Thursday there were about ten regulars hanging out in the place and I was starting to get my head on when the big guys came in. They plop down at the far end of the bar and I wander over. These guys are genuinely big; even sitting on the stools, they loom a little. But big means nothing, I'm more curious about the way they're dressed. Both guys are wearing Nike tracksuits: one in black, one in white. They are sporting several gold chains each, which go well with the gold-rimmed Armani sunglasses they both have propped up on their shaved heads. These guys are not our usual crowd. I take them for Poles or Ukrainians left over from the old neighborhood before the East Village went Latino and then arty and now yuppie. They order an Amstel Light and a cosmopolitan. Each. They have Russianic accents. And this is still far from the weirdest pair we've ever had in the place, so I fix the drinks and take the cash and they say thank you.

As I walk back down the bar to get my own drink and resume my game of movie trivia on the MegaTouch, I hear cursing behind me. I turn and the guy in the white tracksuit is holding his cosmo like the glass is full of vomit.

—This is shit.

He turns the glass upside down and spills it on the bar. The guy in black tastes his and promptly spits it back up, also on the bar.

—This is also shit. I cannot drink this.

To prove his point, he takes another sip and spits it on the bar, then he stands and walks to the trash and drops the drink, glass and all, into the can.

I don't like to fight. I have fought very little in my life, but what I have noticed is that even when you win, you get hurt. I work out four days a week and take boxing and self-defense on the weekends. I have steel-toed boots and a Buck knife. I have an ax handle behind the bar. None of this will help, because I don't want to fight and these guys clearly do. I smile. I walk down the bar to the two tracksuits, a smile plastered on my semidrunk face, radiating joy and love. I am Martin Luther King. I am Gandhi. I will ask these gentlemen if they would prefer another drink or their money back. I will carefully wipe their spit off the bar and all will be at peace, because I don't want to fight. They sit at the end of the bar, Amstels untouched, the one upturned cosmo glass before them and, as I approach, they both slip their sunglasses over their eyes like they've been blinded by my smile. And that is when I notice the small, girlish and simply beautiful hands they both have. I am not afraid. These men are lovers, not fighters. These men are concert pianists with graceful digits made for music, not pugilism.

I reach the end of the bar and open my smiling mouth to offer them a round on the house as compensation for their disappointment. They grab me, drag me over the bar, and beat the crap out of me. Then they leave.

I've been beat up before and had it hurt a lot worse. I don't even look that bad. But I do close the bar early and spend the next several hours drinking and holding an ice pack to my ribs while Tim, a couple other regulars and I tell fight stories: the high and low moments of beating and getting beat. We have chalked up the tracksuits as psychos and, hey, what more can you say? A few hours later the blood shows up in my piss.

I give Bud's blanket a gentle tug and I can feel that it's caught on something. I reach in and feel around, expecting to find a flange of molded plastic or some other deformity in the case itself. There is a flat object taped to the bottom of the box and the corner of the blanket is caught under a bit of the tape. What I took for tearing blanket was tearing tape. I untangle the blanket and, in the process, I detach the object. It is a tiny manila envelope that feels like it contains a key. I look at the envelope. The key feels odd, a bit bulky in some way. This is not mine. This is not my business. This is the spare key to Russ's apartment or his safe deposit box or something. It is not for me and I suddenly feel nosy. I untangle the tape and reattach the key as best I can, trying to get it exactly right. I also put the blanket back in. If the blanket is clean, Russ might figure I saw the envelope and it could make him uptight. This is what I'm thinking. Then I think about having a drink and this reminds me about the laundry. I pick up the sack, say good-bye to Bud and leave. I never put two and two together and, after all, why should I?

I moved into the East Village about ten years ago, when I first came to New York. There was a little grocery downstairs from me where you could walk up to the counter and buy crack or dope or coke. It's a nail salon now and there's a sushi restaurant across the street. There are still plenty of junkies and burned-out storefronts and a handful of hookers, but the wild wild west feel the place had when I got here is gone. Condos, boutiques, and bistros are popping up like fungus. But murders, muggings, and rapes are way down, so when people bitch about gentrification I usually tell them to fuck off. I like sushi fine and the Japanese girls in the salon hold my UPS packages when I'm not home. And, hey, the place still has color.

I come out of my building with my buzz on and stand for a moment at the curb and enjoy the fall sun. Jason is sprawled at my feet. Jason is a wino who has lived on this block from before I ever got here. He's a real old-fashioned wet-brain drunk. He is also the barometer of my own drinking habits and this moment is a good one for me to see Jason sprawled on the sidewalk at midday, utterly unconscious, with a shortdog of T-Bird still in his hand. I step over him and head for the laundry.

The truth is, I'm pushing it a little bit here. The doctor who yanked my kidney told me to take it real easy, going up and down the stairs with garbage and doing my laundry is probably not what he had in mind. I think he had more the lounging-around-on-the-couch kind of easy in mind. But I need the action, so I separate my darks and lights and add my detergent and bleach and softener and pump quarters into the machines at the Korean laundry. The place is pretty much empty, so I sprawl across two seats, pick up a *Daily News* someone has abandoned and check some scores.

This is what is left of the season:

The Giants will close a series against the Rockies today, then have three games on the road against the Dodgers.

The Mets will finish off the Marlins and play three home games against the Braves.

I will not cry when the Giants lose. I just don't have it in me anymore.

I move my clothes to the dryer and flip through the rest of the paper.

The dryer stops drying and I get my clothes. Everything is piping hot and I'm tempted to change jeans right there just to get that toasty feeling on a chilly day. I settle for slipping on a warm sweatshirt. I fold everything and pack it all back into my bag. I haven't thought about a beer in about an hour or at least no more than once or twice. Mission accomplished, I balance the laundry bag on my shoulder and go home.

Outside my front door I shift the bag from my right shoulder to my left to dig for my keys. This is a mistake. I no longer have a left kidney. What I do have is a big hole held closed by a bunch of staples. When I stretch my left arm up to hold the bag on my shoulder, my staples also stretch. Or rather the flesh stretches and my staples stay right where they are. I gasp and squeak a little at the pain and drop the bag, spin around and do a little pain dance. Then I get my shit together along with my keys and put the bag back on my right shoulder.

As I do this, as the bag is settling onto my shoulder, I register something in the window of the pizza place next door. There is a counter that runs along the front window of the place and people sit there to eat their pizza and you can't see their faces and they can't see out unless they hunch a little because the front window is plastered with

Italian movie posters down to about a foot above the counter. The owner of this place is a huge movie fan. I know this because I get all my pizza there and we talk movies sometimes. He's a nice guy and I always tell him he should take those posters down so people can see out and in through that nice big front window. But right now I love those posters. I love those posters because of what I just barely glimpsed on the counter: four beautiful, small hands, dressed to the wrists in Nike tracksuits—two in black and two in white. I feel certain that the pizza those hands are clutching is being shoved into the mouths of two huge Russianic thugs with a fondness for light beer and foofy pink cocktails.

I drop my keys. I drop my keys in such a way that anyone sitting at the counter of the pizza place will be able to see me if I bend to pick them up. This is so fucked up. Careful to keep the laundry bag positioned in front of my head, I squat, bending at the knees, and pick up the keys. I have not moved the bag from my right shoulder since I caught my glimpse. I do not know what the hands are doing. Nor do I know for certain that they are the hands I think they are. But I am freaked out. I hurry to get the door open and drop the keys again. Fuck this. I squat again and this time I shift the bag just enough so I can peek up into the window of the pizza shop and see who exactly is at the counter and get this over with. It's them. They don't see me. I stand, work the key in the lock and am inside very quickly.

Weird shit happens in New York. I have run into people on the street here who I knew once in elementary school back in California. It is not impossible that these boys live around here and just happen to like Muzzarel's Pizza. But I'm scared anyway because this is so fucked up. I am walking up the two flights to my floor and I am repeating a mantra to myself:

—This is so fucked up. This is so fucked up. This is so fucked up.

And that's why I don't really register the sounds coming from the hall just outside my apartment until I'm a few steps away.

The knocking I hear coming from my hall might just be the exterminator, or a friend, or Federal Express with the bag I lost at JFK three years ago. But the presence of the Russian goombahs downstairs makes me think otherwise. My feet are carrying me into view of whoever is there, and my sense of self-preservation makes an executive decision. I shift the laundry from my right shoulder to my left so that it will hide my head from anyone at my door. I ignore the pain this causes and step onto the landing. I do not stop. I turn and take the next flight up without ever looking at my door. All knocking and conversation has ceased and the only sounds are my steps and breathing and the ridiculous pounding of my heart. As I mount the stairs to the next floor and climb one, two, three, four, five steps, the noise behind me begins again. When I reach the top floor of the building, I stop. There are now three floors between me and whoever is down there.

My side is screaming. But what really sucks, is that for the first time in days my feet hurt.

The building I live in is no palace, but when I first moved in it was in *really* sorry fucking shape. A few years back, when the real estate boom finally reached Alphabet City, my landlord decided to spruce up a bit so he could jack up the rents on new tenants. For the purpose of making these improvements, he hired a group of retards who I'm sure were quite affordable. The way it worked out, this crew of mongoloids went through the building destroying all that came within their grasp, while Carlos, the building super, followed them around and redid all they had undone. I needed a few bucks and Carlos needed an extra pair of hands, so I helped him with some things, including tarring and papering the roof. This is how I came to have roof access in the building when no other tenants do.

I'm standing in the hall on the top floor and I can hear the guys outside my door as clear as day. That is, I can hear that they have stopped knocking on my door and now there is only some shuffling and whispering. And then I hear what sounds like a door opening and more shuffling and a door closing and total silence. And I think, I really do, that those fuckers are in my apartment. What I want to do is, I want to call the cops. In this situation, there is no reason not to call the cops. People break into your apartment, *people who seem to be associated with people who beat you bloody a few nights ago break into your apartment,* and there is just no good reason not to call the cops.

No reason except for the huge bag of grass sitting on my coffee table and all the paraphernalia it's hanging out with.

The door to the roof has a combination lock. I know the combination. I climb the half flight of steps to the roof door, work the lock and step outside. I finally put down the laundry bag because it's really fucking killing me. I have to leave the door just a bit ajar, otherwise it will latch and if I open it, I'll trigger the fire bar and set off the alarm for the whole building. I did this once when I was working up here with Carlos. He spewed out every curse word he knows in English and Spanish and a few in Tagalog that he'd gotten from his Filipino wife. Afterwards, I bought him a beer or three and he forgave me, but it was a pain in the ass. Fire trucks, tenants in the street, traffic jammed up and all because I needed to go inside to use the john.

So I leave the door a little ajar.

I have no plan. I can still call the cops, but I figure the pot is a good enough reason to take a wait-and-see approach, at least for the moment. Especially since I have no clue what these guys are doing. I do not have nice things. There is some cash in my place and a couple standard appliances, but other than that, the weed is probably the most valuable thing I own right now. So I'm on the roof and I have no plan.

I walk to the front of the building and, when I get close to the edge, I go down on my hands and knees and peek over. Good call. Black tracksuit and white tracksuit have moved across the street. They are standing in front of the tattoo parlor there and doing the "look how damn inconspicuous we are" thing. One is talking on a cell phone and the other is drinking a bottle of Yoo-hoo through a straw. They are both avoiding looking at my building. I have entered new territory. These guys are looking for me. I feel confident that they have my place staked out and are looking for me, acting as lookouts for the guys in my apartment. This has never happened to me before and I'm at a bit of a loss for the next move. And that is when I realize that it's time to cut the crap because this is potentially a very dangerous situation and I should just call the damn cops. I creep back from the edge of the building, stand up and head for the door, which the nice fall breeze has apparently blown shut.

For a moment, I think about just opening the door. Trigger the alarm and that would surely bring this whole thing to a swift conclusion. Bad guys dash out, fire trucks and cops show up, I tell the simple truth and, if I get snagged on the pot, well, so be it. Sometimes you just have to be a grown-up and bite the bullet. Instead, I turn into Spy Boy and decide to climb down the fire escape to get a closer look.

I used to break into houses. I was seventeen and couldn't play ball anymore. My leg was so messed up I couldn't play anything for a while. In gym I rode the bench with the burnouts and watched my jock friends play and thought about how I'd like to beat the shit out of their healthy bodies. After about a week, I started sneaking off with the burners to get baked behind the equipment shed. That's how I met Wade, Steve, and Rich.

Breaking into a house in the suburbs is easy. Unlocked doors are common and unlocked windows are universal. No one had an alarm back then. Rich and Steve only did houses they knew were empty. That was fun. You hop a fence and usually just go in the back door. You run the house quick, looking for cash or jewelry or drugs, just what fits in your pockets, then you get out. Wade liked to hit houses when the people were home. I liked it too.

You pick a house. What you're looking for is no lights at all or lights in one room only. A house where all the people are sleeping is a charge, but a house where someone is awake is unreal. You test the side garage door and go in there. Once in the garage, you can get a feel for what's going on in the house. And *no one* locks the house door to the garage. You slip into the house and listen for the TV. Thursday night in the eighties and everyone in America is watching *The Cosby Show*, *Family Ties*, *Cheers*, *Night Court*, and *Hill Street Blues*. For those three hours you could do whatever you wanted. Walking past the open door of the family room, you peek in and see Mom, Dad, and the kids grouped around the set. Even if you asked directions to the bathroom no one would look up. Sometimes it was too easy.

I was at it for a few months until I got busted. The cops stopped me and Wade after we did a house. All they were looking to do was hassle us for being out after curfew, but we smarted off and they got us with cash, a bottle of Valium and some lady's engagement ring. I quit after that. My folks picked me up at the station and I quit. They looked so disappointed. I didn't see much of Wade and Steve after that, but I stayed close to Rich.

The fire escape for my apartment is at the back of the building. I move down it quick and easy, or as quick and easy as I can with the pain in my side. I stop when I get to the floor above mine. The fire escape extends down at a sharp angle, half ladder/half staircase, and dumps you about a foot to the left of my bedroom window. Unless one of these guys is standing right at the window, I should be able to creep down and press myself against the bricks between my place and Russ's. From there I can listen and decide if I can afford to take a peek or if I should just get the hell out.

I relax. I am ready to start down the steps. And the dog in the apartment I am outside of starts to bark bloody murder.

I don't think. I fly down the steps and flatten myself against the bricks. The only way I can be seen now is if someone sticks their head out the window. I wait while I catch my breath and the dog winds down. No one opens my window. I am calm. I settle against the bricks and listen. They are in there. I can hear low voices and what seems to be a great deal of rummaging and low-key destruction. The sound is a bit faint and does not seem to be coming directly from my bedroom just inside the window. I decide to take a peek. I turn so that I face the bricks, inch over to the window and dart my right eye out and back as quickly as possible. And I see nothing. I breathe. Slowly this time, I poke my head out enough to see a wide swath of the bedroom and living area and I see nothing. No people, no signs of search or forced entry. I see only Bud sitting on my bed where he is not allowed and looking at me with an expression that clearly says: "What the fuck are you doing?" Yes, the searching sounds are in fact coming from behind me in Russ's apartment.

I repeat the process. I edge to Russ's window and do the quick peek and get an impression of a big mess and some people. I do some more breathing and go back for a better look. There are three guys in there; I'm not sure what they look like because the blood pounding in my temples keeps blurring my vision. One of them is big, one is small, and one is medium. The Three Bears. Russ's apartment is being broken into by the Three Bears. The thought makes me giggle. I hold it in, and it almost bursts out again. I have to get off this fire escape before I start to laugh. I go back to my bedroom window, which is locked, of course, but my bedroom has two windows and the second one is unlocked. It is, however, a few feet beyond the fire escape. But right now I want to be in my apartment and that's all I know.

I climb over the rail. I plant my left foot on the escape and grip it with my left hand and stretch. If I hadn't had a major surgical procedure in the last week, this would be easy. As it is, it hurts like hell. I bite my lip to keep from shouting and it makes my eyes water, which, for some strange reason, makes me want to sneeze. I plant my right foot on the window ledge. The window is not ajar, so I can't get a grip on the lip. I have to press my palm flat against the glass and push up. I don't have enough leverage. I'm going to have to get lower. I loosen my grip on the escape just a bit and bend at the right knee while I stretch farther with my left leg. My staples dig in and my left arm is sore and I press my palm against the window and push up with my right arm and leg and tears are now streaming down my face and as the window lurches open I sneeze massively and throw myself into my bedroom as my left foot slips from the escape.

The top half of my body flops into the apartment, my hips caught on the sill, my legs dangling outside the window and more searing pain radiating from my side. There are quick footsteps next door as someone runs to Russ's window. I drag my legs inside, shut the window and curl into a quiet ball in the space between the bed and the wall. I hear the window next door open. I hear someone climb out onto the fire escape. I sense someone at my window looking in. I couldn't move if I wanted to.

I stay like that until I hear them leave Russ's apartment about fifteen minutes later. Then I get up, go to the bathroom, and puke. Big surprise: Throwing up makes my staples hurt. But I don't appear to have popped any of them during all this. Adrenaline is leaving my body and in its wake it leaves a huge craving for booze. I drink some water. I straighten up my apartment. I remember my laundry on the roof and decide to leave it there until later, tomorrow even. Then I smoke a roach, flush the rest of my high-grade Virginia pot, make a phone call and play with Bud while I wait for the cops.

I tell them about everything except the grass. First, I tell the uniforms who answer the call. I tell them about getting beat up. I tell them about finding the tracksuits outside my apartment. I tell them the idiotic tale of my climb to the roof and descent by the fire escape. They're pretty nice on the whole and only laugh a little about what an asshole I am. Then Detective Lieutenant Roman of Robbery/Homicide shows up.

If the job description for a great cop said "dark, brooding, efficient as hell, and looks great in a black suit," then Detective Lieutenant Roman would be your guy. He asks me all kinds of incisive questions as we sit around in my apartment and all he ever looks at are my eyes and his little notebook.

—How many people did you actually see?

—I think five, altogether.

—Why "you think"?

—I didn't get a very good look through the window, so there might have been more. But I know there were the two guys downstairs and I definitely saw three in Russ's apartment.

—Russ is Mr. Miner, your neighbor?

—Right.

—Tell me about the guys downstairs.

—Two big guys, they were in the pizza place next door and when I got to the roof they were watching the building from across the street.

—These are the two who beat you up last week?

—Right.

—And when they came into the bar that night, did they ask for Mr. Miner?

—No. They didn't ask for shit except a couple drinks. Then they went haywire.

—OK. The guys in Mr. Miner's apartment, what can you tell me about them?

—Uh, one guy big, even bigger than the two Russians.

—Russians?

—The guys who beat me up, the guys in the tracksuits, had accents. I think they were Russian or Ukrainian or Polish.

—You said Russian.

—Or Ukrainian or Serbian for all the fuck I know, just Russianic.

—OK. What about the big guy in the apartment?

—Big. And I think he was Latino or something.

—He was, what, dark?

—Yeah, dark skin, but lightish. I mean he might have been black, but not dark black.

—Brown complexioned?

—Yeah.

—Hair?

—Lots of it, I think. Long hair, black. That's what I think.

—OK, who else?

—A small guy with bright red hair.

—Carrot topped?

—No, *real* red, might be dyed kind of red.

—Fire engine?

—Almost.

—Good, that's good.

—Yeah?

—What about the third?

—Uh, not much. Averagish size, dark hair, and wearing black, I think.

—You think he was wearing black?

—He was definitely in black or very dark blue.

—OK.

He looks at his notes and waves one of the uniforms over. Without saying anything, he takes the uniform's notebook and flips through it, looking for something. He hands the book back to the uniform and takes another look at me. And he *really* looks at me, I mean, he looks me up and down like he's sizing me up for a secret mission or something.

—Can you tell me, this is difficult and I don't want to compromise you, your friendship with Mr. Miner, but can you tell me, is Mr. Miner involved in any illegal activities?

Well, fuck, what do I do with that?

—Fuck, I don't know.

—This is crucial. You understand that, yes? If your friend is in danger, we need to know everything there is to know.

—I understand.

—Good. Now do you have any reason to believe that.

And I just cut the guy off.

—For chrissake, no. Frankly, I don't know what the guy does. I think he's trying to be an actor or something, I think he works at a club in the meat-packing district, but I'm not sure what the fuck he does. And as much as I like him, I'm not so much worried about him being in danger since I'm the one got the shit beat out of him.

I'm spazzing a little here and I know it, but honestly I've been under a lot of pressure and I just snap. Detective Roman doesn't even blink. As far as he's concerned, we're having a lovely tête-à-tête over tea and fucking crumpets.

—OK. That's good to know. As far as danger goes . . .

—Yes?

—I wouldn't worry too much. Figure the guys who beat you up came into the bar looking for Mr. Miner and you must have pissed them off somehow. And if they are looking for him, not you, they probably have no idea that you're his neighbor. So take it easy and we'll get this all sorted out.

Color me reassured.

—Thanks, that helps.

—And you're certain you don't have a number where Mr. Miner can be reached?

—No.

—When he left the cat, he gave you no phone number and no address?

—No.

—OK.

—It's just, he was in a hurry and I was a bit loaded that night, so . . .

—OK.

—But he always talked about his dad being upstate somewhere. Rochester, I think.

—OK.

—And I'm pretty sure about the place he works, where it is and all.

—OK.

The way Detective Roman says "OK" this last time makes it clear that I'm just babbling now, so I put a sock in it and he makes a last note in his book.

—Let's get to it.

He stands up, pulls out a pair of thin rubber gloves, and goes across the hall to Russ's door, which he can't open because, of course, the bad guys locked it behind them. But that's OK because whoever looked out the window while I was flopping around left that wide open. One of the uniforms goes through the window and opens the door.

I stand in the hall and watch Roman do his thing and I am thoroughly impressed. He goes through the place like a machine, telling the uniforms what to touch and what not to touch. He pokes and pries into every corner and dusts for prints and gets the job done in a way that makes you happy to be a taxpayer. Then he's finished. He closes the door to Russ's apartment and slaps a police seal across the jamb. He gives me his card and tells me to call right away if anything else happens and to have Mr. Miner call him immediately if and when he returns. Then he and the uniforms leave and I sit down on my couch and wish I had a cocktail and Bud jumps up in my lap and I remember the fucking key in his box.

I can't sleep. I lie in bed and think about Russ and the tracksuits and their pals. I think about Detective Roman telling me not to worry. I think about not having a job and I think about the money I owe. I think about the key. I think about the key a lot.

When I remembered the key, I froze. The cops had just left and part of me was screaming to go after them with the key, but I froze instead. Who knows what the fucking thing is and why Russ put it there? But he entrusted it to me. Granted, he didn't tell me about it, or the fact that some guys might be looking for it and I might be getting beaten up. So fuck him. And so I grabbed the key and ran after the cops, but they were gone by then. In the end, my head was in too many knots to do much good thinking, so I put the key back in Bud's box and, since I was so beat, I tried to hit the hay.

But with all the shit I've been through today, I can't get to sleep. Or keep from thinking about a drink. I haven't gone to bed without at least a nightcap in quite a while and I'm not sure how to go to sleep without it. I try to read a bit. I try to watch TV. I end up back in bed, staring at the ceiling.

I can't take it. I get up and dig in a desk drawer and take out an old brass pipe. Carefully, I break it down into its several component parts and scrape the weed resin from each one. I collect the resin on a fold of paper, reassemble the pipe, form the resin into a gummy ball, drop it onto the screen, and light up. A resin high is not an up high. There just isn't much helpless giggling involved. Likewise it is not a lightweight high. It is not for amateurs. Fortunately, I'm not looking for laughs and I have years in this business: I am an experienced professional.

I take the smoke in extra deep and hold each lungful for as long as I possibly can. If this doesn't work I'm screwed for sleep and I don't feel like taking any chances. I put *Shotgun Willie* on the CD player, turn off the lights and hop into bed to finish smoking. Bud hops up on the bed and I let him stay. His food thingy is empty. I'll need to fill it in the morning. Willie has the greatest voice for getting high to. I can't believe the shit that happened today. I'm starting to drift; the resin is doing its job. I suck down the last hit, put the pipe on my nightstand and burrow in under the covers. I always sleep on my side in a little curl, Bud settles into the space between my knees and my stomach and we both fall asleep.

The nightmare is always the same. I play center field for the San Francisco Giants. It's my rookie season and we're playing in game seven of the World Series against the Oakland Athletics. I have excelled all season long, batting over .300, hitting 34 homers, knocking in 92 RBI and competing for a Gold Glove. I am a shoo-in for Rookie of the Year. We're playing in Oakland, it's the bottom of the ninth and I just sacrificed in the go-ahead run in the top of the inning. Now the A's have runners at second and third with two out. Our one-run lead is hanging by a thread.

I roam center field. My teammates range around me. I feel safe. I have that great big-game feel in my stomach: half tight, half loose. In the dream, I know everything about all the guys in the game, not just the ones on my team, but the A's as well. I know everything about the whole league. I have a season's worth of memories, all 162 regular season games plus the postseason.

The batter steps up. His name is Trenton Lane. I played against him in the minors. He's a beast, a right-handed third baseman that loves to hit heat. On the mound we've got our left-handed closer, Ed-uardo Cortez. Eddie throws nothing but fire and hasn't given up a run in the playoffs. The crowd loves it. The guys on the field love it. I love it. This is baseball.

Trenton has arms like an ape. Anything outside he's gonna pound, so Eddie will try to drill him inside. Out in the field we're all shading to left, hoping for a pop-up. The play is at first. The A's have speed on the bases, a single will score both the tying and winning runs, so if Trenton hits anything playable, we'll go for the out at first and get this thing over with.

Trenton is in the box. Eddie goes into his windup, a huge, slow de-livery to the plate that takes forever. Then the ball explodes from his hand at ninety-eight miles per hour. And it moves. Eddie's pitch is per-fect; it bursts out of his hand looking like it will hit the outside of the plate, then darts inside. To hit heat like that, you have to guess where the ball will be when it reaches you and start your swing just as the pitcher releases it. Trenton starts his swing in time and his guess is dead-on. He's leaning back in the box with the bat choked in tight against his body and he lays wood right on it. The guy is a monster. Even handcuffed by a pitch like that, he launches the ball skyward.

It's coming at me. When it flys off the bat, it shoots up at the kind of angle that screams pop-up and on any given day, it's a ball that should fall just short of the warning track in right-center. But today the wind is up. It's blowing out from behind the plate and as I start drifting back to the wall I can see the ball get caught up there, danc-ing and blowing out on the currents. The left fielder, Dan Shelton, is moving in. But I call him off: I have the ball. This is my ball. I know the runners are streaking to beat out a single. I know that cocky bas-tard Trenton is moving slowly down the first base line, waiting to break into a home run trot. But this is no home run ball, I can see that. This is no homer. It's gonna be close because the wind is really moving it around up there, but this is no homer. The play is gonna be right at the wall. If I'm not perfect I'll flub the catch, it'll drop in, and we'll lose the game.

The ball carries farther than I thought it would. It's going over. It's a homer. The crowd is screaming, willing the ball over the wall. I have sudden visions of Carlton Fisk waving his arm, willing his home run fair.

I put on a burst to the wall and jump, stabbing my glove into the air, and feel the comfortable thump of the ball coming to rest in the woven pocket of my glove. I drop to the ground, cradling the ball, my ball, my World Series–winning fucking ball. And the Oakland Coliseum goes berserk. I am mobbed by my team. The rest is a blur leading to the champagne-drenched locker room.

There are microphones and celebrities and a call from the president and Eddie wins the Series MVP and drags me up to the podium and says he wants to share it with me. Someone brings my folks back to my locker and they're both crying and we hug and laugh and gradually things start to settle down a bit. I'm twenty-two. I've spent four years as a Minor League phenom and now I'm a star in my Major League rookie season. I have everything I ever wanted and my whole life is waiting for me and it just sparkles. My parents head for home, the strangers clear the locker room and I start to get undressed.

I am unbuttoning my jersey. As I turn to my locker, Rich is standing there right in front of it. He's still seventeen. He has beautiful long brown curly hair that drops to his shoulders and this goofy smile that chicks just eat up. He's wearing sneakers, black jeans and his favorite Scorpions T-shirt. I am so happy to see him.

—Hey, Rich, man. How'd you get in here?

—Just snuck in, man.

—Wow! Wow, you look great. How are you, man?

—Good, I'm good. But you! Hey, talk about wow.

—Can you believe it?

—Sure, man, everybody can. There was never any question. I mean, come on.

—Thanks. Thanks, man, that means a lot.

—But hey, that catch! Nobody, nobody could have called that. Fucking outstanding, man.

—That was. Man, I can't, I can't describe. That just felt.

—Cool, right? It just felt cool.

—Yeah, that's it, man. It felt so fucking cool.

—Awesome, just awesome. So what now, what do you do now?

—Well, there's a thing, you know, just a huge bash all night. Come, man, you should come.

—No, man, I'd feel weird.

—No, really.

—No, I'd love to, but it's not for me, you know?

—Sure. Well, look, man, it's so fucking great to see you, man. I can't believe you're here, you look so fucking great.

—Yeah, well, clean livin', right?

—Right, man.

—Well, I better blow. But, man, it's great to see you and, man, I'm just so blown away, so happy for you, the way things worked out.

—I can't believe it. It's my life, you know, but I can't believe it.

—Right. Well, take care, man, and I'll see you around.

—You too, man. Just come around, OK? I mean, I'm really happy to see you, so come by anytime, OK?

—Sure, I'll see you soon.

And he hugs me and I watch him join the other folks leaving the room. And I think to myself, Fuck, Rich, I haven't seen him in forever. When was the last time I saw fucking Rich? And it all starts to fall into place and I remember the last time I saw Rich and I remember his face as we flipped through the air and he looked into my eyes and I know this is all a dream and this is not my life and I gasp for air, trying to make a sound, any sound. And I wake up shouting.

It's somewhere around 2:00 A.M., the nightmare has my heart pounding and my head disoriented and it takes me a few moments to sort out where I am and realize the implications of the sounds in the hallway: Someone is knocking on Russ's door.

I have an aluminum baseball bat in the closet; I've had it for most of my life. I hear the knock again. I pull on a pair of jeans and go to my door with the bat in my hands. At the door I try not to breathe as I slip open the peephole and look out. Three feet away, two men are standing in front of Russ's door. One is big in a hard-as-a-rock kind of way; the other is quite a bit smaller, but also in a hard-as-a-rock kind of way. They're both black and appear to have shaved heads, although I'm not sure about that because of the matching black cowboy hats they wear. This seems to be a theme for them. In addition to the hats, they both sport black leather vests over black T-shirts and black jeans, which I'm willing to bet lead down to black cowboy boots, but I can't tell from this angle. The smaller one nods and the larger one lifts a hand wrapped in silver rings shaped like skulls and knocks again on the door. They wait. I wait. Nothing happens. The cowboys look at each other, they both wear black wraparound sunglasses. The smaller one reaches into his vest and takes out a notepad and a pen. The big one turns and faces down the hall and the small one places the pad against the big one's back and starts to write. His fingers are covered in silver rings shaped like naked women.

I'm sweating. It's very cool in my apartment, but I'm sweating because these freaks three feet away from me are scarier than anything else that's happened today. The little one finishes writing, tears the page out, tucks the pen and pad away and turns back to the door. He slips the note into the crack between the door and the jamb, but the gap is too big and the note drops to the floor. Both he and the big one bend to pick up the note at the same time. They don't bump heads, but it's close. They both straighten and look at each other, waiting; then they bend again at the same time. This time they bump. They straighten again and stare at each other. The big one finally picks up the paper. The little one grabs the paper from the big one, pulls up a corner of the police seal on Russ's door and sticks the paper underneath. Then they leave.

I wait a half hour before I go out and read the note. It says, "Russ, just stopped by to say hello. Deeply concerned. Please call. Ed and Paris."

And the number of a cell phone. I don't touch the note, I read it as it hangs there on the door and as soon as I finish I dash back into my apartment. I have a feeling that these guys aren't really deeply concerned about Russ at all.

* * *

I'm drunk. I'm at Paul's and I'm drunk and I'm not sure how I got here. It had something to do with cowboys and being scared. I know I've done something stupid, several somethings stupid, but one big thing in particular. I'm just not sure what it is.

Edwin is working the bar. Wait, that's wrong, I'm the bartender, I should be back there. I stumble off my stool and try to circle around the bar and someone takes me by the arm and sets me back down. It's Yvonne. She's telling me to take it easy and putting a glass in front of me. I take a drink. It's water.

—What the fuck? What the fuck's with the water? Yo, Edwin, let's have a beer.

Edwin ambles over (he does that, he really ambles) and plops a Bud down in front of me. I take a pull and nothing comes out. I take a look at the bottle. The cap is still on.

—Yo, Edwin. The cap. Pull my cap.

—Get that cap off and you can drink that beer.

I wag my finger at him. That Edwin, he's a crafty fucker. There's something in my hand; it's a beer. I try to take a drink, but the cap is still on. I twist the cap and it doesn't pop off. I put the lip of the cap on the edge of the bar and give it a good rap with my fist. I rake my knuckles across the bar and the bottle pops out of my hand onto the floor, spritzing beer. I stuff my bleeding knuckles into my mouth.

—Yo, Edwin, I need another brew here.

—Yvonne, can you put a lid on him?

—Who the fuck are you calling Yvonne? Let's have a beer, huh?

I feel something against my feet. I look down and Yvonne is leaning down, cleaning up a beer some numb-nuts has spilled on the floor. Fuck, that pisses me off. I bend to help her and slide off my stool and someone catches me before I bite it. It's Amtrak John.

—Amtrak John, thanks for the save, man.

—Sure.

—You're a big motherfucker, Amtrak.

—Yep.

—Big fucker.

—Yep.

—Wanna fight?

—Sit here.

I'm on my stool and Edwin is passing me a glass. He gives it to me with his right hand, the one with RUFF tattooed across the knuckles in ink blacker than his skin; the other hand reads TUFF. I laugh as I drink the water and most of it sprays.

—You're a funny fucker, Edwin. A fun-ny fuck-er!

—Thanks, man.

—Those fucking tattoos, man. Fun-ny!

—Thanks.

—Ya wanna fight?

—Nope.

—Shit. Nobody wants ta fight. What's with that?

I lift my head from the bar. The bar is empty and all the lights are on. Edwin is stacking stools. I get off mine and start to help him. He looks at me.

—Take it easy, man, I've got it.

—It's cool, I'll help, I can help.

—Just chill. Sit still.

   I've got a jacket. I'm not sure if it's mine, but it fits.

—Edwin, this my jacket?

—Yeah, that's it. Just hang on and me an' Yvonne will get ya home.

—Is Yvonne here? When'd she get here?

Yvonne is holding my hand. We're on the curb. Edwin has just climbed into a cab and taken off and now Yvonne is trying to get me into a cab.

—Come on, I'll take you home. You can stay over; I'll make some breakfast.

—Naw, I'm gonna walk.

—Then I'll walk with you till you get home.

Yvonne is such a sweet girl. She loves to look after me, but she just doesn't realize I'm not safe to be around. I mean really, who knows what's waiting for me at home?

—Nah, nah, I'll just walk. I gotta call Rome.

—You gotta call Rome?

—Roman, I gotta call Ro-man. About the fucking cowboys.

—Jesus, are you betting football? I thought you hated football.

—Football is a bitch's sport. Baseball, that's a fucking game. That's a sport.

—Come on, get in the cab.

—Nah, gonna walk home.

—Then I'm coming with you.

—Nah. Gonna walk alone. Safer that way for you.

—I don't need you to fucking protect me from myself, for chrissake. Fucking go home alone. Fucking get home safe, will you.

I'm walking home. It's tricky. I push off with my right foot and drift for a moment, balancing on my left. I swing my right foot out in front of myself and lurch down onto it with a jolt. Then I push off with my left and repeat the process. The walk around the block from Paul's to my building is revealed in snapshots, a picture taken every time I plop down on my front foot. I stutter home and it feels like the very early morning darkness is illuminated by strobe light. I have a picture of my key in my hand, a picture of flipping a light switch, a picture of struggling out of my jacket and a picture of collapsing into bed. And no dreams at all.

I wake up just a few hours later and I feel wrong. I'm not sure where or who or what I am. Bud is meowing up a storm. I look over the edge of the bed and am pleased to see I didn't throw up on the floor in the middle of the night. I'm wearing all my clothes and the lights are on and something about my pants and the way they fit is off. I don't need to look. I can feel it. I've pissed myself in my sleep. I've pissed myself and crapped myself.

I try to get up without sitting. I try to roll off the bed because I don't want to sit in the crap in my pants. I roll off and stand. I'm half-drunk and half-hungover. My stomach is a pile of nausea and my head feels like it's floating painfully a foot above my shoulders. I stumble to the shower and get in with my clothes on. I run the water hot and strip off my filthy pants and underwear. I push my clothes into a pile in a corner of the shower and clean myself in the scalding water. Then I turn the water to cold and stand in the icy blast as long as I can. Shivering badly from the booze and the cold, I towel off. Bud is still making a racket while I dress in clean jeans and a sweatshirt. The blankets on my bed are untouched, but the sheets are urine stained. I strip them off. I bundle the sheets into a black plastic garbage bag and stuff my dirty clothes on top. I pull on some sneakers and limp painfully downstairs to the street.

Outside I dump the bag of filth on the curb with the rest of the garbage. I stand hunched against the bright morning sun and the alien feel of my body. I look around and Jason is standing a few feet away, leaning against a wall mumbling to himself. And the shame I feel overwhelms me. I have no reason, no right, to do this to myself. Life has been good to me. Life has been good to me. I say it out loud:

—Life has been good to me.

I know it's true, but I don't believe it. I look at New York. I don't want to be here anymore, in this city. I'm just tired of it, I'm tired of my life here. I want to go home, and I'm not sure how to do that.

I go to breakfast. I go to the diner and order bacon and eggs and lots of water and OJ. My kidney, the one still there, aches in a hot, swollen way, but I don't know what to do about it. The missing kidney just hurts in an open wound sort of way. I woke too early and now I'm getting the best of both worlds: the nasty end of my drunk and the leading edge of the hangover. Nothing seems quite real; it's all fogged over and I'm having trouble putting last night back together. My food comes and, as I eat, I try to figure it all out.

I panicked. I was very scared and wanted out of my apartment and I ran to Paul's just a block away. I smoked a joint in the can with someone and at some point I just went ahead and had the first drink. But first I talked with Edwin. We talked about the job, but I also asked him a favor. Did I ask him for a loan? No. Did I ask for help finding another job? No. He's doing something for me. I feel in the pockets of my jacket for clues and come up with Detective Roman's card.

Did I call him last night after the cowboys left? Did I tell him about the note? Fuck, was the note still there this morning? I can't remember. I'll have to call him. Fuck, I'll have to call him and tell him I can't remember if I called him last night. That should do wonders for my credibility. Fuck it, I'm gonna call him, I'm gonna call him and tell him about the cowboys and the key and just get this the fuck over with. But first I'm gonna go home and feed Bud because I just realized that's what the little shit was making all the noise about. On my way out I see a paper on the counter flipped open to the box scores. The Giants took another one from Colorado, and New York choked in extra innings. One back, three to go. And as sad as it sounds, that makes me feel better.

When I turn the corner onto my block, I freak out. Down the street, just past my door, two guys are fucking with Jason. The hangover is so bad, everything about my body feels detached and my brain has given the whole day a wash of unreality, but seeing these two cretins pushing Jason around sends a blast of adrenaline into my veins. I pick up my pace and start toward them. As I get closer, I break into a little trot and all I want to do is fling my body onto these guys. I hate cruelty. I hate brutishness. Jason is as helpless as they come and I'm gonna fucking disassemble these dickweeds.

I know I should have a strategy, but I don't. I'm seeing red and any rationality I might usually possess is strangled by the hangover and my rage. I see a bottle on the sidewalk ahead of me. When I get there, I will pick up the bottle and smash it across the backs of their heads in a single brutal swipe. I have a vision: I see the first one's skull dent a little as the bottle smashes down, the scalp tearing as I sweep it across at his friend's head, the jagged rim of the broken bottle lodging in the fat head-skin and ear of the second one. So much for strategy.

I am almost to my door. They are a few yards beyond. They are so engrossed in bouncing Jason off the wall that they have no idea I am almost upon them. I shove my hand in my pocket and dig out my keys, open the door of my building and dodge inside.

They have traded the tracksuits in for baggy jeans and Tommy Hilfiger jackets, but it was them. The Russians.

I don't care about Jason anymore. I care about me. I head down the hall to the foot of the stairs and pause to listen. I don't hear anything coming from my hallway on the third floor, so I start up. At the landing to my floor, I stop to listen again. My breath is heaving in and out and my heart is knocking against my swollen brain, but I don't think I hear anything. I step into the hall. All clear. I move as quietly as I can to Russ's door. The note from Ed and Paris has been torn off, leaving a little corner of paper trapped in the police seal. I try to steady my breathing and listen very closely at his door. Nothing. Relaxing a bit more, I hear someone cough behind me in my apartment.

I start to head back down to the street to get to a pay phone and I remember the creeps outside. I think about Carlos, the super, but he has a day job and won't be home. I think about the three cool Welsh girls down the hall who keep a spare key for me in case I lose mine, but I don't want to get them involved, so instead I head back to the roof. I run up the stairs and everything is drenched in déjà vu. I could swear I just went through this. The hangover makes the confusion worse. My body still feels like someone else's, like my bones and skin are detached from anything they actually do or feel.

I dash out onto the roof and trip over the bag of laundry I left here yesterday. I curse. The rest is old hat. I assure myself the door won't be blown shut this time and head for the front of the building. I crawl up to the edge and look down. The Russians have left Jason alone and taken up their spot in front of the tattoo parlor.

This is stupid. I cannot afford to be stupid. The people in this building know me because of the work I did with Carlos and because I'm a nice guy. I have lived here for ten years and am well known and trusted. I will go down to the top floor and start knocking on doors until I find someone home. I will explain through the door that my apartment is being broken into and ask to use the phone. If they refuse to let me in, I will read Detective Roman's number from the card in my pocket and ask them to please call him quickly. I will repeat this process until I achieve success. One of the Russians looks up from the street and straight at me.

I duck. That is, I drop to my belly and squirm back from the edge of the roof. He didn't see me. He could not have seen me. I repeat this to myself for a while until I get my nerve back. I worm up to the edge and peek over the ledge. He didn't see me. They are both as before: Black Hilfiger with White Trim and White Hilfiger with Black Trim, not looking up at the top of my building, pointing at me and hustling across the street. All is well.

Someone grabs me by the ankles and yanks me backward. My hands slip out from underneath me and my face lands in the grit of the rooftop. My staples scream and so do I.

My apartment is small to start with and has been made claustrophobic by the sheer number of toughguys milling about. The Russians are in the tiny kitchen area. Whitey poking in the fridge and Blackie on the cell phone he used to call the guys in the apartment to tell them there was someone on the roof. The huge guy, who looks Samoan rather than Latino and who wears black leather pants and a motorcycle jacket, is using my crapper and I'm hoping he lights a match when he's done because he's been in there for a long time. There's the skinny redheaded Chinese kid in plaid pants, a green polyester disco shirt, and a red vinyl jacket that matches his hair. And then there's the guy in the black suit. He's the scariest one of all because I know his name.

Detective Lieutenant Roman.

The Samoan was the one who grabbed me on the roof. He took me on a ride through the gravel for about ten feet, then he twisted my legs around each other so I flopped over on my back. He's much bigger than the Russians and his hands are dinner plates. He dropped my legs, bent over, grabbed my belt and lifted me to my feet. Then he wrapped one of those hands around my throat and put a finger to his lips.

—Shhhhhhhh.

Then he marched me down here and dropped me on the couch and I held very still and tried not to think about the oozing I could feel coming from my wound. I'm scared shitless. Then I hear Bud.

I can't see Bud, I can just hear him. He's somewhere over in the bedroom and every so often he makes a weak, plaintive meow, the kind of sound I would make if I were a cat in a great deal of pain. I seem to be the only one in the place worried about this, and why not? These other guys are clearly assholes.

Roman has been checking me out this whole time in much the same way he did when I thought he was just your basic supercop rather than your basic supercop gone rotten to the core. Now he sits down in the same chair he used yesterday, picks up a slip of paper from my coffee table and holds it in front of my face. It's the note from Ed and Paris, the two cowboys. I can tell he's going to start asking questions and I'm just praying to Jesus that I know the answers so I can tell him every fucking thing he wants to hear.

—When were they here?

He is clearly referring to the guys who left the note. I am composing an answer, trying to determine what time exactly I woke from the nightmare and what comes out is:

—What did you do to the cat?

I really don't fucking want to say this, but all I can hear is the pathetic sounds Bud is making in the bedroom. The Russians are paying no attention to the drama taking place a few feet away. Whitey has found some cold cuts and now appears to be looking for bread, Blackie is deep in conversation on the phone, speaking what I would definitely now bet is Russian. The Samoan tower is still out of action. So that leaves Red and Roman to look sharply at each other when I ask about the cat.

—Don't worry about the cat. The cat is fine. Right now you need to tell me when the men who left this note were here.

—The cat is not fine. I can hear the cat and that is not the sound of a fine cat. That cat is fucked up and I want to know what you did to it.

Red and Roman look at each other in a way that screams, "So it's gonna be like this, is it?" Red sits on the couch next to me and I try to scoot away, but I'm already pressed against the armrest. He just sits there while I stare at him and cringe a little. Roman shakes the paper so it makes a soft rattle.

—What time were these men here?

Bud is probably under my bed. If they hurt him, there are only so many places to hide. So he's under my bed and he's hurt and scared and hungry because I didn't feed him this morning because I was too messed up. I suck.

—What time?

If I could see Bud and see how bad he is, I think I could concentrate to answer. I really want to answer. But as it is, I just keep picturing the poor bastard under the bed. Red slowly reaches out his fist until it is inches from my nose. It hovers there hypnotically for just a moment, then he pops it into my face. The cartilage in my nose gives a crack, blood pours across my mouth and tears flood my eyes. I snap out of it.

—Last night. I think two or so. But I was asleep. I got drunk. I'm not sure.

I'm cupping a hand under my nose, trying to catch the blood. Red puts a hand on my forehead and pushes my head back against the couch. Roman says something in pretty good sounding Russian and Blackie, still on his phone, comes in from the kitchen with a dishcloth and stuffs it in my hand. I put the cloth to my nose and try to slow the blood. I'm thinking to myself that this is just starting. Right now, this is just starting.

Roman asks a few more questions about the cowboys and I tell him everything I can and things seem to be going swimmingly. Red fetches some ice from the freezer for my nose, to keep it from swelling up like a squishy tomato. Whitey finds the bread and is feasting quietly on an enormous Dagwood in the kitchen while Blackie carries on with the phone. The Samoan remains behind locked doors. Roman calmly asks very precise questions. And Bud keeps getting quieter and quieter. Then Roman asks the only question that really matters.

—Where is Miner?

And I just don't have a suitable answer to that question.

—We really need to find Mr. Miner.

—And I really, really wish I could help you guys out. I mean, you have no idea how much, but I just don't fucking know.

Roman leans back in his chair and closes his eyes. He rubs at his forehead like he has this massive pain shooting through his brain. With his eyes still closed, he starts to talk.

—There is an object, something valuable. The ownership of this object is in some dispute. Be that as it may, these men and I can rightfully lay claim to this object, and we intend to do so. We have formed a profit-sharing enterprise, but if we do not find the object, there will be no profits to share. And I assure you, these men value nothing so highly as profit. Therefore, they are inspired in this situation to use means and go to lengths they might not otherwise. This is the nature of motivation. The object in question was last known to be in the possession of Mr. Miner. Now, in a moment, I will ask you a question regarding Mr. Miner and no matter your answer, it is essential that I be certain you are telling the truth. If there is any doubt in my mind, I will allow these men to do with you as they wish until that doubt no longer exists.

Which, I suppose, is one way of saying, "Tell us what we want to know or we're going to kick your ass."

—Where is Mr. Miner?

And as truthfully and sincerely as I possibly can, I answer.

—I don't know.

Roman's eyes remain closed. He sighs a little.

—But he left a key taped to the inside of the cat's carry box, if that's what you're looking for.

And Detective Lieutenant Roman opens his eyes right up.

I have a secret. I have a secret these guys know nothing about. I have a dirty sock stuffed in my mouth to keep my screams from shattering the whole building, but I also have a secret.

I told them where the key was and they looked in the box and just as I was getting ready for my life to get normal again, Red, who was looking in the box, popped his head out with a frown.

—No key.

And those two words revolved around and around in my head. They meant something, but I wasn't sure what. So they just kept plowing through the smog of my hangover, looking for a place to land while my apartment got quieter and everybody could hear Red say, again:

—No key.

And that's how I end up facedown on my bed with a mouth full of sock and Red sitting on my legs, pulling out my staples one by one with the needle-nose pliers they found in the toolbox under my sink. And I have a secret. The secret is, I don't know where the key is. So these guys can do whatever they want and I just won't talk. Because I have nothing to say. Lucky me.

I'm having trouble breathing. I have the sock in my mouth and my nose is clogged with blood, so I'm having trouble breathing. The bad guys seem to be aware of this, so they have developed a system. The way it works is, while they're actually hurting me they leave the sock in to muffle the screaming, and when they ask a question they take it out so I can answer. Every time the sock comes out, I gasp a bit to get as much air as possible before I tell them I don't know anything and they stuff it back in and I start to suffocate again.

I've got about fifty or so staples. The first few they yanked out real quick, without asking any questions at all, just so I'd get the idea, I suppose. Now, they're getting serious about it. Red sits on my legs to keep them from thrashing around and digs the tips of the pliers into my wound until he gets a good grip on one of the staples, then he starts to pull on it, slowly. The Russians have my arms pinned down, stretched straight out from my shoulders to either side of the mattress. Whitey has the right and Blackie the left. They feel like they might pop out of their sockets at any moment. I know Roman is standing near the bed off to my left, because that's where his voice comes from every time he asks another question I don't know the answer to. The Samoan has yet to make himself known to me, so I assume he's still on his own clogging up my toilet. Bud is definitely under the bed; I know this because every time I scream through the sock, he starts to yowl along with me.

They started with the easy questions.

—Where's the key?

To which I mostly spluttered.

—But I left it right there, it was right there. I don't know what could have happened to it.

Then the questions start getting a little weird.

—What is the key for?

The sock comes out.

—Gasp! Gasp! Gasp! What? Gasp! What is the key for? Gasp!

Roman pauses for a moment and I'm expecting the sock to come back, but it doesn't.

—What is the key for, what does it open?

What the fuck?

—Gasp! How the. Gasp! How the fuck should I. Gasp! Know? It's *your* fucking key. Gasp! Your fucking *object*.

This is not a state-approved answer. The sock is stuffed in my mouth. I'm in the middle of drawing in a lungful of air and the sock cuts it off. I get sock fluff lodged in my throat and I start to choke. I feel like I might vomit. I don't want to vomit. Please, God, don't let me vomit. Please, God, I don't, I just don't want this. Please make this stop. Please. Red gets a grip on the next staple and starts to tug. The original wound was sharply defined, a pain that had carefully designated borders. As Red pulls at the staple, I feel the wound stretch. The original pain is distorted and twisted and a new pain, more crude, takes its place. Just as the flesh around the staple starts to tear, I feel a pop and the wound snaps back.

The Beach Boys' *Pet Sounds* has always been one of my favorite albums. When the Russians grabbed me and started dragging me toward the bed, I made a bit of a scuffle. To help cover the noise, someone, Red I think, put on a CD: *Pet Sounds*. I don't know if this represents personal taste or if it was simply at the top of the stack. In any case it was a really good idea on their part, because even with the sock in my mouth, I'm making a fuck of a lot of noise, but then I guess it should come as no surprise that these guys know their business.

The sock comes out and I vomit onto my pillow.

—What is the key for?

I'm coughing quite a bit now, trying to spit up the puke and breathe at the same time, but I manage to give him an answer.

—I don't. Gasp! Choke! I don't know. I don't know. Choke!

—What did Miner tell you about the key?

—Nothing, he didn't say. Gasp! He didn't say. Choke! Nothing about the key. I don't know about the key.

—You knew where it was.

—Gasp! Accident. I found it by accident.

I get the sock again. Red is having trouble getting at the next staple, he's really digging in. The pain is making me even more nauseous than I was with just the hangover and I think I may vomit again. Please, please, God. My throat is clenching and hitching and the blood in my nose is running back in. The coppery taste of the blood is blending with the bile of the puke. Please. Oh, God, please. The staple gives way and I scream again. They yank the sock and I spill out another flood of puke, this one tinted pink with blood.

—What did he tell you when he asked you to hide the key?

I can't talk, I just can't. I heave and blubber and beg and Roman sticks the puke-and-blood-soaked sock back in my mouth and Red hurts me again and I realize then that they are going to kill me just as soon as they can.

Roman is a cop. Despite what you may have heard, the behavior he is now engaged in, not even an officer of the NYPD can get away with. They will finish asking questions and, when I have no more to offer, they will kill me. And, having had this realization, I start trying very hard to think as clearly as I can, because I don't want to die.

—What did he tell you about the key?

—Gasp! Gasp! He. Didn't. Tell. Me. Anything. Gasp! About. The. Key.

—Why did he give you the key?

—He. He. Gasp! He didn't give me the key.

—Why did you say you had the key?

—He. Fuck. He gave me the. Gasp! The cat. The key was in its box. I didn't know. He didn't give me the key. Gasp! He stuck me with it. I didn't know.

—What is the key for?

Think. Think. I don't want to die. I need to think. I'm trying to think of ways not to die, but the pain and the hangover keep getting in my way and I can't keep my thoughts together in one place long enough to make them work for me. I try to keep answering the questions without saying something that will make me dead.

—I don't know.

—What does it look like?

—I didn't see it.

I get the sock and another staple goes. I think I black out for a couple seconds, I can't really tell for sure.

—How do you know there was a key if you didn't see it?

—It. Gasp! It was in an envelope. Gasp! I felt it. It felt like a key. Gasp! It felt like a lumpy key. Big. Lumpy.

—Where is the key now?

Fuck!

—I. Don't. Know. I just don't.

And the sock. And another staple.

—We did not come here looking for a key, but if Mr. Miner gave you a key, then we want it. Where is the key?

—Gasp! I just. Fuck! Gasp! I just don't know. I put it back in the box yesterday. Gasp! And last night after those guys were here, I got drunk. Choke! I got real fucking drunk. I fucking blacked out. I fucking shit my pants, for God sake. I don't know where it is now. I left it in the box.

The sock. A staple.

—Where is the key?

I say nothing. I try to get as much air as I can. I breathe. I try to figure out a way to live. And Roman says something odd:

—Chew the fat.

I have no idea what that's about until Blackie releases my arm and starts scrabbling under the bed and I hear Bud crying. Then I realize he meant to say, "Get the cat."

In all fairness, he probably did say "Get the cat" and I only heard "Chew the fat." Bud is giving Blackie hell under the bed and the bastard is grunting and cursing in Russian. My left arm is free now, but the circulation is all messed up and it hurts so bad that I can barely move it. Not that I'd know what to do with it if I could move it, but it's nice not to have someone pulling at it for the moment.

—Man, just. Gasp! Just leave the cat. Just leave it alone. Gasp! Don't hurt the fucking cat.

Aren't there rules about this kind of thing? I mean, there are rules, right? You can do whatever you want to people, but you don't hurt fucking animals.

As if on cue, the toilet flushes, the door to the bathroom opens and the Samoan returns. Enter the torturer of animals.

—Sorry, guys, I had ta drop a deuce. Hey, you got air freshener or what?

Sooner or later, even the most profound events of your life are reduced to concerns like this.

—Under the sink.

—I looked there.

—The kitchen. Not the bathroom sink, the kitchen sink.

—Fuck you, who keeps freshener under the kitchen sink?

—I do.

—What, your shit doesn't stink? You don't need no freshener in the bathroom?

Meanwhile, Blackie has got hold of Bud and is dragging him out of his hiding place, but the fur is flying. Bud comes into the light of day howling and clawing at Blackie's eyes. As the Russian stands upright, I get my first look at Bud. He's writhing this way and that, trying to get a piece of someone, but his left leg is twisted up real weird and he's not moving it at all.

—What the fuck? What, man, what did you do to the cat?

Suddenly the Samoan reaches over and grabs Bud. He wraps those huge hands around the struggling cat and locks him up. Bud's legs are all trapped, just his head sticks out of the Samoan's grasp. And then Blackie hits him, the fucker makes a little fist out of his little hand and hits Bud in the face.

—I kicked this shit cat, this fucking shit cat I fucking kicked. This fucking shit cat, I tried to pet and it fucking bit me and I fucking kicked the shit cat. So fuck you, Mr. Bartender, can't make a fucking cosmopolitan. Mr. Fucking Shitty Drink Maker with the Shitty Cat.

He punches Bud again. They get the sock back in my mouth before I can finish screaming at Blackie.

My head is clearing. The few minutes I had to breathe helped and the adrenaline has cut some of the haze and I'm starting to think a little more clearly. They want the key. I don't know where the key is. As soon as they feel sure I don't know where the key is, they will kill me. If I did know where the key was and I told them, they would get the key and then kill me. I have no idea what to do. Done battering the cat, Blackie gets a fresh grip on my left arm and stretches it back out.

Roman twists my head to the left so I can get a good look at the Samoan and whatever he's gonna do to Bud. Red is still on my legs and he resettles himself, getting comfortable for the next round. Roman is getting cute.

—If you were the key and you had mysteriously disappeared, where would you be?

The sock is still in my mouth, but I grunt so he knows I'm following him.

—Where would you hide if you were a key?

Breathing is starting to be a problem again.

—Would you hide in this apartment?

Bud now has a scrape on the side of his face where he was hit. I can't really tell if he's awake or not. The Samoan tucks the cat into his left armpit, keeping all his limbs pinned except for the broken left leg.

—Would you put yourself in an envelope and send yourself somewhere?

Very gently, the Samoan has taken hold of Bud's injured leg. He extends it until it's fairly straight. I can see the little bend where the bone is broken. I can hear Bud give a mew of protest, but he's clearly run out of fight.

—If you were a key that wanted to hide itself, would you give yourself to a friend for safekeeping?

The Samoan starts to twist Bud's broken leg. He twirls it around and I can see the loose skin bunch up on itself at the break. Bud comes back to life for a moment, yowling and trying to wrestle free, but the Samoan has him pinned tight. A thin stream of urine is leaking out from under the Samoan's arm, but he doesn't notice or care. Bud is shaking now and probably going into shock and dying. I'm jerking around on the bed, but I can only move a couple inches in any direction and the boys dig in and hold me tighter. Black speckles are filling the corners of my eyes and that's OK because I really don't want to see what it looks like when the Samoan gives Bud's leg another twist. If I were a key, where would I hide? I guess I would hide with a friend, yes, that sounds like me. Fuck, yes! I start screaming it.

—I took it to the bar! I took the fucking key to the bar! I gave the key to Edwin to put in the safe! The key is in the safe at the bar!

They pull out the sock so they can understand what I'm saying.

—On the roof, the key. Gasp! It's on the roof. Gasp!

There is a pause. I breathe.

—Where on the roof?

—My. Gasp! My laundry bag is up there. Gasp! I did, I did my laundry yesterday. I. Gasp!

—Why is it with your laundry?

—I put it, I put the key in my pocket when I found it. And. Gasp! Later I did the laundry and I washed those pants. Gasp! It's. It's gotta be on the roof. I left it there.

—Why on the roof?

—Yesterday. When I saw you guys yesterday and I went to the roof. Gasp! I had it with me. I left it there. I forgot about it.

The Samoan still has hold of Bud's leg, but he's not twisting it anymore. Roman lets go of my head and I breathe and breathe. He turns to the Samoan.

—Go check.

The Samoan drops Bud. Just lets him flop to the floor into the little puddle of cat pee. Bud lies there, like me, and breathes. The Samoan is heading out the door.

—There's a lock.

Roman looks at me.

—Where?

—The door to the roof has one of those push-button lock things.

—And?

—Three-nine-eight-nine-two.

Roman looks at the Samoan to make sure he's got it and the Samoan nods once and goes out the door. Roman drifts into the living room and this seems to indicate a time-out. The Russians let go of my arms and light cigarettes and Red climbs off my legs and walks around, stretching his own. I watch Bud. He doesn't look very good.

A couple minutes pass.

That's when the Samoan pushes in the wrong combination for the door to the roof, tries to force it open, and sets off the fire alarm for the building.

Things go about as well as you could hope for I suppose. Roman looks at me. He just stares into my swollen eyes as he tells Red and the Russians to get out. They leave just as the Samoan is coming back down the stairs and, over the alarm, I can hear them shouting at him to get out. I can hear people starting to drift out into the hall as Roman pushes my door closed and comes back over to the bed. He is careful not to step on Bud, which I appreciate. He sits on the edge of the bed. I can move a bit, so I roll onto my right side to look at him. Everything hurts. People are talking in the halls, but no one seems to be evacuating the building. This is the nature of New York City: alarms go off so often that no one wants to respond to them until things start burning down or blowing up in front of their eyes. Nonetheless, the NYFD should be here in a moment and that gives me comfort. Roman rubs the back of his neck.

—Is it up there, the key?

I would like to smile at him enigmatically. I would like to rip off some cunning bon mot or scintillating repartee. I settle for spitting up some blood.

—If you know where either the key or Mr. Miner is, you should really tell me now.

I look at Bud. He's a mess. I look back at Roman and keep my mouth shut. He gets off the bed and heads for the door. He opens the door and takes a last look around the apartment like he's reliving fond memories from his wistful youth of bygone days.

—I really do need that key. So get it and call me or I'm going to start hurting your friends. Don't call the police. It won't help. I know everyone. Good-bye.

And he waves as he goes out, the door swinging shut behind him.

The alarm turns off, which means the fire guys must be out there now. I could yell. I could yell for help and they would come and take me and Bud to a hospital and make us better. And then someone would ask questions and someone would call the cops and I won't know who to trust. I need to get up and help Bud. And I will in just a second. The phone rings. I let the machine pick it up.

—Hey, it's your mom. Are you there? OK, I just called to say hi and check up on you. We didn't hear from you yesterday when you got home from the hospital. . . . Anyway, give us a call when you get in so we know you're all right. Dad's at a soccer game today, but I'll be around. Oh, did you get a package? I sent a care package with some stuff to make you feel better while you rest. Just stupid stuff, but let me know when it shows up so I don't worry about it. OK, we miss you, can't wait to see you at Christmas. We love you. Call soon.

I miss you, too, Ma.

Mom and Dad still live in the house I grew up in. Mom is the principal at a continuation school, and Dad has a little garage and spends his days working on specialty cars. I love going back to visit. And I always go home for Christmas. I get my ticket a couple months early because it's cheaper. The ticket is in my desk drawer right now, and I'm gonna use it to get the fuck out of here.

I get off the bed and everything hurts. My legs are stiff and asleep, my arms and shoulders are sore and feel unnaturally heavy. My nose pulses hotly with every beat of my heart. The flesh around my wound feels grated. I stand and I can feel blood running down my side, into the waistband of my jeans. I limp over to Bud.

He's breathing very rapidly and shallowly and his broken leg is still twisted around. I bend over stiffly and, with as much care as possible, I try to untangle his limb. He jerks a bit and makes a slight sound but remains unconscious, which I take as a very bad fucking sign. I leave him on the floor for now and head to the bathroom. On the way, I remember something and grab the air freshener from under the kitchen sink before I go in. Good call; it reeks in here.

I can't get my shirt off over my head, so I take the scissors from the medicine cabinet and cut it off. They ripped out about nine staples and left a tear in my side just above my left hip. I drench a towel in hydrogen peroxide and use it to clean the hole. It's bleeding, but the bulk of the stapling is intact. I get a huge wad of gauze and use it to cover the bad stuff. I have to get some electrician's tape out of my toolbox to hold the bandage in place.

My nose is a real mess. I clean up all the goop to get a good look. It's bright red, squashed, and bent to the left, but it has stopped bleeding. I touch it gingerly with my fingertips until I get a sense of how it has been broken and what belongs where and then I give it a rasping twist and a yank.

—Mother! Fucker!

It gives a little crackle and starts to bleed again. I tilt my head back and stuff some more gauze into the nostrils and that's about all the time I figure I have for first aid.

The fire department has left the building and I have no idea how soon Roman and Co. might return, so it's time to go. Bud hasn't moved, but he's still breathing. I get an athletic bag from the closet. I grab some clothes, my plane ticket, my ID, keys, credit cards, about a grand in cash tips from the bar. I stuff it all in the bag. Then I put in a couple towels, molding them to create a little hollow. I could put Bud in his case, but I'm afraid he'll bounce around in there. I pick him up and tuck him snugly into the little nest of towels and zip the bag about halfway. I have him on his back so the broken leg won't fold up underneath his body and it's easy to imagine he's sleeping peacefully, but he's not. I have to get out of here.

I get a cab right away and sit in there with my head back against the seat until the driver snaps me out of it.

—Where to? This is not a taxi for sleeping in, it is for driving in. Where to?

Which is a great fucking question, I suppose.

I give the driver an address across town just off the West Side High-way. I can't get on a plane yet. I need to get cleaned up, I need to think.

I pass out.

I met Yvonne right after she showed up in New York about six years ago. She was hanging out at Paul's and mentioned she needed a job. Edwin put her to work. She was a few years younger than me, twenty-two at the time, and we hit it off because we were both from California. But she had a boyfriend, so I backed off. One night, I was working and she came in, her boyfriend had just dumped her. She stayed till closing and took me home.

She's an artist, a sculptress. She uses ceramics, old rusted iron, bits of antique wood, and assorted trash to make dollhouses. She popu-lates the houses with handmade glass figures shaped to look like people from her own life or books or TV or movies or whatever. Some-times she sells them, sometimes she breaks them up and uses them in new pieces and sometimes she sets them on fire, takes a picture of that and sells the picture. I have two of her houses in my apartment and last year I gave another one to Mom for Christmas. I think they're pretty cool. I think Yvonne is pretty cool. I'm just not in love with her. Which would be fine if I didn't know she was in love with me. We car-ried on for quite a while, but I cut it off in the end. Mostly.

I wake up and the cabbie is pulling my arm and shouting at me:

—Not for sleeping in. You are here now, so you must pay. Pay and get out. Stop sleeping and get out.

We're parked in front of Yvonne's building. I shake the cabbie off, give him some cash, get my bag and step onto the curb. The cabbie doesn't even wait for me to close the door, he just peels out and crams his taxi into the never-ending stream of cars sweeping past. I stand there for a moment, collecting myself. My side feels damp and the throb in my nose is worse than ever. Plus, the hangover still has my head wrapped in Jell-O. I try to buzz Yvonne, but there's no answer.

She still has my key and I still have hers. I open the door and start up the stairs. She has a small loft on the sixth floor that doubles as her apartment and studio. I climb the steps a half flight at a time. Bud continues to breathe.

I get to the top floor and slump against the wall. I'm losing it. I support myself against the wall and walk–stumble to Yvonne's door. It takes a while to work out the keys and, while I'm tinkering with the lock, the door opens and Yvonne is standing there still wet from the shower, wearing a robe, her hair up in a towel. She looks great. When she gets a look at me, she gives a little gasp and puts her hand over her mouth. One of the clumps of gauze falls from my nose and a stream of blood dribbles out. I smile apologetically.

—Someone hurt my cat.

And. I. Black. Out.

PART TWO

SEPTEMBER 29, 2000

Three Regular Season Games Remaining

—Henry. Henry. Hen, wake up for just a sec, OK?

Henry, that's me. Henry.

—Hen, doll, I have to go to work, OK? Are you with me, doll?

Henry is my name and baseball is my game. Was. Is? What the fuck?

—Henry, please, just for a sec, OK?

Henry, that's me, but most people call me Hank. My mom, my mom calls me Henry.

—Ma?

—Henry, just open your eyes a sec, OK?

My eyes peel open. They feel gummy. It's dark. The room is dark and through the corner of the window I can see it's dark outside. It's dark out. It's night. When is it? Where am I? I feel gummy. Every fucking thing feels gummy.

—Ma?

—No, Hen, it's me.

Me? Well, that's a big fucking . . .

—Yvonne.

—Yeah, babe. How ya feelin', doll?

—Gummy.

She giggles, she actually giggles.

—Good, gummy is good.

—Crummy. I don't feel gummy, I feel crummy.

I'm in a bed on my stomach and my body feels far away. She's stroking the back of my head. I want to roll over and look at her, I want to ask her questions about things I don't really remember, but I can't. I just can't seem to move and my eyes keep falling shut.

—Hen, I have to go out for a while. I'm leaving water and the phone right here and a note in case you forget where to call me, OK?

—Yeah, right.

—Henry?

—Yeah?

—What did I just say?

Oh, fuck, a quiz.

—Henry!

—What?

—What did I say?

—Water, note, call you.

—I'll be back late, so just sleep, OK?

—No problem.

I feel her get up off the bed. I hear her grabbing keys and her bag. I hear the front door open and close and I hear her locking up. Then I hear her walking away down the hall.

I drift.

I wake.

I drift.

Henry, that's me. I'm at Yvonne's. She's at work. I'm supposed to sleep. No problem. Sandbags fall on my head. I shake them off.

—Hey, baby, how's Bud?

But no one is there to answer.

I wake up curled on my right side. The bed seems harder than it should be and that's because it's a futon instead of my mattress. There's a morning kind of light coming in through the shades, a small digital clock next to the futon reads 11:48 A.M. Next to the clock is a phone and, leaning against that, is a note:

Hen, I had to go to work. Sorry. Try to sleep and don't move around. I took care of everything I could. I'll be back in the morning sometime early. Call me at the bar if you need me. Y.

Well, it's morning now. And that's when I realize that the warm thing curled against my back must be Yvonne and the smaller warm thing curled against my stomach is Bud.

He's asleep. His left front leg is stuck straight out from his body, wrapped in a hard cast. Some of the hair on his head has been shaved away and he has a few stitches and a big scab on his snout. He breathes slowly and regularly, and when I shift, he moves a little to press his body against mine. I look over my left shoulder at Yvonne, who is pressed against my back. She's not under the covers and all she's wearing is an oversize Knicks jersey. Number thirty-three, Patrick Ewing. She loves that guy, cried the day the Knicks traded him.

I try to twist around to face her and the sudden flame in my side serves as a reminder that I was busy being tortured about twenty-four hours ago. I gasp at the burst of pain and tears spill out of my eyes. Yvonne's eyes flip open and she gives me a grim little smile.

—Morning, sleepyhead. Ready for a doctor?

After I blacked out, she got me inside and tried to call 911. Apparently, I managed to convince her that was a bad idea and she did the best job she could rebandaging me. She took Bud to a vet with emergency service, left him, and came home to check on me, but all I did was sleep. Eventually she went to work, and when she came home early this morning, she was able to pick up Bud. She told the vet Bud was hit by a car; he told her to be more careful and gave her some little kitty painkillers for him. The stitches are the dissolving kind, but he's stuck with the cast for at least a few weeks. So all in all, it's not such a bad morning. Especially the part about still being alive. But Yvonne's patience with my loose-lips-sink-ships attitude is wearing thin and she wants some answers about what the hell is going on. Welcome to the club.

In the end we make a deal. I'm lying on the bed and Yvonne gently pulls the bandage away from my side.

—You know, I never went to college like you, Henry, but me? I'd say you're pretty fucked up. So, now that you're not all delirious with pain, I thought I might be able to get you to a doctor or something.

I grit my teeth as she wipes more blood away from the wound.

—No.

—Fuck you, Hank. Unless you have a better idea, I'm calling 911 and getting an ambulance over here before you ruin my bed with your fucking blood.

She stands and heads for the phone.

—Baby, wait.

—Don't "baby" me, Hank.

She has the phone in her hand, waiting.

She's right. I do need a doctor. I tell her the number to call.

Yvonne has her loft set up with her studio at one end and the living area at the other. Everything is open except for the curtained-off bathroom in one corner. In the middle she has a little kitchen built around an enormous antique oak table. She uses the table for counter space and dining, it bears innumerable burns and scars from both. She found it abandoned on the street a couple years back and me and some guys from the bar helped her to get it up here. We had to take the legs off and Wayne, this ex-marshal from the bar, tore his groin muscle getting it up the last flight. Yvonne sanded it down and refinished it, then promptly began abusing the hell out of it. I'm facedown on it right now because it's the brightest spot in the room and Dr. Bob wanted as much light as possible to stitch up my side.

This is service above and beyond the call of duty even for the doc. A morning house call to sew up mysteriously brutal wounds on a surly and unforthcoming patient is not covered in the Hippocratic oath. However, ministering to the sick all measures that are required is. For that matter, there's something in there about respecting the privacy of the patient, and the doc is doing a particularly good job on that one. Which makes a lot of sense, seeing as he's made it clear he doesn't want anyone to ever know he was here doing this.

—What I don't want is some emergency room doctor asking for the name of the butcher who sutured you rather than sending you to the hospital. I don't want to suddenly start receiving calls from lawyers regarding malpractice charges. I don't want your buddies popping up at my door in the middle of the night with bullets they need taken out of their guts. I also don't happen to want you slowly bleeding to death as you wander around the city.

He punctuates each statement by pulling the knots tight on each suture. He gave me a shot of Novocain, so all I feel are little tugs against the skin. A wild improvement over Red's technique.

He applies a dressing and helps me to sit up.

—You were lucky the surgery was healing so well. I could probably take out the rest of the staples, but we may as well leave them in. You might need them. The real risk is infection. I'm going to give you some penicillin. Other than that, you need rest and pain management. You've already flunked out on getting rest. So what do you have for pain?

—Vicodin.

—Uh-huh. Take them. That thing is going to hurt like hell. Clean the wound once a day. Get some Advil for the swelling. Have the sutures and staples removed next week.

—Right. Thanks. Anything else?

He's packing his stuff away. Yvonne grabs his coat from the bed and brings it over.

—Anything else. Yeah. Call the cops and stop fucking around. Whoever did this to you needs to be locked up. Before they hurt someone who cares about their life.

I try to give him money. Bad call.

I'm sitting at the table now instead of lying on it, fingering a deep knife scar in the oak grain and watching Yvonne in her Knicks jersey while she makes me a waffle. She's doing a great job of not asking questions, but the way she clunks down the waffle plate on the table in front of me is a good indication that the levee will soon break.

I tear into that waffle. She makes great waffles, warms up the real maple syrup and everything. Besides which, I really don't want to see her sitting across the table from me, drinking her coffee and rolling up a Drum cigarette. Waiting. I finish the waffle and the half grapefruit she cut for me and my water and the O.J. and, man, was I hungry. I look at the empty plates and close my eyes for a second. I want to stay here. I want waffles three times a day and the smell of her cigarettes and the sound of her kiln roaring, firing a new piece, and Bud sleeping on her too-hard futon and just to stay here. I open my eyes, push back from the table and look at Yvonne. She's leaning back in her chair, feet up on the table, staring across the room out one of the windows that looks toward the Hudson. Her jersey has slipped up her thigh just enough for me to see that she has no underwear on and I feel a little horny all of a sudden. She takes a sip of coffee and drags on the cigarette. I make a little throat-clearing noise and she turns her head slowly to look at me and hear what I have to say.

—Baby, I have to get out of here.

She takes another drag. She put a Leonard Cohen album on her old turntable earlier and now "Suzanne" is playing; such a beautiful song. She exhales a cloud of smoke and looks back out the window.

—Fair enough.

I stand up. It's so nice in here, so warm.

—Do you, babe, do you know where my stuff is?

She looks at me.

—Sure.

She takes her feet off the table and the legs of her chair bang down on the floor. She gets up, takes a last drag off her smoke, drops the butt on the floor, and grinds it out with her bare foot. She walks over to the living area and digs around under the futon frame until she comes up with my bag and then sits on the bed and reaches over to stroke Bud where he lies still sleeping. I go sit on the bed too and start putting on my boots.

My body is sore as hell, but my head is pretty straight. A beer would help most of the aches. My boots are tied. I pull an old black sweater from my bag, stand up, and put it on. I'm looking around for my jacket, but I can't find it. Yvonne reads my mind, gets off the futon and walks over to one of those rolling clothes racks you see in the garment district. It's what she has instead of a closet. She pulls an old leather jacket off a hanger and holds it out to me.

—You didn't have one when you showed up yesterday. Take this. It'll fit.

I come over and take the jacket. It fits perfectly and has a nice lining.

—Thanks.

—Sure.

I go back to the bed, get my bag, and zip it up.

—Something else.

—The cat?

—Yeah.

—How long?

—I'm not sure.

—Fair enough. I'll get his stuff from your place, OK?

I look at her. I look her in the eye.

—No. Don't go there, OK? Don't go there at all.

I reach into the bag and take out some cash.

—Don't. Don't even fucking try to give me money.

I toss it on the bed anyway.

—For Bud. For the vet. And he'll need new stuff.

—Fine.

I walk over to her and put a hand on her head and we wrap our arms around each other. Her face is in my chest and her voice is muffled.

—You gonna be OK?

—Sure.

—You gonna be safe?

—Sure.

—You gonna call me if you need help?

—You know it.

She squeezes me and then pushes me away. I take a look at Bud sleeping, then I head for the door. She calls.

—Hey.

—What?

—I've been rooting for the Giants.

I stop with the door half-open.

—Yeah?

—Yeah.

—Well, they'll choke in the clutch.

—I'll keep rooting for them anyway.

—You always like the underdogs.

—Yep.

I leave and close the door behind me. I have to get the key. I have to get the key, get it to Roman and get lost before any of my friends get hurt. I repeat this to myself over and over as I go down the stairs, leaving that warm room farther and farther behind. It's not easy, none of it is easy, because she's so cool. And me? I'm just a fucking idiot.

Out on the sidewalk in front of her building, someone grabs me from behind and someone else punches me in the crotch. They drag my doubled-over body to the curb, throw me in the trunk of a car, and close the lid. I hear the driver's and the passenger's doors open and shut. Then the engine starts and the car pulls away from the curb.

As it turns out, the small one is Ed and the big one is Paris. And I was right, they do wear cowboy boots. Matching black snakeskin boots with rattler heads on the toes.

I'm rolled up in a little ball, blinking up at them from the trunk they've just opened. After about an hour of me bouncing around in here, we stopped. I heard the doors open and close, then the lid popped open and there they were. The little one took off his hat and smiled.

—I'm Ed, this is my brother, Paris. Sorry about the ride.

It's bright out and I can see dozens and dozens of seagulls wheeling in the sky behind Ed's and Paris's heads. There is a terrific stink in the air. Ed puts his hat back on and reaches out his hand to me.

—Let's get you out of there.

I blink. I take his hand and let him help me out. My legs are cramped up and I almost fall over, but Ed catches me and holds me steady while I get my balance. Paris just stands there a few feet away and watches. We're in a landfill. We are way out in the middle of what must be a New Jersey landfill and there is no one in sight except ourselves and the seagulls. Paris reaches inside his vest, pulls out what looks like a vintage .45 Colt Peacemaker revolver and starts walking around the dunes of garbage, shooting rats.

—The Chink do that to you?

CRACK!

—Huh?

—Your face, the Chink do that to you?

CRACK!

—Uh, yeah. The guy with the red hair.

—Yeah, the Chink is a mean motherfucker. No doubt.

CRACK!

Every time Paris shoots a rat, his gun makes a nice firm crack that ripples across the landfill and sends any nearby seagulls leaping into the air. He's emptied and reloaded the revolver twice now and doesn't seem to be getting bored. Ed and I lean against the lip of the open trunk and converse.

—Paris and me, we met him, he was straight out of juvie. Crazy little fucker.

CRACK!

—Who?

—The Chink, the guy busted your nose there.

They know him. And why not? Why shouldn't goons know each other? All members in the goon union, no doubt.

—You know him?

CRACK!

—All of 'em, we know all of 'em.

—All of them?

CRACK!

Paris flips the cylinder on the revolver and dumps the empty shells onto the ground. He feels around in his pockets and, not finding what he wants, walks back over toward the car. Ed reaches behind himself in the trunk, finds something and tosses it to Paris. It's a full box of cartridges. Paris loads up and goes back to work.

CRACK!

—Sure, we know 'em. The Chink, Bolo, he's the Hawaiian-lookin' guy, those fucked-up Russian fags, and Roman. Now *he's* one zombie motherfucker. Yeah, we know all those cats, but we're really looking for our man Russ. You know Russ.

CRACK!

Ed is about five eight or so and has little bowling balls stuck in his arms where his biceps should be. He never turns his face toward me, just stares out in the direction of his brother, his eyes hidden behind his pitch-black sunglasses.

CRACK!

—I know Russ.

—Sure you do. No question 'bout that. But do you know where he is, where we might find him?

—He left a key.

CRACK!

The car is a Caddie. I'm not sure what year it is, but it's from the tail-fin era. It's a black Caddie with monster fins and it rides like a dream. Paris has wheeled up out of the landfill and onto the road back to Manhattan. Ed sits in the backseat with me. He has the window on his side rolled down and the chill fall air blasts into the car as Paris winds it up past eighty on the speedometer.

—Nice ride.

Ed keeps his head turned toward the window.

—You want to drive it a little?

—No thanks. I don't really drive.

—You from California, you don't know how to drive?

—I know how, I just don't.

Paris has tuned in a classic rock station on the radio and Jimi is playing "Voodoo Chile."

—Can't argue with a man don't want to drive, but she drives nice if ya change your mind.

—Thanks.

Ed rolls up the window. He leans back into the far corner of the big bench seat, looks at me, and takes off his sunglasses. He's got sleepy brown bedroom eyes. Beautiful eyes. Crazy eyes. He exhales and gives a little grin.

—So the key was in the cat's box?

—Right.

—And you found it?

—Yeah.

—And then you got drunk and lost it?

—Right.

—That's pretty fucked up.

—Yep.

—And you didn't give it to Roman?

—I did not give the key to Roman.

—He wants it, though, don't he?

—Yep.

—You sure you don't have it?

—Yep.

—Give us that fucking key, you fucking motherfucker!

Paris has suddenly twisted around in his seat to scream this at me. His left hand clutches the wheel while he reaches into the backseat and tries to grab me with his right. I'm pushed as far back into the seat as I can get and his hand flails at the air inches from my face as the car begins to swerve out of its lane.

—Give us that fucking key or we're gonna kill your motherfucking ass, motherfucker! It's fucking ours! That fucking Russ, piece of fucking, backstabbing fucking piece of shit.

The cars around us are blowing their horns and trying to get out of the way.

—Hey! Hey! Hey!

Ed has grabbed Paris's huge right arm and is keeping him from taking hold of my face.

—Keep your eyes on the damn road!

Paris snaps out of it. Ed lets go of his arm and Paris turns back in his seat and gets the car under control. The flow of traffic settles down around us. Ed leans back into his corner and smiles at me.

—We need that key.

They all know each other.

—See, Russ had a very simple job.

We're seated at a booth in a diner just outside Jersey City. Ed and Paris are across from me, eating steak and eggs smothered in Tabasco sauce. I'm having ice water and staring at the sweating bottles of Heineken they both have in front of them. Ed is talking between mouthfuls of food and beer.

—All he was supposed to do was meet us somewhere with something. Instead he fucked around an' got a bunch a people looking for him.

—Uh-huh.

—Yeah. An' in the deal he also got you, his buddy, in some steep shit.

—Uh-huh.

Paris empties his beer, holds the bottle up in the air and waggles it at the waitress, signaling for two more. My mouth waters and I drink more water.

—What did Roman tell you?

—He said there was an object you all wanted and the key wasn't it, but it would do.

—True enough. If the key is what Russ left, it's what we want.

The waitress shows up with the new beers, sets them down, and leaves. Ed finishes his last bite of egg, pushes his plate aside, gets up and heads for the bathroom.

—I'll be right back.

Paris takes a huge swallow of his new beer, pokes at the remains of his steak, looks around to check for eavesdroppers and leans toward me a bit.

—I had a dream last night. I shot my dad. The fucked-up thing, I mean, shooting him was fucked up enough, but the fucked-up thing?

When I shot him, he was dressed like a Nazi, like a SS motherfucker. And I shot him in the back.

He drinks more beer.

—Anyway, sorry I lost it in the car. I'm not like that. Really.

—No problem.

He sticks his hand out across the table. I take it and we shake.

—Sure you don't want a beer, something to eat?

—Yeah, but thanks.

—Sure.

Ed plops back down in the booth.

—Sorry about that. When ya gotta, ya gotta.

The diner is mostly empty, just us and a mixed bag of travelers. Under the table I'm silently clicking my heels together while in my head I repeat to myself over and over, There's no place like home. There's no place like home. There's no place like home.

We cruise around Manhattan, Paris at the wheel. Ed tells me a story.

—When we were kids, me an' my brother, when we were kids we used to hang out at this Boys Club in Queens. We hated goin' there. Kids always wanted to fight, everybody, fightin' all the time. Me an' Paris, we hated fightin'. Every day, we'd tell our mom we didn't want to go, an' every day she'd tell us to get the hell over to the Boys Club an' let her get some damn work done. They had this wood shop; supposed to make things. All they got to make things with is wood an' old tires. No shit. Not even real wood, scrap shit fulla knots an' sap an' nails an' shit. You ever try to make something outa old tires an' scrap wood? A bird-house? Bullshit, no fuckin' way. Kids, what they did, they'd cut long strips of rubber from the tires an' have whip fights up on the roof of the club. Go up there an' whale the shit out of each other. One day this kid, Dex, he gets Paris up on the roof, but Paris, he don't want trouble. Don't fuckin' matter to Dex. Him an' his friends, they go after Paris, they pull down his pants an' whip shit out of his rear end. Leave him up there cryin', snotty, blood all over his butt. I get him home an' our mom flips, wants ta call the club, call the cops. Tells us she's sorry, we never have to go back. Next day, we go right back. We go to the wood shop an' cut us some long-ass strips of steel-belted radial. Have to cut that shit with a hacksaw. Then we break off these little slivers of razor blade an' stick 'em in the tips of our whips. I find that Dex kid an' tell him I'll see him on the roof. He shows up with his boys an' before he can even open his mouth to start talking shit, I rake that whip across his eyes. Fucker went right down screamin'. His boys try to step up an' I just start whippin' all over 'em. Paris, he's all calm an' shit. He walks over to where Dex is on the ground holding his eyes in his head, yanks the boy's trousers down, an' cuts his ass up good. Dex's crew freak out, can't handle the action, so they bug out. But Paris just keeps the whip on Dex till he's pretty much dead. Once he stopped, we were both a little worked up, I guess, knew we were in trouble, but we didn't really know what to do about it. So we just dragged Dex over to the edge of the roof an' rolled him off. Kid was so bloody, he actually splashed when he hit the ground. That's how we ended up in Montana at one of those juvenile camps. Take troubled inner-city youths an' put them in the great outdoors an' make 'em work? That shit. But, man, was it beautiful. Plains, mountains, Big Sky Country. Coulda spent my whole life there. So look, Hank. It's Hank, right?

—Yeah.

—So, what this is about, your role. When we didn't find Russ at home, we decided to take a peek at Roman, see what he's up to. An' what he was up to was you. So we took a peek at you. Followed you to that place on the West Side. Thought we'd take you for a ride. Got it?

—Sure.

—So now, the thing is, Hank, we need that key. I figure Roman, he told you that he'd do something bad if he doesn't get the key, right? Kill you, hurt your people, whatever, right?

—Right.

—But you get him the key, he'll just leave you alone, right?

—Right.

—Well, fuck that, 'cause I guarantee you that zombie fucker's gonna kill you key or no key. That sound about right?

—Yeah.

—So, me an' Paris, this is the deal with us: We don't get the key, we're gonna kill your ass, no doubt. Kill your ass an' your family an' your ancestors, kill your fucking house plants an' all that shit. Right?
—Right.
—But you give us the key, not only are we gonna leave you breathing, but we're gonna give you a nice piece of change. Sweet, huh?
—Sure.
—Know why we're gonna give you a nice piece of change?
—No.
—'Cause after you give us the key, you're gonna help us set up Roman and the rest of his fucking freak show. Then we kill 'em an' they won't be no trouble for us or you or no one ever again. Sound good?
—Good.
—All right. Now you take my card, you get the key, wherever it is, and you call me. Do it quick, Hank, an' everything goes back to normal. OK?
—OK.
—We let you off anywhere special?
—No. Anywhere's fine.
—Good enough.

Ed taps Paris on the shoulder and he pulls the Caddie over to the curb. I try to open my door, but it's jammed. Ed touches my knee.
—Sorry, that door's all messed. Gotta get out on this side.

He gets out on the curb and I slide across the seat and climb out. He reaches back into the car, pulls out my bag, and hands it to me.

He gets into the front seat, closes his door, and gives me a little wave and they drive off. I look at the card in my hand: *Ed,* followed by a cell phone number. I'm on the corner of 49th and Ninth. I walk about twenty yards down the street and into the first bar I see.

The kidney is an organ. It removes wastes from the blood. If your kidneys, or in my case kidney, is damaged and can no longer perform this function, you die. And yet, many people live long healthy lives with only one kidney because they love and nurture and respect that kidney.

One of the best ways to disrespect your last remaining kidney is to raise your blood pressure by engaging in any of a number of activities, including excessive drinking.

I sit on the bar stool and comtemplate the bottle of Bud. The bartender offered me a glass, but I like to drink my beer out of the bottle. There's sweat all over the brown glass and the lower right corner of the label is peeling. I make a deal with myself: If I can peel the label away in one piece, I get to drink the beer. I tease the label a bit, then strip it away in a single smooth swipe and it comes off in one piece. I get off my stool and walk to the back of the bar.

The phone booth is one of those old-fashioned wooden ones, a cabinet built into the wall. I step inside and close the door and a little light in the ceiling flips on. I dial a long series of numbers, listen to some instructions and dial more numbers. Finally there is a ringing at the other end of the line and I sit on the little bench in the booth. Someone picks up the phone at the other end.

—Hello?

—Hi, Mom.

—Oh! Oh, there you are.

—I'm sorry, Mom.

—No, no, we were just. I was worried when you didn't call. Is everything OK? Did you decide to stay at the hospital a little longer?

—No, Ma. I just. They gave me these painkillers.

—Painkillers? Does it hurt a lot? Are you OK, Henry?

—I'm fine, Mom, it just aches a bit, ya know?

—But you're OK?

—Yeah, I'm fine, but the pills they gave me really knocked me out and I kind of turned off the phone so I wouldn't wake up. I should have called right away, but I just listened to your message.

—Well, Dad told me not to worry, but he was worried too and I just.

It's quiet on the phone for a minute. I lean my head against the glass of the booth's door. My mom misses me, she has missed me for ten years since I came to New York. She doesn't understand my life. Neither do I. So I can't help her much.

—Anyway, I was just worried.

—It's OK, Mom. I'm really OK.

—Are you sure I can't come out?

—No, Mom. There's no reason. I'm fine. I'm taking it easy and everything is fine.

—Is someone there taking care of you?

—Yvonne gave me some help, but I can take care of myself.

—How is she?

—She's fine, Ma, but she's not really taking care of me. She just ran a few errands.

—She's so sweet.

—Yes, she is.

—I just wish I could be there.

—I know.

—I can't wait to see you at Christmas.

—Me too.

—Did you ever decide what you want?

—Anything, Mom. I always like what you get me, and besides, it's still a ways off.

—Well, you know I like to get things done.

—I know. So is Dad around?

—He's at the shop today. Do you want to call him there?

—No, I'm pretty tired, I think I'm gonna get some more sleep. Be sure to tell him I love him, OK?

—I know. Oh, did you get the package I sent?

—No, not yet.

—That's OK. It's just stupid stuff I know you like.

—Thanks, Ma. Look, I'm gonna go and I'm gonna probably keep the ringer off. I'm still really tired. So if you don't get me right away, don't worry. OK?

—OK. I love you, Henry.

—I love you, too, Ma.

—I'll talk to you in a day or two, OK?

—Great. I love you, Mom.

—I love you, Henry.

—Good-bye.

—Bye.

I sit in the booth for a while after that.

I sit in the booth and look out at the bar, at my bottle of Bud still sit-ting in front of my stool and the little pile of bills, my change, sitting next to it. I pump coins into the phone and call United. They can change my ticket whenever I like for a seventy-five-dollar fee, plus the difference in ticket price. Would I like to make that change now? Yes, I would, very much. But I need to get the key first, decide who to hand it over to and stay in one piece while I'm doing it. I know where the key is. Now, who do I give it to? I dig out one of the cards I have in my pocket and dial. He picks up himself.

—Roman.

—I have it.

Pause.

—Where are you?

—I don't have it, I know where it is.

—Where?

—I'm not. Look, I'm not going to tell you.

—And so the purpose of this call is?

—I'm not going to tell you where it is. I'll get it and then give it to you.

—When?

—I. I want to leave. I want to leave New York. I'll give you the key right before I go.

—When are you leaving?

—I don't have a flight yet. I'll get the key and I'll call you. I'll meet you, I'll call you . . .

—Yes?

—I don't know how any of this works.

—Well, there aren't any actual rules. But may I make a suggestion?

—OK.

—Get the key. Book a flight. Call me and tell me the airport, but not the flight number, and tell me what time you want me there. Pick a time before your actual flight so that I won't be able to make a guess about which plane you're leaving on. At the last moment possible before you board, have me paged and tell me what gate you are at. I will meet you there, in full view of the public and you can give me the key.

Wow, good plan.

—OK.

—And you might want to book a flight to someplace other than your final destination and fly to . . . wherever, from there. To discourage pursuit.

—Right, that's good.

—Well then.

—Yeah, OK, so, I'll go . . .

—Get the key.

—Right.

I sit there holding the phone.

—Good-bye.

—Oh, yeah, good-bye.

I hang up. Then I walk straight to the beer and pick it up. Before I can take a drink, I catch a glimpse of the TV. I look again. The Mets game has just concluded: Atlanta 5, Mets 3. I put the beer back down. I don't need it. Besides, I'm going to another bar right now.

Now that I've made a decision about what to do, I'm in a hurry. I flag a cab and tell the driver where to go. I close my eyes, try to ignore all the places my body hurts.

I'm glad I called Roman. Roman is definitely the one I want to deal with. I mean, he may scare me, but he doesn't freak me out like Ed and Paris, who are obviously crazier than a sackful of assholes.

The cabbie drives like all New York cabbies, which is to say he guns it flat out as soon as the light turns green and slams on the brakes at the last possible second when it goes red. I have my seat belt on, which keeps me from slapping my forehead against the Plexiglas sheet that separates the driver from the passenger. Our progress downtown is measured in a series of jumps and lurches. I take a quick look around at the cars behind us, but I don't see any signs of a black Caddie. The cab pulls over and I pay the driver and hop out.

I walk into Paul's. Lisa, the day bartender, takes one look at my face and lets out a little scream.

—Jesus fucking Christ, Hank, you look like yesterday's shit on last week's paper.

When I first came in here looking for a job ten years ago, Lisa was behind the bar. She was about thirty or so back then, six feet tall and built. Just big everywhere. She nailed me about a week or two after I started behind the bar. I never went back for more, but I never had any regrets. She's a big, happy woman and about the only thing she does that pisses me off is getting shit-faced on the job when I'm working the shift after hers. Trying to pick up the pieces for a drunk-off-her-ass bartender is a pain. She's sipping on a greyhound right now and I can see trouble ahead for whoever's on tonight.

It's just about 4:30, so it's a light crowd at the bar. Happy hour starts at 5:00, and things will pick up then. For now it's just a few of Lisa's hard-core regulars. I don't know this bunch too well, but Amtrak John and Cokehead Dan are in. Everybody in this fucking place has a nickname.

I plop down on a stool and put my bag on the floor. Lisa comes over and brushes her fingertips across my forehead.

—Oh, Hank! They told me those guys left your pretty face alone. I specifically asked and everybody told me those assholes didn't touch your pretty face.

—They didn't, this is brand new.

—New! Oh, shit, Hank, what are you up to? You're a lover, baby, not a fighter.

—Just lucky this week.

—Well, shit, baby. Let me get you some medicine.

She reaches into the cooler, pulls out a Bud, pops the top and puts it in front of me before I can say no. But I don't want to say no; I don't want to say no at all. Lisa raises her glass to me and nods at the beer.

—Drink up, Sailor.

That's my nickname here, Sailor. Sailor Hank. I don't know how it got started. Edwin picks your name and it just sticks.

—Drink up.

—Not right now, babe. I really just need to see Edwin, is he around?

She tosses off the rest of her drink and shakes her head.

—Naw, he's been picking up your shifts till he can find someone he likes. So he's takin' a lot of naps to keep up with the hours.

—He'll be in later?

—Should be, he's been comin' in around, say, six or seven to do the cash, gets behind the bar about nine.

Edwin trusts me. It took about a year for me to become his top bartender, we never used the word *manager*, but at some point, I just started helping with inventory, ordering stock, and training new employees. But with Edwin, trust is a matter of degrees. So my problem right now is that while I'm pretty sure he put the key in the floor safe in the office, I don't know the fucking combination.

—So you gonna have a drink with me or not?

—Doctors say no, babe.

—No shit?

—No shit.

—Not even beer?

—Not even beer.

—Well, shit on that.

—Shit on that indeed, babe. Shit. On. That.

—Well, you mind if I carry on myself?

—Don't mind me, babe, it is no longer my problem.

She laughs as she builds another greyhound. She puts it in a beer mug and really lays on the vodka. I've got to give it to her, she may end up drunk as a monkey, but it takes her all day to get there. She takes a sip from her glass.

—Aaaaahhh! Still mother's milk to me, Sailor.

—Well, thank God for that. Look, I'm gonna run out to the store for a few things. Can I grab you anything?

—Yeah, get me a pack of smokes, will ya? Marlboro Lights. The hundreds.

—Yeah, I know.

She tries to hand me a couple bucks for the cigarettes, but I wave her off.

—Just keep an eye on my bag, will ya?

—Sure.

I pass my bag over to her and she tucks it into one of the cupboards behind the bar. I've got the cash in my jeans, but everything else is still in there. I head for the door and she cruises back down the bar. I turn to take a quick look at her ass. Time has been kind to Lisa. But then, she really is built for the long haul, not the sprints. The beer is still on the bar where she put it and I just can't believe this is the second one I'm gonna walk out on today.

—Sailor! Hey, Sailor!

It's Amtrak, waving to me from down the bar.

—Hey, Sailor, you watchin' this?

He's pointing at the TV and I look up just in time to see the first-inning scores from the day games out west: Dodgers 9, Giants 0. Amtrak cackles and tips his Mets cap at me.

—One back with two to go; stick a fork in you, pal, you're done.

I wave my middle finger at him and walk out the door.

I'm at the Love Stores at 14th and Third. The bandage Dr. Bob stuck on my side got rubbed half off during my ride in Ed and Paris's trunk and I want to fix it. I grab a basket from the pile next to the door and head down the first aisle. I get a bunch of gauze pads, some surgical tape, a bottle of hydrogen peroxide, Band-Aids, and some Advil. I take everything up to the counter and ask the girl there for a carton of Marlboro Light 100s. I figure I'll get Lisa a little going-away present. The girl is ringing it all up and putting it into a bag and I'm just kind of letting my gaze drift around when I catch a bright flash of color through the window behind the counter and I just say it:

—Shit.

—What?

—Nothing, sorry. How much?

—Fifty-nine forty-nine, and you best watch your language in here.

—Sorry, I just remembered I forgot something.

—Fine, forget all you like, just watch your language.

—Sure. Look, I know this sounds fucked up.

—I said, watch your language.

—Right, sorry.

—Yeah, you're sorry. Now that's fifty-nine forty-nine.

I take three twenties and a hundred from my pocket and spread them on the counter.

—What I'm trying to ask, I know this is weird, but is there a back way out of this place, and can I use it?

I push the C-note toward her and look at it significantly. She looks at the bill and back at me.

—No, there ain't no back door to this place and you couldn't use it if we had it and can't you read?

She gestures to a sign taped to the cash register.

Due to a recent wave of counterfeiting, we cannot accept bills over $20.00.

—That's fifty-nine dollars and forty-nine cents. Please.

I take the hundred off the counter and slide her the three twenties and she passes me my change.

—Fifty-one cents. And next time, watch your language.

I'm at a loss for words, so I just take my money and watch my language. Besides, I'm busy looking out the window behind her to see if I can catch another glimpse of Red on the sidewalk across the street.

I am not a rocket scientist. And yet this does not explain why I didn't realize that someone was bound to have Paul's staked out. Then again, in my own defense, I've never really done this before and I'm playing with professionals. Although whoever it was that sent Red to spy on me could stand to brush up on the basics of subtlety. I can see him out there, same red hair, same flashy clothes, except the pants are now bright blue polyester and the shirt is gold. He's also wearing an enormous pair of yellow-tinted goggles. So at this point I'm not overly concerned about losing sight of him.

—Hey, foulmouth, you mind making room for customers ain't gotta swear to express themselves?

I'm still standing at the counter and the girl is staring at me and pointing to the older woman behind me patiently waiting her turn.

—Sorry.

—Man, you just full of sorrys. Now get out the way.

I shuffle a few steps to the right. I don't really have any options. I'll just go out the door and try to lose him on the street. I start out the door and the security guard steps in front of me and puts a hand in my chest.

—Sir.

—Yes?

—Sir, may I see the bill you had at the counter?

—The bill?

—The hundred you had at the counter?

—You must. Look, it's not. I'm not passing bad paper.

—May I see the bill, please.

I'm not scared. I mean, really, a drugstore security guard just doesn't have much leverage with me today. But I want to get moving, so I pull out the hundred and hand it to him. He takes it, holds it up to the light, gives it a long look, then looks back at me.

—OK.

He tucks the bill into the breast pocket of his little security blazer and takes hold of my arm.

—What the fuck?

I jerk my arm back, but he's got a pretty good grip on it and pulls me in close.

—Fuckin' take it easy, man, and just come on with me.

And he starts leading me toward the back of the store. The girl at the counter stops in the middle of her transactions.

—Martin? Martin? Where you goin' with that foulmouth?

—Cheryl, just mind your own fuckin' business.

—Don't curse me, don't you curse me.

—Yeah, yeah, fuckin' yeah.

—Oh, oh!

—Just work the register, Cheryl. This is a security matter, so you just work the register.

—You busted, Martin. You soooo busted.

The rest is lost as Martin takes me back into the stockroom.

—OK, man, come on.

He lets go of my arm and starts leading me through a series of twists and turns, around piles of boxes, and through a couple very short hallways to a door with about eight locks. Martin stops and looks at me.

—OK, man, this is the stock entrance. I'm gonna open it quick, so you just jump out, 'cause I got to get back out there and chill Cheryl. OK?

—Sure.

The whole time, he's twisting dead bolts and sticking keys from a big ring into locks until there is just one left to open.

—You ready?

—Ready.

He snaps the last lock open, pulls the door inward and I jump out. The door is exactly ten yards down the street from the store's main entrance and, as I hear Martin relocking the locks, I look up and see Red, who has spotted me immediately and is waving at me, a big fucking smile on his sadistic little face. And I run away as fast as I can.

As alcoholics go, I'm really more of a dedicated amateur than a true professional. I tend to be more of a bingeing, life-of-my-own-party kind of drinker rather than a steady, dying-an-inch-at-a-time kind of drinker. And even in the middle of a bender, I still get myself over to the gym most days. It gets the heart started and sweats out the worst of the booze and helps me to hide from the hard core of desperation that has somehow become my life. I've jogged, lifted weights, and even sparred while still fully plowed from the night before. It's part vanity, but mostly I'm fighting a holding action against my lifestyle, convincing my mind that I'm not really trying to kill myself. I stay in shape. But even at my best, stone cold sober, well rested, well fed, with two kidneys and no recent beatings, even at my best I am not a shadow of what I once was.

I'm running west on 14th Street. Two lanes of traffic running both east and west, the sidewalk crowded with pedestrians checking out the discount shops. The bag from the store is in my left hand and, as I run, it swings crazily and keeps bouncing off the wound in my side and it's all I can think about. After the first twenty yards I drop it. With my hands free, I try to focus on my stride, try to find the point where I can slip my legs into gear and let them carry me along, but it's hard because I keep snapping my head over to the right to catch a glimpse of Red, to see how far back he is. He's not far back at all; in point of fact he's just about parallel to me, but he's sticking to the north side of the street and seems satisfied to just keep pace. I catch a break at Second Avenue, a green light that lets me shoot across the crosswalk and onto the next block.

These days when I run, it's really just jogging. I'll open it up a bit every now and then to work out the kinks, but I never really kick it. I don't like to feel what I lost. They talk about burst: the ability to explode into full speed from a dead standstill. I had burst. Against the guys at school and in Little League, I stole at will, and when the scouts came to see me play, they just clicked their stopwatches and shook their heads.

I'm about halfway to Third Avenue. My stride is uneven, I've got a stitch starting beneath the real pain of my wound, and the muscle where my leg broke is a stiff little ball in my calf. I snatch a look at Red and, from the way he's reading the traffic, I can tell he's getting ready to cross over to my side of the street. I figure I need to make a move.

At Third the light is green for me, but I cut left and head downtown instead. I don't look back, but the horns and brake squeals tell me all I need to know: Red is crossing 14th Street to stay behind me. I more than slightly hope to hear the dull thud of a car hitting a human body. No such luck.

Thirteenth Street comes up quick; these north-south blocks are much shorter than the cross-town blocks. The light is red for me, but there's a big hole in the traffic and I plunge through it no problem. I race the length of another block and across 12th, just in front of a bicycle messenger going the wrong way down the street and, behind me, I hear a neat little collision and a lot of cursing.

I twist my head around to confirm it. Red is all jumbled up with this Jamaican dude and his bike. I dodge traffic to the north side of Third Avenue and down a block to the multiplex movie theater on the corner of 11th Street.

A ticket window is open just around the corner, off the avenue, and out of Red's view. No one is waiting in line. I have a twenty in my hand. I shove it under the glass, panting.

—One.

The guy in the booth is reading a magazine and he doesn't look up from it.

—For what?

—What?

—What movie do you want?

—Anything, I don't care.

This time he looks up at me.

—Well, ya gotta pick something.

—I'm telling you, I don't care, I just. Just anything, OK?

He puts down his magazine.

—Look, don't give me a hard time, just pick a movie.

—Man!

I look at the movies. They've got eight screens and only three pictures playing on them and they all suck. The ticket booth is built into the corner of the theater with windows on both 11th and Third. Through the glass, behind the booth guy, I can see a block up the avenue where Red is getting untangled from the Jamaican and his bike.

—Just give me a ticket for anything you like, OK?

—Well, I like *Shell Shock*, but it started a half hour ago.

—I'll take it.

—But it started a half hour ago, you missed the best part.

—One for *Shell Shock*, please.

—OK, man, but it's not my fault if you don't like it or you don't know what's going on.

—One! Please!

—Yeah, yeah, cool it.

He punches out my ticket and pushes it through the glass along with my ten dollars change and three or four coupons for monster servings of soda and popcorn at the concession counter. I take the ticket and the change. Inside, I watch the street through the tinted glass of the lobby doors. Red is looking around for me, and the Jamaican is in his face; a few people are standing on the sidewalk watching the altercation. Red does something to the Jamaican. I can't really see what he's done, but the Jamaican drops straight to the asphalt and I think I see a few of the spectators flinch and they all suddenly find better things to do and start to walk away. Red takes one last look around and heads down the street in my direction, but still on the wrong side of the block. I give my ticket to the ticket guy and he looks at it.

—You know this started a half hour ago?

—I know.

—You want to wait? There's another starting in twenty minutes.

—I'm in a hurry.

—OK.

He tears the ticket and passes my half back to me.

—Two levels down on the escalator, concessions on the right.

I step onto the down escalator.

—Thanks.

—Sure, but you already missed the best part.

I've seen *Shell Shock*. I know that I have indeed already missed the best part, which speaks volumes about an action movie that runs over two hours. The bathroom is on the first level down, so that's where I stop. It's empty. I go into the stall, take off Yvonne's jacket and my sweater and pull up my T-shirt and, sure enough, the peeling bandage is stained with a bit of fresh red. I take a seat on the toilet and rest my head in my hands.

I'm thirsty.

I get off the can, leave the jacket and sweater in the stall and go over to the sink. It's one of those where you push the knob down and it turns itself off a moment later. I push it down and hold my cupped hands under the water and it shuts off before I can fill them up. I hold the knob down with one hand while I fill the other, but I can't really get a proper drink that way. Finally, I just hold the knob down and stick my head in the sink and drink straight from the faucet. I'm really thirsty and I'm taking in huge gulps and the water is rushing right next to my ears, which is why I don't hear it when the door opens and Red comes in.

I don't even realize he's there until he steps past me and into the stall. At which point he sees my jacket and sweater hanging off the hook on the back of the door and I guess he realizes that the bum in the T-shirt drinking from the faucet is actually the fuck he's looking for. Which is the exact same moment that my eyes flick up to the mirror and see the back of his shocking red head in the open door of the stall.

The element of surprise is an amazing thing and, as has been documented many times, can be the decisive factor in even the most lopsided conflict. In this case, we get the drop on each other and it produces a kind of tableau. I straighten, water running down my chin and onto the front of my T-shirt, but I haven't had time to turn, while he has spun neatly on his heels to face me. So I look at the mirror, straight through the yellow lenses of his goggles and into the reflection of his eyes. He stares back. There's a cut on his chin and scuff marks on his otherwise flawless red jacket and, somehow, I just know that he's more pissed about the condition of his vinyl than his face. I slowly wipe water from my mouth and chin. We are in a bathroom. Someone could walk in at any moment.

—I talked to Roman. I told him I was getting the key. I told him I'd call him.

He blinks behind those goggles. Slowly.

—Fuck Roman.

I spin and backpedal at the same time. I'm bigger than he is, but for it to do me any good I need room. He dances in toward me as I lift up onto the balls of my feet, tuck my chin, and bring my fists up. He skips back just a bit, keeping his hands loosely balled down by his hips. I want to stay mobile, but the boots I'm wearing slow my feet down, so I'm doing my dancing with my head and upper body, keep the target moving. The tight space plays to his size, but if I can keep some distance between us, I might have a chance. He darts in, trying to come inside my guard and I pop out a jab to keep him away. Before my arm is fully extended he hits me three times.

They're tight little punches that pepper my lower ribs. And that's about it for boxing. I flinch back, ducking and turning, and he just plants a good one right on my wound. I give a sound halfway between a scream and a gasp and my body twists back toward the pain, and he flattens his hand into a spear point and drives it into my solar plexus. I fold. He grabs me, puts me into some kind of hold, spins me and drives me back into the stall, kicking the door closed behind us.

—Fuck Roman. *I* want the key.

He's got me pressed face first against the wall across from the stall door. He's knotted the fingers of his right hand into the fingers of both mine in some fucking Shaolin Super Death Grip. And as a bonus, he's digging the thumb of his left hand into my wound, living up to all the clichés of the Asian torture master.

—I want the key.

—Yeah, I got that part.

He digs the thumb in a little harder and I bite my lip.

—The key.

—Yeah, look, I told Roman—

He gives me the thumb and does something to my hands and I swoon. My knees buckle and all the air goes out of me, my vision blackens and I only stay up because he keeps me there.

—I'm just gonna kill you right now. Right now, just kill you and find the key on my own. Now fuck Roman. I want the key.

—I don't have it. I didn't get it yet.

—Where is it?

—I gave it to a friend.

—What friend? We know all your friends. Which one?

They know all my friends.

My boxing instructor, he's a badass. He also teaches street fighting. When I came to him to start boxing, he asked me why I wanted to study and I told him that I had trouble in the bar from time to time and wanted to be better equipped to handle it. He took me on for the boxing but suggested I take some of his other classes as well. He thought they might serve my needs better. And you know what? He was so right.

I shift against the wall and gasp like I'm trying to get room to breathe. Red moves his feet back a bit for better leverage and I lift my left foot and rake it down his shin and slam it onto his instep. His upper body lurches back, but he keeps his grip. I snap my head straight back. I'm too tall to plant it in his nose like I'd like to, but I catch him a good one on the forehead. And before I can think about the pain that shoots through my own skull, I crack him again. This time his face is turned up and something goes mushy against the back of my head and he lets go.

I lurch to the right and turn. He's slumped against the stall door and his eyes have gone funny. I've evened the score on broken noses. His looks pretty munched and it's streaming blood as he slides all the way down to the floor. I take a quick step across the stall and kick him once in the head to make sure he doesn't get up and hurt me again.

I grab my sweater and jacket, push him aside and take off. On the escalator, I pull my clothes back on and then I'm in the lobby, heading for the door. I pass the ticket guy and he waves at me.

—Hey! Hey, if you're looking for your friend, he just went down looking for you.

And I'm through the door and back out on the street.

I feel great. I hurt. My wound hurts, my nose hurts, my ribs and gut hurt, my hands hurt, my feet hurt. Man, I hurt everywhere. But I feel fucking great. It's close to 5:00 now, just starting to get a little dim here in the city and I bounce down the sidewalk, heading back to Paul's. There's some blood trickling down the back of my neck, but it's not mine and that makes me feel even better. If Red was working solo today, then my plan with Roman still holds. And I'm gonna just assume that's the case. Like I have a choice.

When I get to Second Avenue, I head up to 14th Street and then turn east toward Alphabet City. And how about this? There's my Love Stores bag still on the sidewalk where I dropped it. I pick it up and everything is still inside. I stand there on the sidewalk with a big shiteating grin on my face. Sometimes, baby, you just eat the bear.

I trot happily down the street to Avenue B, take a right and cruise into Paul's. A few more folks have come in to warm up for happy hour and I get a nice chorus of greetings. I nod and smile as I head for the bathroom in the back and toss the carton of Marlboros to Lisa behind the bar, still sipping her drink.

—What took you so long, Sailor?

—Just had to stop in somewhere, baby. Just had to stop in.

—Hey, I only needed a pack, Hank.

—No problem, baby.

—Well, thanks. When you get out of the john, I'm gonna buy you a soda or something.

I smile at her and go into the bathroom and lock the door. Out in the bar the jukebox is playing Joe Cocker, his cover of "With a Little Help from My Friends." I hum along while I check myself over. First,

I clean Red's blood off the back of my head. Then I strip the bandage from my nose and take out the little gauze plugs I've been using to prop it up. It looks stable at this point, so I just clean up the flakes of dried blood and leave it alone. My wound is another matter. It's oozing blood again. I clean it and dry it off as best I can, slap some gauze over it and tape it down. I look at the bottle of Vicodin. I can have two an hour, but they'll make my head foggy as hell. I take one out of the bottle, bite it in half and dry-swallow it. The adrenaline is wearing off and I'm starting to crash from the fight high, but I still feel pretty damn good. I look myself over in the mirror; no doubt about it, I'm a wreck. But I'll hold together for now.

Back in the bar, the bell for happy hour has rung and things are starting to cook. Tim is down at the end of the bar, getting a quick one in before he does his evening deliveries. Some of my other regulars are around now, too. I get a lot of back pats and commentary about the nose.

—Ali! Hey, Ali!

—What's the other guy look like?

—Did you get the license on that truck, Sailor?

I laugh it all off and pull up a stool next to Tim. He gives me the once-over and shakes his head.

—Jesus.

—Yeah.

—Jesus.

—I know.

—Man, you need to make some healthy life choices but soon.

—I'm making them, Timmy, my boy, I'm making them.

—Damn.

Lisa comes over and passes me my bag and I stuff all my new first-aid crap into it.

—Ready for a drink yet?

—Naw, just get me a . . .

—Yeah?

—Fuck. Get me a seltzer.

She chuckles and gets me my seltzer. Tim tosses back a shot of Tullamore Dew and shakes his head.

—Seltzer! Now *that*! *That* is what I call a healthy life choice.

Lisa plops the soda down in front of me and I pick it up and raise it in Tim's direction.

—To healthy life choices.

He lifts another shot and clinks it against my glass.

—To health.

We drink. He slams his empty shot back down on the bar and Lisa tops it right off. With Tim you don't have to ask, you just keep him full and put another mark on his tab. The seltzer's not bad, not bad at all, kind of refreshing and I feel good, here in the bar with people I know and like, with friends. And in my head I hear a voice telling me, *We know all your friends. Which one?*

I don't say good-bye. I just pick up my bag and leave.

It's rush hour. Impossible to find an empty cab. I start jogging west. I could call, but if someone is there, it might freak them out or something. Fuck, I don't know. I jog and keep looking at the traffic, searching for an in-service cab. At Third Avenue I strap the athletic bag on tight and start to run. I reach, I stretch for my stride and, this time, I find it. I blow down the street. It's too far to keep this up all the way. Across Union Square, on University, a guy is just getting out of a cab and the cabbie is flicking on the off-duty light. I cram myself through the door and into the backseat. The cabbie starts yelling something at me in whatever his native tongue is. I push a big wad of cash through the Plexiglas shield and he shuts up.

—West Side Highway and Christopher.

He looks at the money I've dropped on the front seat. It's well over a hundred dollars and he pulls away from the curb. We don't talk. He looks at me from time to time in the rearview, but we don't talk at all.

He stops on the highway where it meets Christopher, I climb out and he drives off. The traffic is too dense for me to try to cross, so I have to wait for the lights to change. When they do, I run over to the building, let myself in and run up the stairs. None of the locks to the apartment door are fastened.

Just inside there is a grocery bag full of cat stuff spilled out over the floor. I don't want to look up from the mess, but I do. She's all over the table, spread-eagle with her limbs strapped to its legs. Lying in the same space I occupied a few hours ago. They've done something horrible to her. The kiln is still on and the whole room smells like burning. I approach her with my head turned away. Then, with my eyes closed, I place my ear against her chest to hear that she is dead. I run to the futon for a blanket and cover her. Then I crawl under the table to hide.

In action movies, there is a moment where the hero is just pushed too far. The bad guys have stolen his money, taken his good name and beat him up and he's swallowed it all. But then they go that one step too far: they kill his partner, his wife, his kid, whatever. This moment is indicated by the hero tilting his head back and releasing an agonized scream: NOOOOOOOOOOOOOOOOOOOO! Then he gets mad.

I don't feel like that at all. I want to sleep. I want to roll over and die. I want to give up and lose. I don't care. I just don't care.

They followed me. They followed me from my apartment to Yvonne's and then they waited. They watched her come and go and kept waiting until they saw me leave and saw the cowboys throw me in the trunk. Then maybe someone followed us, and Paris lost them or maybe fucking not. But they waited until she left again and they went up to look for the key and when she came back they asked her where it was and she didn't know what the fuck they were talking about because I didn't tell her anything that might have saved her life.

I hear a soft, regular thumping on the floor and look up to see Bud coming towards me. A cat walking in a cast. He manages to get into my lap and curls up there and promptly goes to sleep.

This is it, this would be the time to finally call the police and let them sort it out, take my chances with Roman, and have it over with. But I find that it really is too late for that because, just as I'm thinking about it, several officers of the NYPD come running in and stick their guns in my face.

They find I have no record in New York. They find I was once arrested as a juvenile in California for breaking and entering and burglary, that I pled the case, served a year of probation, and did over a hundred hours of community service. They find these things out without my help because I'm not talking.

My eyes have become little glass windows at the ends of two dark, narrow tunnels. I sit at the other end of the tunnels and look at all the things happening out there. People talk to me and it sounds like voices traveling between paper cups tied together by long pieces of string. Deep inside, back behind the tunnels, I am aware that I am in shock. And at a deeper level I realize that I am also thoroughly fucked.

They have me in one of those little rooms with steel screens on the windows, where all the furniture is bolted to the floor and the wall opposite the door has a small one-way mirror. They think I'm a tough-guy. They think I'm giving them the freaked-out-psycho-killer-silent-treatment. The fact is, I just can't talk. Words form in my mind and I send them to my mouth, but they never get there. What I really wish they would do is take the pictures off the table in front of me because, no matter how hard I try not to look, my eyes keep getting dragged back. They beat her. They didn't cut her or burn her or strangle her or rape her. They beat her until she was dead.

Yvonne shared the top floor of her building with a guy. He lives in a loft at the end of the hall. He came home and saw the door of her place wide open and, like a good neighbor, he took a quick look to see if everything was OK. When he saw the covered thing on the table and me sitting under it, he crept back to his apartment and called 911. Nice guy. A lot of people wouldn't have bothered. He told them I was a guy Yvonne saw sometimes and there I was, catatonic, holding a cat, all bruised up with blood still on my clothes from the fight with Red. It sounded perfect to the cops, some kind of freaked-out sex/violence jealousy crime. Case closed. Except I gather now that there's a problem because people keep coming in here to whisper stuff to the cops who have been questioning me.

The two detectives in the room with me both drink coffee and smoke cigarettes. They are both balding, paunchy, and ruddy and have matching mustaches. I can tell them apart because one has a terrible cold and keeps blowing his nose and hawking and spitting into the wastebasket. He's clearly pissed at me because he wants to be home in bed. The other cop is pissed at me because he thinks I'm a "sick, murdering fuck." They tried a little good cop, bad cop at first. Then they tried bad cop, bad cop. Now they're really just Sick Cop, Bored Cop. They keep asking questions though and, through it all, I keep trying to say the same thing and stopping myself just before I say it because I just don't know what will happen when I finally say the words *Roman did it*.

Sick Cop launches a lung oyster into the trash and Bored Cop stubs out his cigarette. Then they look at each other and have one of those cop telepathy moments and Bored Cop lights another smoke, looks at me and tells me what's fucking up their case.

—So, OK, so we know something. We know that more than one person did this. We have hairs, right. We have fibers and scuff marks and bruises on the body and we know this was two, maybe three people. We know you didn't do this alone. So fine, so paint the picture: It wasn't really *you*, *you* were just there. OK? Something got out of hand with you and your girl and some friends. You were just there and you didn't do anything. That's fine, that's OK, we can live with that. So paint that picture and tell us how it happened, how it wasn't you, and tell us about the guys who did do it. Tell us about your friends.

The strings snap. I race down to the end of the tunnel and the glass over my eyes shatters. I reach out and flip the pictures over. I look directly at the one-way mirror because I know who's on the other side.

—They're not my fucking friends.

And Roman walks in.

Sick Cop and Bored Cop look over and nod at him. Sick Cop takes out a tissue from the little plastic pack in his shirt pocket and blows a hole in it.

—Lieutenant.

Roman makes a little grunt noise and waves the two detectives over to where he stands by the door. The three of them huddle up with their heads close together and suddenly burst into laughter. Sick Cop laughs and chokes on his own phlegm while Bored Cop guffaws and slaps his knee. Roman chuckles and pounds Sick Cop on the back and they all settle down. Then Sick Cop and Bored Cop start picking up their stuff and getting ready to leave. Roman holds the door open for them and, as they exit, he says something else to them I can't hear and they start laughing all over again. Roman closes the door. He walks over to the table, picks up the full ashtray, takes it to the wastebasket and dumps it out. He walks over to the intercom box next to the door and makes sure it's off. Then he comes back to the table and sits across from me. He reaches out, scoops the pictures together, taps them into a neat stack, flips through them, places them facedown back on the table, looks me dead in the eye and nods at the pictures.

—I didn't do this.

Roman is a very good driver. He obeys all traffic laws and, more than that, is courteous to a fault toward other motorists and pedestrians. I admire that. I sit in the passenger seat of his unmarked police car while he drives. My hands are uncuffed and Bud is in my lap. I have not been charged with murder.

I am being held for suspicion of murder, but no official charge has been made. In the meantime, Robbery/Homicide has put me in Detective Lieutenant Roman's custody because of my connection to a case he is already working on. Any assistance I can give him will only help the disposition of my own situation.

Roman has driven into SoHo. He cruises around, turns onto one of the little cobbled streets, parks and shuts off the motor. The clock in the dash says it's 1:57 A.M., about eight hours since the cops found me. Roman rolls his window down a bit. The street is very quiet and the loudest noise is Bud's purring. The animal control people hadn't arrived at the station to pick him up and, as we were leaving, I saw him curled up on a desk. Roman got him for me along with my personal belongings, which are now in my bag in the backseat. Roman loosens his tie a bit and undoes his top collar button.

—I have a "Contact Officer" attached to your name.

I look at him.

—Anytime your name, the name of one of your associates, or one of a few key addresses pops up on the computer, it's tagged and they let me know. Same thing with Miner. That's how I ended up at your apartment in the first place. Miner's address came in associated with a disturbance and, eventually, someone let me know.

—Clever. I thought it was because you were the one who had just broken in there.

—That too, that too.

He reaches into his jacket, takes something out and hands it to me. It's Ed's business card. The one I had in my pocket when I was arrested.

—Did you tell them much?

—Everything.

—The key?

—What about it?

—Do they have the key? Did you give it to them?

It's another beautiful fall night in Manhattan. The air is clean and there's a lover's moon in the sky. It's Friday night or Saturday morning, depending on your point of view and people are out. Back on my street, things are probably in full swing right now. I like to go out alone on my nights off, play some pool, meet new people, have more than a few. This would be a great night for it.

I look at the empty backseat of the car.

—Where is everybody, Roman?

—The partnership has broken up.

—That sucks.

—It was never stable. Frankly, it doesn't alter my own situation. But it does greatly increase the danger to yourself.

—How so?

—There is now a large number of rogue elements at large, all looking for the key and, thus, for you. And I assure you that to the extent any of those elements have ever been able to show restraint in their dealings, I have always been the one holding them back. They are violent men and you are going to need an ally against them.

—Yourself?

—I nominate myself. Events like these have a momentum. Brutality lends itself to greater brutality and without realizing it, one can be swept along in its wake. If you wait too long, you might find yourself someplace you never knew existed. Doing things you never thought possible. I can both protect you and help to return your life to normal. I would like to do that.

He squeezes his eyes shut for a moment and pinches one earlobe with the fingers of his right hand.

—I would like very much to do that.

All the running around has my feet hurting again. I stroke Bud and feel my feet throb in time to my heartbeat. Yvonne would rub my feet sometimes, not always, but every now and then. She always made me wash them first.

Roman reaches into his jacket again. He flips on the car's interior dome light and shows me what he has. It's one of the pictures. A close-up of a bruise pattern on her neck. Roman traces a finger over the bruises.

—Look here. See how the bruises are knobbed and distinct? The skin is abraded in each of the bruises. Torn. This kind of bruising you get when someone wears brass knuckles. Or sometimes, you see it if the perpetrator wears several rings.

I think about Ed and Paris in the hall outside my apartment. I think about them knocking on Russ's door, knocking with their hands covered in silver rings. Naked women and skulls. Roman puts the picture in my hand. I look at it and think about Yvonne in her Knicks jersey, spooned against me on her futon.

—Your legal problems are significant, but not insurmountable. I can help you there. More importantly, you have enemies, enemies who are fierce. I can help you there as well. To get away or to get revenge.

I think about the first time I slept with Yvonne, how drunk we were, how we laughed. I think about her hands, callused, scarred and covered in small burns from her work. I look again at the picture of her sweet neck mottled, red, black and blue. Roman watches me.

—Did you give them the key?

—No.

—Did you tell them where it is?

—No.

—Where is it?

—It's at the bar. It's in the safe at the bar.

—Let's go get it.

I'm staring at the picture, feeling the pain in my feet and listening to the rushing sound in my ears, and really, I'm just not that surprised when Bolo opens the car door, pushes me over and climbs in, wedging me tight between himself and Roman just like Red is now wedged into the backseat between the Russians, who are wearing their tracksuits again. In the rearview, I can see Red's face, a huge gauze pad over his nose held in place by a big **X** of white tape. He looks at Roman, who is starting the car.

—I told you it was the bar.

Bolo adjusts himself in the seat to settle his bulk and looks down at Bud.

—Hey, man, how's the cat?

—Spalding Gray.

—What the fuck, Spalding Gray? Who the fuck?

—Spalding Gray, he's a, a, whaddayacallit, a performance, a monologist. He talks.

—Actors, fucking actors only.

—He is a fucking actor. He's in movies, too.

—Bullshit.

Bolo and the Russians are playing Six Degrees of Kevin Bacon. Bolo is kicking their asses. Tempers are flaring. Bolo looks at his watch.

—Come on, man, Spalding Gray.

—I don't know fucking Spalding. Fucking Spalding is a fucking ball.

—So forfeit the point.

—Fuck you.

Red is leaning forward against the back of the front seat. The Russians put their heads together behind him and whisper to each other. Bolo grins.

—Come on, forfeit, you don't even know who the fuck he is.

—Fuck you.

Red flicks the back of my ear again. He's been doing it for a few hours now but doesn't seem to be getting bored. Sometimes he just moves like he's going to do it so he can watch me flinch, then he laughs a little. The car smells like the coffee they keep getting from the grocery across the street and about a half hour ago someone started passing gas. Fortunately, Roman makes the Russians get out of the car when they want to smoke; otherwise it might be unbearable in here. Roman just sits there behind the wheel and keeps his eyes on the front door of Paul's down the block and across the street.

—How much longer, do you think?

It's getting close to 5:00 A.M. and a handful of folks are still in the bar and Roman wants them out soon.

—I don't know, sometimes Edwin will hang out partying till almost noon.

Roman runs his fingertips around the steering wheel and nods.

—Spalding Gray, Spalding Gray, Spalding Gray.

—Fuck you, fuck you, fuck you. Fucking, fuck, fuck, Spalding, fuck.

—Hey, man, is that your own rage you're choking on or just bile?

—Forfeit, we fucking forfeit. Our turn.

Red also whispers into my ear from time to time, the same thing over and over.

—Pussy bitch, pussy bitch, pussy bitch.

—Christopher Lee!

Bolo laughs.

—Christopher Lee? Are you sure about that?

—Fucking Christopher Lee.

—OK. Lee to Peter Cushing in *Horror of Dracula*, Cushing to Carrie Fisher in *Star Wars*, Fisher to Billy Crystal in *When Harry Met Sally*, Crystal to Robin Williams in *Father's Day*, Williams to John Lithgow in *Garp*, and, of course, Lithgow to Bacon in *Footloose*.

—Fuck! Fuck!

And again in my ear.

—Pussy bitch, pussy bitch, puuuuuuuussy bi-tch.

Bolo is still laughing.

—Christopher Lee! That your big gun, boys? Christopher Lee?

—Quit! Fucking fuck you, we fucking quit this fucking shit game.

—Yeah, fucking, yeah. Quit, you always fucking quit.

Right in my fucking ear.

—Pussy bitch, pussy bitch, pussy bitch.

I clear my throat.

—Hey, Roman, did Red mention that when he ran into me earlier today, not only did I kick his ass, but he tried to get the key for himself? "Fuck Roman," is what he said. "Fuck Roman." That was it, wasn't it, Red? "Fuck Roman"?

The whispering in my ear stops and everything is really very quiet as Roman swivels around, crams the barrel of a small automatic in Red's mouth, and pulls the trigger. There's a muffled pop. A flashbulb goes off inside Red's face and smoke shoots out his nose. The car is quiet and stinks and then I start screaming like a girl until Bolo clamps one of his hands over my mouth and shuts me up.

The Russians wrap what's left of Red's head in some old newspaper, dump him in the trunk and stay on the sidewalk to smoke as Bolo goes to the grocery. Me and Roman sit in the car with the windows rolled down to let out the stink of cordite, blood, and crap from Red's bowels letting loose as he died.

5:23 A.M. Saturday morning on Avenue B and the streets are empty; no witnesses, except maybe a junkie or a squatter, and who cares anyhow?

Roman looks at me and taps his upper lip. He points at my face and taps his lip again. I get the idea and wipe my lip with the back of my hand; it comes away bloody. Roman shakes his head and taps his lip again.

—No, there's still some. Here.

He takes out a handkerchief and wipes it across my mouth and chin a couple times.

—There. Sorry about that. Messy.

He folds the bloody handkerchief and puts it back in his pocket.

—You're sure you don't know the combination?

—I'm sure.

—Well, I guess you're going to have to go in and get the key.

The blood is still on the back of my hand, drying. I rub it against the seat to get it off.

—No. I don't. I don't want any more. I can't do. I can't. I'm so.

I'm trying to say something. Fear robs my voice and I gasp out half-finished words. Bud is getting squirrelly in my lap. All the action and noise and smells are riling him up and I'm trying to calm him, but it's not working because he can feel how scared I am. Roman reaches over and takes him from me.

—Here, let me.

He holds Bud tight and starts scratching him behind the ears. Bud starts to settle and rubs his head against Roman's chin.

—Give the cat back.

Roman stops and smiles a little.

—Sure.

He passes Bud back and I settle him in my lap. Roman leans forward, crosses his arms over the top of the steering wheel and rests his chin there.

—You see it happening, don't you? Circumstances spinning out of control, out of your realm of experience. The world you know is receding. I know. I know that the further you travel down this road, the less likely it is you will ever return to home. So.

—So what, man? So fucking what?

—So, if *you* can't go in to get the key, then I guess *we'll* have to go in and get the key.

Bolo opens the rear door and climbs in with a bottle of Formula 409 and a roll of paper towels and starts cleaning up Red's brains.

The plan was that we would wait for everyone to leave the bar, then I would let us in with my key and one of Roman's crew would open the safe. After that, things got vague about what happens to me. But I still thought it was a pretty good plan since it didn't involve any more people I care about getting hurt. I liked the plan just fine until Roman blew his safecracker's brain all over the backseat of the car.

Roman explains to me the relative advantages of my going in alone to get the key over him and his minions going in to get it.

—You have the advantage of being able to go in and simply ask your friend to get the key for you. If we go in, we'll have to resort to threats and the use of violence.

I start to hyperventilate and Roman puts his hand on the back of my head and bends me forward until my face is between my knees.

—Just breathe.

I breathe while Bud squirms out of my lap and jumps down into the car's footwell. Roman gives my shoulder a little squeeze.

—Good. Now, I would just as soon not go in there. Too many variables, too many risks, and the most likely outcome would be bloody. But it's getting light out and someone has to be going in there very soon. I need that key, I really do.

I sit up and look out at the graying sky. The dash clock is at 5:34.

The street is still empty, but soon early morning stragglers will appear. In the backseat, Bolo is still cleaning, humming a song under his breath. I think it might be "Car Wash." Roman stares out the front windshield, eyes still focused on the bar's front door. I try to picture happy endings and all I get is the nightmare image of Yvonne. There is no happy ending anymore and all I want now is to go home. I want to leave New York, I want to be with my family and be safe again and forget.

—Will you help me?

Roman is silent.

—Will you still protect me from Ed and Paris and get me off the hook with the cops? Will you still protect me?

Roman scratches his earlobe and nods.

—Nothing changes. Get the key and bring it out and I will help you. But do it now and do it quickly. Dawdle, and we'll have to come in.

I pet Bud, climb out of the car, and cross the street over to Paul's.

They're listening to Black Sabbath. Edwin loves Sabbath. He has all the CDs from the original lineup loaded into the jukebox. It's his party music. I take a look through the little window set into the door and, sure enough, it's a party.

Edwin and Lisa are on the bar. Edwin is doing push-ups and Lisa is sitting on his back. A small group of regulars is gathered around them, keeping count, shouting out the numbers as Edwin pumps up and down, showing no sign of strain or stopping. From the door I can see Wayne, the ex-marshal, and his hippie girlfriend, Sunday. Also Coke-head Dan and Amtrak John. It's an after-hours party and, by the huge lines of coke Dan is cutting on the bar, I'd say it's not ending any-time soon.

I look at Roman's car. The Russians have gotten back in, and I can't really see anyone. I give a little wave and the headlights flash back at me. I take out my key, unlock the door and go in.

* * *

Paul's was a Thai restaurant until Edwin bought it. He gutted the whole thing and rebuilt from the floor up. The place is just a long hallway, about four yards wide and twenty deep, with a bar running down the right wall, an elbow-high ledge running down the left and thirty stools scattered between. The bar itself is an antique Edwin bought at an auction, as is the mirror behind it. He put in hardwood floors and an old-style tin ceiling with insulation and another plaster ceiling above it so the noise wouldn't bother the landlady, who lives right upstairs. It works great. *Master of Reality,* Sabbath's second album, is pounding at full volume and no one seems to be complaining. I close and lock the door behind me.

Edwin is a bit past fifty but still built like a tractor. I've watched him carry a full beer keg on his shoulder up and down the cellar stairs. He's still grinding out push-ups as I walk down the bar, apparently going for a personal best. The crowd is reaching a crescendo with the count and Edwin is finally slowing down.

—Forty-three! Forty-four! Forty-five!

His record with Lisa on his back is fifty-three. He did around fifteen once with Amtrak on his back, but Amtrak weighs about 280. With nobody on his back Edwin can do push-ups until everyone just gets tired of counting.

—Forty-nine! Fifty! Fifty-one!

The natives are really whipped up. "Children of the Grave" has just started screaming out of the juke and Lisa is giggling uncontrollably on Edwin's back. She tries to take a sip of her greyhound, spilling it down her chin. Edwin is now shaking and grunting. Sweat is racing down his face and arms.

—Fifty-two! Fifty-three!

Edwin gulps air and Lisa gets down a big slug of vodka and grapefruit juice as he ratchets himself up again and again and again.

—FIFTY-FOUR! FIFTY-FIVE! FIFTY-SIX!

The record is shattered and Edwin collapses on the bar. He rolls to his back, tumbling Lisa to the floor behind the bar, where she lands, still giggling. Edwin gasps and shouts.

—Reward me! My just due! Reward me!

The gang applauds and cheers. They pour beer into Edwin's open mouth and dig bills from their pockets to throw at him.

It's a good party.

Edwin spots me when he boosts himself back up on the bar.

—Sailor! There ya are, ya fuck!

Everyone turns to see me, and they send up a new cheer.

—SAILOR!

They all toast and take a drink.

—Sailor, how goes it?

—Hank. How's it hangin', Hank?

—Did you see the fucking Giants game, man? Mets, man, it's all about the Mets now.

Edwin vaults down from the bar and rushes me. He wraps his arms around my middle, lifts me from the floor and squeezes. All the air rushes out of me and I make little squealing noises.

—Ya little girl, ya little fucking girl. Get the beat shit outta ya and ya quit! Ya little fucking girl.

His arms are locked around the wound and my arms are pinned to my sides and I can't get enough air to tell him to let me the fuck down.

—What's a matter, little girl? Looks like he's gonna cry here.

Edwin starts to swing me around and around. Everyone is crazy, laughing. Amtrak shakes up his beer and sprays me with it while someone else pelts me with peanuts. Lisa picks herself up from behind the bar and sees the action.

—Edwin! Edwin, for chrissake, Edwin, put him down. EDWIN!

She walks over to the juke and pulls the plug.

—Edwin, for fuck sake put him down, he just had surgery.

Edwin stops spinning and sets me gently on my feet.

—Oh, fuck! Fuck, Hank, I'm fucking sorry, man. I wasn't thinking, man, I'm just glad to see you, man.

—It's cool, Edwin, I'm, man, I'm really glad to see you, too. It's great to see all y'all.

This sets off another round of cheers and Edwin grabs me by the back of the neck and shakes me a little. He's totally fucking loaded. He's got booze-sweat pouring out of his skin and his pupils are pinned up tight from the coke and the whole place reeks of weed. He steers me over to the bar by my neck and waves to Lisa.

—Set 'em up, Leez. Gobble gobble, Wild Turkey all around, all around.

Lisa grabs the bottle of Wild Turkey 101 and starts filling shot glasses while everyone packs around us at the bar. Someone turns the music back on, but it's not Sabbath anymore. There's a wind sound and a bell and the opening organ notes to Elton John's "Funeral for a Friend" fill the bar. I put my mouth close to Edwin's ear.

—Edwin, man, I need a favor.

He looks at me and nods and smiles.

—Sure, sure, man, anything.

—No big deal, but that little envelope I gave you to put in the safe the other night, I need it now.

—What?

—The envelope, man, I need it.

—Here, drink. Drink!

He shoves a shot glass into my hand and pushes it toward my face.

—Edwin, man, I can't really drink anymore.

—"Can't really drink." Hear that? Motherhumper was in here falling off his stool other night. Now he can't drink.

—Seriously, Edwin, I need to get into the safe, man.

—Fucker quits on me without, I might fucking add, the traditional two weeks' notice and he won't have a drink with me.

The group is into it, egging him on and yelling for me to drink.

—Edwin, man! This is important and I'm kind of in a hurry.

Edwin looks to his audience.

—The man is in a hurry. A hurry! Well, you better hurry up and drink that drink, man.

Another cheer. Everyone is holding their shots aloft, chanting.

—DRINK! DRINK! DRINK! DRINK!

—Edwin, please.

—Drink first, then business.

I toss down the shot. Everyone hollers and knocks their own back.

It hits my stomach and I almost choke it back up. It stays down. And I wish for another. Edwin hugs me again, puts an arm around my shoulder and moves me a few feet down the bar away from the group.

—OK, man, OK. Now, what's up, what do you need from the safe? Hope you don't think ya got any money comin' to ya 'cause I'm dockin' all your pay till ya come back.

—No, man.

—Seriously, though, you need cash? You need it, you can have it.

—No, Edwin, man, I need that envelope, that envelope I gave you the other night.

He looks at me.

—Envelope?

—The envelope I gave you to put in the safe. It has a key in it, I need it right now, man, the envelope with the key, fast.

He puts a hand on my shoulder.

—Hank, man, I'm sorry, but you didn't give me no envelope the other night, no envelope and no key.

The music segues into "Love Lies Bleeding." How long have I been in here? Five minutes? Ten? Not ten, between five and ten. How long will Roman sit out there? How much time will be too much?

—Edwin, don't fuck around, I know I gave you that key.

—And I know you didn't give me shit that night except a pain in my ass from being so fucking drunk, which is why you can't remember what you gave me or didn't fucking give me. Your key is not in the safe. Period.

The bar hounds are all singing along to the jukebox, Lisa behind the bar leading them. Edwin and I are at the very back of the bar, where there are four doors. The two doors on the left are bathrooms, the one straight back is for the little box of an office where the safe is and the one on the right opens on a little courtyard. The yard is shared with most of the buildings around the block; it's clogged with garbage and the only way in or out is through one of the other buildings' back doors or up the collection of rickety fire escapes.

—Edwin, I'm in trouble.

—Yeah, I kinda figured that.

—Big trouble, Edwin.

—What is it?

—Guys are looking for me, Edwin, coming for me.

—Those fucks that beat you up?

—Yeah, but worse. Edwin, they're here, they're coming here. Oh, God! Oh, fuck! Edwin, I'm sorry, man. Big trouble, Edwin. It's big trouble.

—No problem.

His little coked-out eyes are shining. Edwin likes to fight. Back in the late sixties, early seventies, he rode with a gang in St. Louis called the Sable Slaves; picture a cross between the Hell's Angels and the Black Panthers. When he takes his shirt off, Edwin's black skin is covered in a mixture of tattoos and scars. Tattoos of naked women, spiders, daggers, skeletons, dragons, and a big one on his back of a Klansman strapped to a burning cross. Scars from motorcycle timing chains, knives, baseball bats with nails driven into them, broken beer bottles, and at least one from a bullet. Edwin is the toughest fucker I've ever seen, and he likes to fight. He smells a good fight right now.

—Trouble's no problem, Hank. Bring it on. Bring. It. On.

—Edwin, no, no. No! We, we, we. Listen, man, we need to go now, we need to take everyone out the back door and get the fuck out of here.

—The fuck you say. The fuck I'm gonna chase my friends out, get run out of my own bar.

I've started opening the locks on the back door. Edwin is trying to stop me, grabbing at my hands, but not wanting to hurt me.

—EDWIN! HEY, EDWIN!

Sunday is at the front door, looking out the little window. She yells over the music again, still looking out the window.

—EDWIN, THERE'S A BIG GUY OUT HERE WANTS IN. SHOULD I LET 'IM?

We stop wrestling with the locks and look at Sunday. There is only the sound of breaking glass as the window in the front door shatters. Sunday's head snaps back and she drops to the floor with a little black hole drilled in her nose. Bolo's huge brown hand smashes through what's left of the window and starts groping around for the dead bolt. Edwin has started running in that direction as I flip the last lock and open the back door. Blackie and Whitey are standing there, their tracksuits dirty from coming over the rooftops. They're holding the kind of pistol-size machine guns that look like toys but aren't. Bolo gets the front door open and steps in and Edwin barrels into him sending the gun he used to kill Sunday spinning to the floor. Bolo does the easiest thing: he lets himself fall forward, pinning Edwin between his own enormous mass and Sunday's corpse. Edwin can't get a limb free to strike at him but keeps trying until Roman steps in, closes and locks the door, picks up the fallen pistol and sticks it in Edwin's ear. "Love Lies Bleeding" ends. No more music plays on the jukebox.

—You have to jiggle it a little.

Roman is trying to open the safe. Edwin has repeated the combination to him several times backward and forward and from the middle, but Roman can't get the safe open.

—I told you, you have to jiggle when you spin right. It's fussy.

Roman tries again.

—No, don't jiggle on the number, just between and not when you go back to nine.

Roman tries again.

—Jiggle, not shake. Jiggle.

Roman tries.

—Just, fuck, will you just let me fucking do it?

The safe is set in the floor under the desk that is against the wall opposite the door. A little panel in the floorboards flips up and you have to cram yourself half under the desk to reach over the trapdoor and spin the tumbler. Roman is squatting down there, sweating. Edwin and I are pressed against the wall next to the door and Bolo stands just outside, unable to squeeze into the room. The Russians have everybody else packed on the floor behind the bar, keeping them covered with their nasty little guns.

The sound of crying carries clearly into the office. I can hear Wayne saying Sunday's name over and over and Lisa trying to shush him.

Roman tries again.

—Just. Let. Me. Do. It.

Roman looks at Edwin and wipes the sweat from his forehead. They came in about six minutes ago and it's clearly five more than he intended to be here.

—You gave me the right combination?

—It's fussy, I told you that. So just let me open it.

Roman unfolds from the tiny space.

—You will work the combination. You will open the safe. You will step away. You will not reach into the safe or I will kill you. Am I clear?

—Fuck, yeah. Now let me open the fucking thing.

Roman and Edwin swap places in the tiny room. Edwin fits much better under the desk. He reaches into the space hidden by the trapdoor and starts to spin the dial. Bolo leans in the open door, his gun in relaxed fingers at his side. Roman is between us, his own gun still holstered. He takes out the handkerchief he used to wipe the blood from my face and blots the sweat from his own. I don't tell Roman the key isn't in the safe. I don't tell because I know what is in the safe and I want Edwin to have it.

—See, just jiggle and it opens right up.

There's a little clank as Edwin turns the bolt and opens the safe. He moves to climb out from under the desk, bumps his head and ducks down from the impact.

—Fuck!

He grabs his head with his left hand, but his right is still hidden behind the trap. Roman starts to reach into his coat and Bolo shifts in the doorway.

—Your hand, let me see your hand.

—Yeah, yeah.

The safe is a deep cylinder set in a concrete block. Edwin told me once that it took him a while to find one deep enough to fit the Remington 12-gauge, even with the sawed-off barrel and the pistol grip. He drops his left shoulder, rolling onto his back as his right hand arcs out of the safe with the shotgun. I jump as far to my left as I can and fall to the floor. Roman is trying to step back out of the room and stumbles against Bolo, who is trying to step forward for a clear shot. Edwin sprawls on his back with the stubby barrel of the .12 pointed up at them and pulls the trigger. It's loaded with birdshot, but from a few feet away the load has little room to spread. Roman takes it in his upper chest and it shoves him back into Bolo and they both fall into the hall. From out in the bar I hear the sudden rattle of the Russians' tiny guns. Bullets rake the office. Edwin twists on the floor, kicks the door shut and from his knees shoots the twin bolts, locking us in. The door is wrapped in steel, with a mail slot cut into it so you can make cash drops on late nights. Bullets ping against the door but don't penetrate. Edwin stands up, crams the barrel of his gun through the mail slot and unloads several rounds.

The office is clogged with smoke and tears flood down my cheeks. Edwin grabs a box of shells from the desk and reloads.

—Cocksuckers must die. All cocksuckers must die. Gonna kill all those cocksuckers.

The mail slot flips up and the barrel of one of the machine guns pops through. It waves around and makes a sound like a minibike and everything in the office explodes. We press against the door while wood splinters and shattered glass pepper us. A bullet ricochets and embeds itself in the wall next to Edwin's head.

—Fuck! Cocksuckers die!

Edwin shoves the Remington through the slot and opens fire again. He empties the gun and starts once more to reload. We huddle against the door and wait, but the machine gun doesn't come back.

—Fuck! OK, fuck! OK, we go. Fucking Butch and Sundance in Bolivia, OK, Hank? Let's do it, let's go.

He's filling his pockets with extra shells.

—Edwin, man, the cops, wait for the fucking cops.

—Fuck that, man. Butch Cassidy and the Sundance Kid, that's us, man, that's us. We're goin'. Go, let's go!

There is no way I'm gonna go, no way I'm gonna run out there screaming to die. There is the rip of a machine gun again, but no bullets bang against the door. Instead we hear muffled screams from behind the bar.

—That's our song, Hank. Open the door! Open the fucking door!

I do it.

I stand next to the door and we both scream at the top of our lungs as I pull the bolts and jerk the door open and Edwin's body collapses in on itself as dozens of bullets seem to strike him at once.

I shove the door closed, shoot the bolts and huddle against it, trying not to sit in too much of Edwin's blood. Outside the door, Roman starts talking.

—That didn't go well at all, did it?

Not far away, there are sirens.

I wait as long as I can before I go out. The sirens are getting very close and I need to get out of here. Roman, Bolo and Whitey are gone. Blackie is just outside the door to the office, his head dangling from his torso, unprotected by the body armor I can now see beneath his shredded tracksuit. They must all be wearing it.

Everybody is behind the bar. All of them. In a big pile.

Amtrak John used to let me ride the train for free when I went upstate to see friends. Wayne helped to move that big table into Yvonne's place, and Sunday would make me little herbal remedies whenever I was sick. Dan would bring his pirate cable box into the bar on big fight nights and we'd watch them for free, then spend the rest of the night watching porn.

Lisa.

Edwin.

The sirens are just up the street. I go out the back door and up one of the fire escapes. I cross over the rooftops to Avenue A, my street, just a block from the bar. I climb down and cross the street. Jason is up and digging through the pile of garbage on the sidewalk in front of my building. I walk past him and take out my keys to open the front door. I stop and look back at Jason. He's carefully untying the bags, picking out the aluminum cans and retying the bags. I walk over to him and start looking through the piles. Jason looks at me resentfully but goes about his task undaunted. I toss aside several bags until I find the one that smells more like crap than the others. I open it up and pull out the jeans I shit in. It's right there where I forgot it, stuffed in the back pocket, waiting for me to give it to Edwin to put in the safe, except I got drunk and forgot about it and all those people are dead because I couldn't remember where it was. I take the key out of the envelope, put it in my pocket and let myself into my building, leaving Jason to his work.

My door has police tape sealed over the jamb, just like Russ's. The cops must have been through here after they picked me up at Yvonne's. I don't want to cut the tape, so I go up to the roof. My laundry bag is still up there, so I take it with me down the fire escape. I have to climb over the rail again to get in the window. Once inside, I reach out and pull in the laundry.

The cops did a pretty good job on the place, but I don't really care at this point. The light is blinking on my answering machine. Mom is there three times, but I don't listen to any of her messages. I can't. I sit on the couch and look at the key. It's notched along both edges and the base is a big square of blue plastic with the number 413d cut into it. It's for a storage locker. This is a key to a rented storage locker. I know because I keep stuff stored at one of the big warehouses on the West Side and have a pink key similar to this one right on my key ring. I sit there and stare straight ahead and suddenly realize what I'm staring at. It's Bud's carrying case. Bud is still in Roman's car. Outside my door someone tears the police tape and starts picking the lock.

I get the aluminum bat from my closet and stand to the side of the door and wait. The lock snaps open, the knob turns and someone comes in.

It's a man. I plant the bat in his gut and as he folds over I whip it up and clip him across the back of the head and he drops flat. I ram the door shut with my shoulder and lock it before anyone else can get in. No one tries. I look at the guy on the floor, shove my toe under him and flip him over. It's Russ.

I tuck the bat under my arm and walk over to the sink. I take a big plastic cup from the dish rack. It's an old souvenir cup from Candlestick Park. Willie Mays is on the side. I fill it with cold water, walk over to Russ and pour it out on his face. Some of it goes in his mouth and up his nose, making him choke, and that brings him around. He rolls onto his stomach and coughs and catches his breath. He reaches up and feels at the lump on his scalp where blood is slowly trickling out. He looks up and sees me for the first time.

—Hank! Oh, man, Hank! Good, good. Look, man, I need my cat.

I hit him with the bat until he's unconscious again, but I stop before I kill him.

*Two Regular Season
Games Remaining*

They're talking about me on TV. A block away, NY1 and all the other local stations are live on the scene of the worst massacre in recent New York history and, from time to time, they replay the official police statement.

A cop in a fancy uniform with a lot of medals on his chest for catching criminals stands in front of Paul's and reads from a piece of paper. —This is. Excuse me, please, I have a statement and I will read it just once. This is a very preliminary statement. As of now, we know, we believe, that a short while ago a gun battle took place between the owner of Paul's Bar and an unknown number of assailants who appear to have been attempting to rob the establishment. We have . . . we have seven confirmed dead, including one of the assailants. We are asking that anyone in this area who may have seen or heard anything suspicious in the early morning here to please contact us. We are . . . we are also seeking a former employee of Paul's for questioning in connection to this tragic crime. That is all.

The cops are not stupid. They arrived at my apartment a little over an hour ago, saw the broken seal, burst in with guns drawn and found it empty. Russ and I stayed very quiet in his place across the hall while they searched mine high and low and eventually taped it back up and split.

Russ sits on the couch with an ice bag on his head and watches the TV at very low volume while I shave my hair down to fuzz with his clippers. I've already shaved my face clean to get rid of the stubble I had when the police took my booking photo last night.

Sooner or later, the cops will have to bite the bullet. Some clever reporter will sniff around and the cops will have to explain how a man already in their custody in connection with one murder escaped and got involved in mass murder. Then my picture will be everywhere. I'm hoping for at least twenty-four hours' grace.

Over on the couch, Russ is a little dopey from the shots he's taken to the noggin, but I don't think he'll make any more trouble now that I have his gun.

When he came round the second time he was a bit confused.

—Fuck, Hank. What the fuck?

—Roman's looking for you, Russ.

—Roman?

—Roman's looking for you, Russ.

He touched the wound on his head and flinched.

—Fuck, Hank, I don't know any fucking Roman. What the fuck, man, like, why'd ya hit me, man?

—Red, the Chinese kid, he's dead. So's one of the Russians. Roman, Bolo, and the other Russian are looking for you and me and the key, Russ.

—Russians? Like, what the fuck, man?

—Russ, Ed and Paris are looking, too.

He looked at me, blood from his head running down his neck and staining the collar of his shirt.

—Ed and Paris?

—Yeah.

—Fuck! Oh fuck! Oh man, oh fuck, oh man. Fuck, fuck, fuck.

—Yeah Russ. Oh fuck indeed.

Around then I got my shit together enough to get us out through my window, onto the fire escape and into his place through his window before the cops could show. They came up the stairs pretty stealthily, but once they saw the ripped tape on my door they went in like gangbusters. I watched from Russ's peephole until they left. When I turned around, Russ had a little chrome .22 stuck in my face.

—Sorry, man, but I gotta go. So just give me the key, OK?

I nodded at my jacket on his couch.

—In the pocket.

He glanced to the right and I swept my left hand up to slap the gun away from my face. I kept a hold on his wrist as I grabbed his shirt with my right hand, stepped in and kneed him in the crotch. He sank to the floor and I covered his mouth to make sure he wouldn't groan too loud. I took his gun, flicked on the TV to check the news and, just like it happens in old gangster movies, they were talking about my "crimes" on the news. That's when I went in the bathroom and started shaving.

I think I gave Russ a concussion when I nailed him with the bat the second time. I wouldn't care except that I'm having trouble getting him to focus and make sense.

—I'm sorry, man, I'm so damn sorry. This never. Oh, God, I'm sorry.

—Russ, we need to talk now, man, I need to know things. Russ!

—No, man, no more, you don't, like, want to. Oh, I'm so sorry. I'm such a sorry sack of shit.

—Russ. Russ, calm down and talk to me, OK?

He stays on the couch, holding the ice bag on his head, rocking back and forth and looking away whenever I try to catch his eye and get him to focus.

I've traded my jacket for one of his, a lined windbreaker with a Yan-kees patch on the back. Fucking Yankees. They think they own the world. Nothing else of his fits me, but I did find a pair of wraparound sunglasses that hide the bruises around my eyes pretty well. I also grabbed his little Walkman radio. I can stay up on the news and the headphones will help my disguise, such as it is.

—Russ, Russ! Come on, man, it's time to go. Come on.

—No. No, man. I'm gonna stay here.

—Russ, the cops aren't that dumb, they'll be back and, if not, then Roman will.

—Fuck that, I don't fucking care. Oh, I'm so fucked.

—Russ, Ed and Paris have already been here once.

He stops rocking and looks up at me.

—Shit, Hank, we gotta go.

We go out the window again.

We use the rooftops to avoid the cops on the streets below and circle the block to First Avenue. There's a chopper cruising the area, but it seems to be focused on the blocks east of Avenue A, over by the projects. We catch a big break when we see some guys working on one of the roofs. They're patching holes in the tar paper, their backs to us. We just sneak in through the roof access door they've propped open with a piece of brick. Down the stairs and we exit onto First. We walk right past two of New York's finest, I flag a cab and we're gone. So much for police gauntlets.

Russ slumps in the seat and lets his head loll back. He's worse than I thought. I get him to look at me and I cover his right eye with my hand, then pull it away suddenly and watch how his pupil dilates, then do the same thing with his left eye. The right one is OK, but the left dilates irregularly. He must be pretty fucking scrambled in there. On top of that, blood is starting to leak out of his cap. I didn't have time to patch him up at the apartment and all my first-aid stuff is in my bag in Roman's car. I took a huge wad of toilet paper, soaked it in some vodka I found under his sink, stuck it on his head, and crammed a ski cap on him to hold it in place.

The cab is just cruising north and the driver wants a specific destination. I give Russ a little shake.

—Russ, hey, Russ. How about it, man? Why don't you show me what it's all about?

—What what's about? What?

—Russ, where to, Russ?

The cabbie is getting testy just driving up First. I tell him to head for the West Side Highway. I shake the blue storage unit key in Russ's face.

—How 'bout it, Russ? Let's go take a look.

He focuses on the key.

—Hey, man, that's my key.

—What's it for, Russ? What's it for?

—Fuck, man, how'd you get my key?

—What's it for?

—It's, like, my unit, man.

—Where?

—Mini Storage. Chelsea.

I tell the cabbie to take us to Chelsea Mini Storage. Russ flops back in his seat and I go through his pockets for cash so I'll be able to pay for the cab when we arrive. Along with Bud, my money is in Roman's car. I find seventy-eight bucks, some credit cards, the jimmy tools he used to pick my lock and a pack of Big Red. I take his wallet and the gum.

They want you to sign in before they'll let you go up. Russ is still too shaky to trust with other people, so I sign his name and give the guy in the booth the unit number. He doesn't ask for ID or anything, just gives me two passes, tells us to wear them at all times and points to the elevator.

The elevator operator asks for our pass numbers. I tell him both. Russ just stands there and shakes his head every now and then. The elevator guy keeps glancing at us. Between Russ's lumpy head and my nearly bald white scalp, we look like we just escaped from the terminal cancer ward. The elevator stops on the fourth floor and we get out.

Corridors and corridors of doors, perfectly identical except for the numbers. Russ is no help showing the way, so we wander until we find 413d.

I have to rattle the lock to get it open and then the bolt sticks, but finally there we are, looking into a fifteen-by-fifteen cubicle with a huge black hockey bag sitting in the exact middle of the floor. I lead

Russ in, turn on the fluorescent light, shut the door behind us, go over and unzip the bag.

When Roman told me they were all looking for an "object," I had visions of jewel-encrusted black birds, little gold statuettes, or the Ark of the Covenant. Apparently, what he meant to say was that they were all looking for a bag stuffed full with bundles and bundles and bundles of cash.

I stare at all the twenties and fifties and hundreds and Russ gestures at the room.

—I could have gotten the five-by-five unit for cheaper, but I wanted the bigger one so I'd, like, have more room to count it in.

Russ counts the twenties and fifties while I handle the hundreds and it's a good thing he got the extra floor space because once we start spreading out all this cash, it takes up a lot of fucking room. It's the kind of money that makes a man stupid, very stupid. Russ, for instance, has been very stupid.

He met Ed and Paris at the youth camp in Montana.

—We hit it off, me and Ed and Paris, cuz we were all, like, into comic books, like, the *X-Men* and *Fantastic Four* and the *Avengers* and shit. We got to go into town every now and then on, like, weekends and I was good at boosting stuff, so I'd, like, boost all these comics and share 'em with Ed and Paris. That shit, those comic books, they're just more fun when you can talk to someone about 'em, so me and Ed and Paris, like, talked comics. We were all due to go home about the same time and we figured to hook up, cuz I was, like, planning a move to the city. But, like, one of the counselor guys, he took a shine to Ed and tried to, like, get over with him, like, tried to rape him and all and Ed and Paris cut his throat, so they ended up getting shipped out to do real time.

I hit five hundred thousand dollars and stop counting for a minute. The pile of uncounted money is still huge.

—Anyways, I went home, but, like, I kept sending comics to them cuz

I felt sorry for 'em in the juvie facility when all they fucking did was kill a fucking, like, child-molesting raper. We were, what, like twelve or thirteen when it all went down and they didn't come back for a while until they were eighteen and by then they had gotten all into the weights and had studied and gotten their high school diplomas. But they were really grateful I had, like, stayed in touch and sent them the comics and shit. Their mom had written them off after they sliced the counselor guy, so they didn't really have, like, a home anymore and I had a flop in Spanish Harlem. So they came and stayed with me.

At first I tried to count all the bills, but now I just rifle each pack to make sure they're all hundreds, assume it's a full ten grand and stack them up. I put another one on the stack and I take a break and chew a piece of Big Red while Russ talks and stacks the smaller bills.

—By that time, I was already boosting stuff pretty much left and right. Mmm. I was, like, into a little B and E, but mostly it was real harmless stuff. But Ed and Paris, they had, like, they had, like, got a higher education doing that hard juvie time. They were, like, right into the strong-arm stuff: mugging, a little muscle for the loan sharks, carjacking, some hijacking, like, liquor and cigs and stuff. Then they moved into armed robbery. Mmm.

Little pauses start creeping into Russ's story. From time to time, his eyes fuzz out for a moment then he shakes his head, gives a little "mmm," and gets back on track. He's still stacking bills, but he's starting to have trouble keeping them in the right piles. I move over and begin straightening things out. He nods a little thanks and I point at the wall. He leans back and continues his story.

—So they get picked up again, this time it's a pretty heavy beef. They pistol-whipped the security guard at this, like, ATM place. Mmm. Uh, then they were so convicted, but get this: They're getting transferred out of town from Rikers to upstate and, like, the van they're in, this is in winter, it slides on a patch of ice and flips. Now, the deputies. Mmm. The deputies, they were, like, required by law to put seat belts on the prisoners, but they didn't wear their own. So the van flips, the deputies go flying, both DOA, and Ed and Paris, they unbuckle and walk away with bruises.

I've got the bills restacked properly now and I stop for a second and stare at them. I think about car accidents and seat belts and, in my mind, Rich flies past me and through the windshield. I start counting again.

—So this, like, Good Samaritan stops to check out the wreck and Ed and Paris, they clock the dude, take his keys and cash and they're rollin' back to the city, still in chains and coveralls. They show up at my place and we get them all squared away. They jack another car and blow town. Mmm. We're all still basically kids at this point. It's, like, '89 or '90 or so and we're all, like, twenty or so. They cruise down south to Florida, where they end up doing wicked shit for these Cuban gangsters. Me. Mmm. Me, I just go along doing my thing, except I catch that acting bug, so I start taking, like, these classes and shit. The fucking New School. I did, ya know, I did, like, day player stuff on *As the World Turns* for a while and some downtown theater stuff, too. Hey, man, did you know I was in a Richard Foreman play? No shit, took my clothes off. But, like, I still stole an' shit. That was my day job. Mmm.

The money is piling higher and higher. I think I've done the twenties and fifties. All that's left are the hundreds. The many, many remaining hundreds. By looking at those counted piles and comparing them to what's left in the bag, I'm starting to get a better idea of just how much money is here. My hands are shaking a bit and I make tight little fists until they stop.

—So they stayed down there in Florida for a few years, but they, like, got into some kind of beef with the Cubans and it ended pretty ugly. I'm not really up on all the details and such, but from what I gather, it was one of those, like, scenes with a bunch of guns, piles of coke, and a machete. *Scarface* kind of shit. Mmmm. So they had to blow and some, like, time had passed and they decided to come home and headed back up here. They, like, gave me a call out of the blue and I helped 'em to get a pad. Mmmm. To get a pad and, like, all situated and stuff. They were cool for a bit, but then they started this gig doing stickups at, like, high-stakes poker games and drug deals. They figured they could keep a lower profile if they, like, restrained their activities to the criminal community. Like, who's gonna give a fuck, right?

I keep counting.

—For a while I helped out a bit, being, like, a technical adviser on a few jobs. I'd, you know, pick a lock or whatever. But the action was really just too fucking hot for me. High returns, but the risks were, like. Mmmm. I didn't like the odds. Normal crime, the cops catch you and you're just busted. The kind of shit they were pulling, other cons catch you robbing them and they're gonna just fuck you all up. Anyway. Mmmm. Anyway, that's about when I hooked them up with Lum. The Chinese kid. The one with the, like, red hair.

Russ is still sitting on the floor with his back against the wall, his eyes closed.

—I had met Lum through friends of, like, friends, and he was this kind of kid criminal prodigy. He wanted to be getting into heavier shit, so I set him up with Ed and Paris and they took him under their wing, sort of. Mmmm. So, at some point it all had to get, like, fucked up, and sure enough, it did. What happened was people, people in the life, got wind of what they were up to and some disinformation was floated their way through, like, usually reliable channels. They went in and hit this card game, thinking it was a bunch of bookies. Turned out it was a cop game.

And counting.

—Ed and Paris don't even, like, blink. They just pull the job like it's business as usual while all these cops are telling them how dead they are. Then, like, it gets messy, cuz one of the cops goes for his ankle piece. Ed and Paris aren't fools. They, like, don't want to kill any cops, but they bust the guy up bad and split with the kitty. Now they're just red fucking hot and they're trying to decide if they should blow town or, like, what, and that's when Roman pops up. Mmmm. Roman, he was like this hotshot hero cop way back. Some kind of Serpico with a real hard-on for the law. 'Cept, story is, he had a bad gambling jones. So things happen, right? He makes a bet here and there, gets some debt, makes a couple small moves to clear it up and next thing you know, he's a hard-core player. That's the way the system works. Mmm-mmm. At this stage, he's a robbery dick and he's already, like, dirty as hell. He tracks Ed and Paris down, I mean like a bloodhound. He just goes right to 'em. There's this big Mexican face-off and he ends up showing all his cards. Turns out he's been on to Ed and Paris for a while. Turns out he's, like, this big fan, he's, like, recognized their talents and wants to, like, manage them. And so that's what he does. Takes over and makes them into stars. Mmmm.

Counting.

—First, he pins the card game heist and all their other jobs on these niggers up in the Bronx. Those chumps get the Amadou Diallo treatment, so they don't dispute any claims made against them. Next, he starts picking gigs for them, using his scoop from being on the force and all. He starts local, then pretty soon he's got Ed, Paris and Lum working all over the tristate, right. Mmmm. I have my hand in, too, like, fence this or get that tool or ditch a car or whatever, nothing too big. Every now and then, Roman comes up with something superheavy and for those he sends in, like, his right-hand man. Bolo. Bolo was a longshoreman. Roman busted him for jacking cargo and then put him to work for the cause. Made Bolo his enforcer on the street. Mmmm. Tell you what. Seeing Ed, Paris, Lum and Bolo go into a room and work it over? That was, like, something else. Pure fear. Those boys all together just radiated fucking fear. People just gave them whatever the fuck and if they, like, got belligerent or some shit, then the hammer came down and that was that. Like, woe betide the motherfucker.

I look at what's left uncounted in the bag. I'm in the home stretch.

—Mmmm. So, so, this goes for years, right. They work a handful of jobs a year, then lie low, then go at it again. All is well. Roman spots a potential job, does the research, sends in his team, they knock it down, he chills any possible heat and all the rest is profit. Roman, he still suffers from that gambling bug. So he's, like, investing his share in Atlantic City stocks and bonds, if ya get me. Bolo and Lum, they're all about good times, so they just party down. Ed and Paris, they live like fucking monks; I mean, the duds and the wheels aside, these are very simple men. They go in for booze and whores, but no drugs, no gold, no bling, no fucking Lexus, no palace. Just that Caddie and the best guns money can buy. They stockpile their cash, like, not in a bank, but under a damn mattress or some shit. Mmmm.

I finish counting, lean against the wall next to Russ, stare at the money and chew more gum while he finishes the story.

—At some point, there's a brouhaha. The boys are doing a chip heist. Silicon chips. The markup on that shit is, like, unreal. That tech shit, it's, like, changed the whole economy. Anyway, turns out some other crew is already there making the same fucking heist. Gunfight, man. All hell and then some. Cops roll up on the scene and Ed, Paris, Bolo and Lum end up shooting their way out and this time they kack three officers. Mmmm. Well, that's the kind of mess even Roman can't clean up, so it's time for the gang to, like, disband. Roman keeps Bolo stashed in Jersey so he can still use him if he needs to, but he, like, cuts Lum and the boys loose. Fine with Ed and Paris. They, like, pack their bags and head south again. Mmmm. They, like, stay mellow for a year, but then they get an idea and they give me a ring. See, Ed and Paris, they, like, want to retire, but they don't figure they have quite enough put away, so they want to do a series of jobs, cash in their chips and head down to Mexico or someplace.

Mexico. I think about Mexican beer with a squeeze of lime.

—Mmmm. Mmmm. Ed, now Ed, he's been, like, learning from Roman, so he's got this plan. He wants to loop through the South and back up through the Midwest doing bank jobs. No major branches, he just wants to hit a whole shitload of little, like, farmers' and merchants' banks in all those little towns. They hook back up with Lum so he can be their wheelman and take care of any alarm action and technical issues. What they want from me is help with the cash. Mmmm. Bank cash is all dirty cash, so it has to be, like, cleaned off. They know I can't really do that on my own, so that's when they call Roman back in. Mmmm. Roman has all the connections, including, get this. Mmmm. Including the Russian Mafia, which is how those thugs Bert and Ernie got into this shit. Mmmm.

Bert and Ernie. I see Blackie on the floor in the bar almost headless. I wonder which one he was.

—The deal is, Ed and Paris, they, like, ship the bank money to me, just, like, Federal Express it, man, if you can believe that shit. I pass it on to Roman, who moves it through the Russians till it's washed and he hands it back over to me, at like which point I put it in safekeeping. Ed and Paris get caught, they don't want to be holding the bag, right. For my services, I'm paid a flat fee. The Russians slice a big percentage out of the gross, Roman takes a cut of the, like, net and the boys and Lum will split the rest. And it goes fucking perfectly. Mmmm. Ed and Paris go on a full-out crime spree, straight-out holdups, real, like, Dodge City shit. They are fully notorious and on the FBI Most Wanted, but they're, like, uncatchable. Just so fast and mean they can't be caught. They pull those hit-and-runs for almost two years and the money piles up and up and, well, man, look at it.

He opens his eyes and we both look at the money. There's a lot.

—A couple weeks back they say, that's it, they're coming to town to pick up their jack. They send the dough from the last bank, I have it laundered, bring it here, pack it with the rest and I guess that's when I, like, started getting, like, sick thoughts and, well, you know, things got all, like, fucked up. But, man, it's just, it's just, like, so much fucking money, ya know? It just, it just made me, like, stupid. Mmmm. Man, I don't feel too good.

He passes out. I lay him out on the floor and check his eyes again. The left one is still kind of funky. I take off his ski cap. The toilet paper mostly falls right off, but some of it is sticking to the wound on his scalp. I try to pick it out, but he winces a few times in his sleep, so I just leave it as is. It needs to be cleaned out and stitched up, but for now the bleeding has stopped and that's gonna have to be good enough.

I park myself in front of the door and stretch out with the Yankees jacket as a pillow. I haven't slept since I first showed up at Yvonne's, whenever that was. Once I'm still, I realize just how bad the pain my wound is and I have to take a full Vic.

I lie there and stare at the money as the fog rolls into my brain. It's just over four and a half million and I know exactly what Russ is talking about. I'm starting to feel stupider by the second.

* * *

It comes as no surprise when the nightmare wakes me up. Cold has begun to creep up out of the floor and into my bones, I sit up slowly, stretching out the kinks and shrug my way into Russ's Yankees jacket. He's still asleep, his breathing is deep and even, I leave him alone. Sleep is certainly the best thing for his head right now. Looking at him, I realize for the first time the slight resemblance he bears to Rich. Same color of curly brown hair, though not nearly as long. A similar toothy grin. The same wiry build. They couldn't be brothers, but perhaps cousins. I leave it alone and look at the cash instead.

I do some math in my head. Four and a half million divided by nine comes out to five hundred thousand. As far as I know, nine people have died for this money at a price of half a million each. I think about Yvonne's family. Her crazy philosopher father and yoga-teaching mother. I think about Wayne's daughter and Amtrak's ex-wife that he still lived with and loved. My stomach flops. I can't want this money. And yet I do. I have the key and Russ and the money. For the first time since I was seventeen I have everything everybody wants, and I don't want to lose it this time.

I close my eyes and, yet again, Rich shoots past me, through the exploding windshield and into the tree. The mediocre years of my life pile up around me. This money is not mine. It is not meant for me, but for someone either more deserving or more ruthless. For me, it is a tool that will allow me to rebuild what is left of my life. I inhale, exhale, until my heart stops jumping and I feel I am myself again.

I open my eyes and see that Russ is awake. He's looking at me with a little smile on his face.

—Makes it hard to think clearly, doesn't it?

Russ packs the money back in the hockey bag while I find some news on the radio. His concentration is better, but the left eye is the same and he still phases out a bit in the middle of talking. I keep a close eye on him to see that he doesn't start pocketing any of the cash.

Paul's is all over the local stations. My name is still out of it, but they continue to mention the "former employee." Then I hit NPR and they're breaking the story nationally.

—A botched robbery attempt at a bar resulted in seven dead in New York City this morning.

I switch off the radio as sweat breaks out all over my body and tears try to well up behind my eyes. How could I be so fucking stupid not to see it coming?

—Russ, we gotta go.

—Wait a sec. Mmmm. I'm almost done.

—We gotta go now.

—Just a sec.

I grab him and pull him to his feet and push him toward the door.

—Now, fucking now!

—OK, man, OK.

I start to step out of the unit, then go back in. Most of the cash is in the bag, but some is still scattered on the floor. I grab a pack of twenties and a pack of hundreds and follow Russ out.

We stand by the elevator, waiting.

—What's up, man?

—I have to make a call.

—What about the, like? Mmmm. What about the money, man?

The elevator is taking forever. I push the button again, leaning on it hard, and hear the bell ringing loud down the shaft.

—Man, what about the money?

I jam the button down and squeeze my eyes tight. What is taking so fucking long?

—MAN, LIKE, WHAT ABOUT THE MMMMONEY?

I take my hand off the button and put it on Russ's throat and slam him back into the wall. His eyes spin around and the concrete scrapes part of the scab from his wound and it starts to bleed again.

—Fuck, man. Fuck, fuck, fuck.

I squeeze his neck and he stops cursing and starts gasping.

—There is no money, Russ. There is no fucking money! My friends are fucking dead, they're fucking dead! There is no fucking money be-with one of Russ's credit cards. When he sees that I have his wallet, he starts to say something but stops himself before it can get out. The sales guy keeps offering me this and that. To hurry it along I tell him to give me deluxe everything and never mind the cost. It takes about twenty minutes in all and I end up with one of those phones where the antenna is angled away from your head so you don't get tumors from the signal.

Back on the street, I drag Russ to a quiet doorway off the avenue and make my call.

It's Saturday. They're both home.

—Hi, Mom.

—Henry! Oh, God, Henry! Oh, God! Oh, God!

—Mom.

—Henry. Oh, my God, Henry.

—Mom! Mom, I'm OK, Mom. I'm. Listen to me, I'm OK.

—Henry, We're so, just so. People called, and the news, we saw the news, we saw the bar. Oh, Henry, the police and all those people.

—Mom, it's OK, I'm OK.

—We've been so, so scared, Henry. Oh, God.

She cries and can't get any more words out. I hear the phone being fumbled around and my dad comes on the line.

—Henry?

—Hey, Pop.

—Jesus, Hank, are you all right?

—Pop, oh, Pop.

—What's going on, Hank? Thank God you're OK, but we just need to know.

—I know, Dad.

—Oh, son. Jesus, I'm glad to hear your voice.

—Dad. I'm in some trouble here, Dad.

—What is it? What do you need us to do?

—Dad, it's big trouble.

—The police called, we're . . . They want to know where you are.

—Big trouble, Dad.

—Tell us.

cause my friends are dead because you gave me your fuck
now there is no fucking money!

His face is going from red to purple. I let him go. He slid
the wall to the floor and sits there gasping and holding his thro.
I lean my forehead against the wall.

—Fuck, Hank. Fuck.

—Yeah, fuck.

We are quiet for a moment, then he slowly climbs back to his fe

—Hey, Hank?

—Yeah.

—Where. Mmmm. Where is Bud, anyway?

I take my forehead from the wall and open my eyes.

—Roman has him.

—Shit.

—Yeah. Russ?

—Yeah?

—You're bleeding again. Put your hat back on.

He puts the hat on, I push the button again, and the elevator doors
open. The operator is standing there.

—Get the fuck off that button, man. I'm here.

On the way down, he takes our passes. I tell him we may be back
later, but he says we'll have to get new ones then. When we get to the
ground floor, I trot right over to the pay phone and pick up the handset
before I notice the little OUT OF ORDER sign taped to the wall next to it.

It's a typical day for New York pay phones. We work our way east, trying to find one that works. At Eighth Avenue, I pick up my fifth phone
and get a dial tone this time, but when I try to punch in the number
none of the buttons produce a tone of their own. I slam the handset
against the phone over and over until the earpiece snaps off and dan-
gles by a couple wires. I'm searching for the next one and Russ grabs
my shoulder and points at the electronics store across the street. I nod
and we cross over.

I pay for the phone itself with cash and open the service account

—Dad, I can't, but I was there, at the bar and the police, Dad, the police think I did it.

—What?

—Dad, they think I did it, but I didn't and I needed to call to tell you I was OK and that I didn't do that. I would never do that, Dad, I would never kill people. But they think I did.

—Why, what the hell is going on?

—I just, Dad, I just fell into some trouble.

—Well, let's get you out.

—It's, uh, it's not that kind of trouble, Pop, and I need you and Mom to just be ready, because I'm not sure how I'm gonna work it all out.

—Ready for what?

—I may, I may need to go somewhere. I don't know, but I may, it's big trouble and I may need to go away and I don't know.

I stop. I can see them standing next to the kitchen counter, my dad with the phone held away from his ear so my mom can listen, leaning against each other.

—What do you need us to do, Hank?

—Just, Dad, I just need you to know I didn't do it. These people, they did it and, oh, fuck, they, they killed Yvonne, too, Dad.

—Jesus.

—And, Dad, I'm trying to do the right thing, Dad. I need you guys to know I didn't hurt anybody, no matter what you hear.

—I know, Hank, I believe you.

—Thanks, Pop.

We both go silent for a moment.

—Hank, what about the police?

—Just don't lie to them. If they ask, tell them you talked to me and tell them what I said, just don't lie.

—Sure.

Russ is leaning in the doorway, trying not to look at me, but I know he can hear everything I'm saying.

—I got to go, Dad.

—Well, you better say good-bye to your mom first.

—Yeah. I love you, Dad.

—I love you, too, son.

He passes the phone to my mom.

—You get all that, Mom?

—Oh, Henry, how could anyone think you'd do something like that? How could they?

—I just. It's just a mess, Mom, that's all.

—I love you, Henry.

—I love you, Mom.

—Be safe, OK?

—I will and I'll call very soon, just, just as soon as I can. OK?

—Be sure you do. Don't say you're going to call and forget. You know I hate that.

—I know.

—We love you so much.

—I love you guys, too, Mom.

—Be careful.

—I will, Mom, I'll be careful.

—OK. Good-bye, Henry.

—Good-bye, Mom.

The line is silent except for her breathing and I know she can't hang up, so I take the phone from my ear and push the little END button and the light on the liquid crystal display goes dark.

At the funeral, Rich's parents had slumped against each other, rocking back and forth. They were alone. They had no other children. Only Rich. And I'd killed him. They didn't blame me. They didn't have to. I blamed myself.

I picture my parents at my own funeral: alone, inconsolable.

I will not die. I will not die for money, or even for another man's life.

I look at Russ and watch him stare at something fascinating on the ground.

—I'm gonna give up the money, Russ. I'm gonna give up the money and I'm gonna give you up, too.

He tilts his head up and looks me in the eye.

—That, like, sounds about right.

* * *

At a Duane Reade, I grab one of those prepacked first-aid kits and a couple Ace bandages. My stuff is still in Roman's car. Russ gets a carton of Camel Lights. At a bodega, we fill two bags with fruit, snacks, cold cuts and soda. Russ wants a six-pack and I don't argue. We walk a couple blocks to 23rd Street and check into the Chelsea Hotel. It may be hip now, but it's still a flop. The desk clerk is so jaded that we don't raise an eyebrow even when I pay with cash.

Russ is pretty quiet the whole time and once we're in the room, all he wants to do is take a shower. I flip on the tube and check out the most recent updates. I don't have to look far. It's all over the dial. Someone's been digging. All the stations are running breaking news about a dishy new rumor. I catch a replay on NY1.

—The suspect most sought in connection to this morning's barroom massacre had escaped from police custody just hours before the murders took place, according to a source within the New York City Police Department. Furthermore, the source claims that the suspect was in custody for another murder that had taken place just yesterday. As of now, there is no response from the NYPD, but a statement is expected at a press conference later today.

It's not really good news, but it makes me just a little bit happy. If questions are being asked about me, then some heat must be getting close to Roman and the thought of Roman in the fire tickles me to no fucking end.

Russ comes out of the shower in his underpants with a towel around his shoulders. His head is bleeding yet again.

—Mmmm. Man, can you do something about this or what?

Russ sits in a chair and drinks tallboys of Coors Original while I take care of his wound. I use the scissors from the first-aid kit to cut away some of the hair, then I bathe the whole wound with hydrogen peroxide. Russ jumps a bit when the burning starts, but I push him back into the chair and he drains his beer and opens another. Once I blot away the blood and clip off some dead skin and scabs, I can see what we're dealing with and it's all fucked up. I tell Russ to keep drinking and get the needle and thread from the sewing kit that comes with the room.

He doesn't like it much, but I convince him that the wound isn't gonna close up on its own. The smell of the beer creeps right up my nose, but I keep my hands steady and focus on not hurting the poor bastard too much. It's not easy. When I thought I might be an EMT, I took all these first-aid classes. Back then, we practiced this on pieces of steak. That was a long time ago and the steaks didn't move around or bleed. It takes a while. Russ finishes his story.

—Once I, like, fuck! Watch that shit, man. Once I, like, disappeared, I knew all bets would be off and they'd *all* be after me. Not just Ed and Paris. Like, the way those other guys think, if I make off with the loot, then it's up for grabs and let the best man win. I didn't figure I'd, like, get too far with that damn. Mmmm. With that damn sack on my back. Plus which, if they caught me with the, like, cash, then they could just waste me and that's that. But if the money is, like, stashed, then I'm thinkin' I might be able to bargain a little. I'll blow town and, fuck! Oww! Fuck! Shit, man. I'll, like, blow town, be mobile for a while, let things cool a bit, then slip back into town for the bag and split for good. So I rented that locker, left the cat and the key with you and took off. Mmmm. Sure enough, as soon as I dropped out, the boys heard about it and, like, sent in Lum to scout for me, seeing as they were still too hot to break cover themselves. Way I put it together from there is that Roman hears I've lit out and that Lum is around, so he, like, makes an offer to Lum to sell out Ed and Paris, hook up with him and take a bigger cut.

You have to stitch the live skin together, otherwise it just won't heal properly. It's gory work, but what has me freaked out is the close-up look I'm getting at the dent I put in Russ's skull. I can see and feel just how crushed the bone is and the picture I'm getting of what's on the other side has my stomach flopping around. But there's nothing I can do about it, so I wipe some sweat out of my eyes and keep going.

—Mmmm. Of course, the Russians catch wind of all this, so they send Bert and Ernie around to take a piece for the workers of the world and Roman fits them into the machine rather than having them out on the street going batshit. Me, I'm, like, taking it easy watching the fall colors upstate, moving around, but laying low. Oww! Oww! Oww. Not good, man. Not good! Watch it! Fuck!

I get him settled back in the chair. He cracks another brew and starts up again.

—Ed and Paris, once they got some info and started putting it together, they must have realized they were getting, like, sold out all over town and it was time to roll onto the scene and take care of some fucking business. About that same time, I, like, pulled into Rochester to check on my dad real quick, cuz, ya know, ya know, he really was sick back there for a while. And when I get there, turns out. Mmmm. Turns out he, like, really has taken a bad turn and how about fucking that for irony, right?

I've got the last stitch in. It's ugly, but it should hold. I start cleaning it up and get a bandage ready.

—He's, like, on his deathbed for, like, real and I. Mmmm. I have to, I can't just leave, so I stay. He's only got, like, a couple days and my mom left the fucker years ago and I don't have any, like, siblings, and there's no one, so I stay. Mmmm. And that's how the Russians get a bead on me. I'm there just two days and I step out of the hospital for a smoke and see these clowns in the parking lot and I know I'm fucked. They aren't Bert and Ernie, but they, like, might as well be, the way they're dressed. I ducked back inside and out the rear and figured the jig was up and if I was gonna get away with the cash, I better, like, make my move. So I, like, came back for my cat.

I finish wrapping the bandage and tape it into place.

—How's your dad?

—Hank, I don't fucking know.

He drinks more beer and falls asleep on the bed. I tend to my own wound. I clean it and dress it and take one of the Ace bandages I bought and wind it around my middle. I want to give Dr. Bob's work a little extra protection seeing as more abuse is likely to be on the way. Dr. Bob. Shit.

He's a good guy. A citizen. He'll be on his way to the police to talk to them just as soon as my picture shows up on TV. "Hey, that guy on TV, the mass murderer? Well, I stitched him up yesterday." He'll be thinking he repaired me just in time for me to go kill a bunch of people. Something else for me to feel like an asshole about. Sorry, Doc.

In the room Russ makes soft snoring sounds while I make a sandwich and eat it. There's one beer left and it keeps staring at me. I get tired of trying not to stare back so I put it in the john where I won't see it or hear it. Russ may want it later.

I pull on my clothes. I've got the TV on with the sound off and the radio tuned to a station I like. Springsteen sings "Atlantic City," and I listen all the way through. Then I take out the cell phone and his card and make the call.

—Roman.

He sounds so normal and professional, no stress, no panic, nothing at all. Just a cop on the job.

—Hey, Roman. How's the cat?

—Yes, well, it is difficult to talk here, right now. Maybe you could give me your number.

—Fuck that. Give me the number of your cell and I'll call you back.

—It would be easier if.

—I have the key now, Roman. I have the key and I have the fucking four and a half million dollars, so give me the fucking number.

He gives me the number.

—I'll call in five minutes, so get yourself somewhere private.

I hang up. I feel good, just like a regular toughguy. I set the phone down, go in the can and stick my head in the toilet until I'm sure I'm not really gonna throw up. When I raise my head, I'm right on eye level with Russ's last beer and that's about all it takes. I guzzle it down and, I have to say, it makes me feel a hell of a lot better, except for the fact that I instantly want about twenty-five more. I splash water on my face and rinse out my mouth and go back in the room to make the call.

—Roman.

—So, how's the cat?

He's quiet for a moment.

—Actually, the cat's fine. Bolo has taken a liking to him and is making sure he's well fed, rested and groomed.

Fuck!

—Roman, let's talk.

—Go ahead.

—I want out and I want to know if that is possible at this point. Can I be put in the clear?

—That would be pretty tough at this point.

—Tough, but possible?

He's silent again. In the background I can hear traffic sounds. He must have stepped outside the precinct house.

—I've been watching the news. Did I mention that, Roman?

—No.

—Well, I have, and I have this theory. See, I think someone is connecting the dots. Connecting the bar to me to Yvonne to me to Russ to me and connecting all of it to you. I think you're getting asked questions about what the fuck is going on. And I think pretty soon, your credibility is going to be shit and you're gonna be needing that money to get lost with. So you better find a way to help me out before I decide to just keep it for myself.

—It will be difficult, but not impossible to get you in the clear.

—What will it take?

—Beyond the money, it will take just one more thing.

I close my eyes.

—What's that?

—We'll need a fall guy.

On the bed, Russ turns in his sleep and makes a little sighing noise.

—Yeah, I've got one of those.

Roman is so very happy to hear that Russ is back in town. We hack out the details. Roman gets the money. I get some semblance of my life. And the cat. Russ gets plugged into the frame that puts both me and Roman in the clear. I have questions.

—What if the rest of the cops don't buy it?

—They will. Miner has a criminal record, he is the subject of an exist-
ing investigation and he's already involved in this case up to his neck.
Now listen: Unbeknownst to you, he left the key. When he came back
to get the key, it had already been stolen from you by persons unknown. He did not believe your story and so began to hunt you across
the city in order to get the key and, in the process, murdered your girl
and instigated the slaughter at the bar.

—What happens when Russ denies it?

—He won't.

   I think about the implications of those two words.

—I don't want him dead, Roman. I won't give him to you just to kill him.

—Not to worry, we need Miner alive to confess. And confess he will.
He'll see that extended police custody allows him his best chance of
survival. It will keep him in good stead with me and away from the
brothers DuRanté.

—The brothers DuRanté?

—Ed and Paris, Ed and Paris DuRanté.

   Great names. I have to give it to these guys: they all have great
names.

—And what about Ed and Paris, what happens to them?

—The brothers are the subject of a national manhunt, they will soon
be forced to flee the area. And if they are ever found by the police,
they will go down in the hail of bullets that is waiting for them.

—What about me?

—You stay in hiding until the news breaks that Miner has been cap-
tured. At which point you turn yourself in and explain that you were
hiding because you were confused and afraid. You turn yourself over
to me and only me. I will then ease your passage through the criminal
justice system with the aid of my good name and a considerable
amount of cash. With luck, we'll both be heroes. Just relax. Soon this
will be over and they'll make you into a movie of the week.

   I'm not stupid. I don't trust him.

—Henry?

—Don't call me that.

—It's your name, right?

—Don't call me that. You want to use my name, you call me Hank.

—Very well. Hank, you must relax. It will all go fine if you do not panic. It's not out of reach, Hank. Your old life, it's not out of reach.

And with no other choice that I can see, I do it. I make the deal and I don't panic. We set up a time and place to make the exchange. He wants me to bring the cash, I refuse and tell him he can have the key, but he'll have to use it himself. He insists and I hang up the phone and let him wait a couple minutes before I call back. He agrees to accept Russ and the key. He tells me to stay hidden until after dark and he tells me to keep an eye on the news. I tell him to make sure that Bud is in one piece tonight and he says good-bye.

I hang up the phone and get some Advil from the first-aid kit. I want to call a grocery and have them deliver some more beer, but when I look at the TV, I realize I'm gonna have to live without. The long-awaited press conference has begun and they're flashing my booking photo from the other night and talking about how dangerous I am.

I watch TV for a while and think about that beer I drank. The clock says 3:15 when I peter out again, tired. I'm so fucking tired. I take a pillow from the bed and toss it on the carpet in front of the door. Now that I have a little time to think, I'm remembering some important stuff. The Giants play at 4:05 P.M. West Coast time and the Mets at 7:30 P.M. EST. I set the alarm for 7:00 P.M. The meet with Roman is at 10:00. We'll have to leave by 9:00 to get set up, but I should be able to watch at least three or four innings. I lie down on the floor and you'd be surprised just how easy it is to fall asleep. No dreams.

My first thought when I wake up is that the alarm didn't go off. I know I'm supposed to be up for something and I can't remember if it's work or a date or a doctor's appointment or what the fuck. Then I see that

I'm on the floor and the pieces fall back into place, including the empty bed.

In my sleep, I've rolled away from the door. Now I see that what woke me was the door bumping lightly into my side. It's closing! The fucking door is being pulled closed from the outside right now! I'm awake.

Still on the floor, I grab the edge of the door before it can close all the way. My fingers get a little squashed, but he's trying to be quiet and gentle, so it doesn't hurt much. I have a good grip now and yank back as hard as I can. He resists for a moment, then thinks better of it. The door flies in at me as he changes his pull to a push. I catch most of it on my left shoulder. It knocks me all the way onto my back and he has a head start. Through the now open door, I see him taking his first big step down the hall toward the elevator.

I lunge up into a sitting position, throw myself into the hall and claw at his ankles. I hook a finger in the cuff of his right pants leg, but he kicks back, freeing himself and knocking me further off balance. I'm trying to go after him and get up at the same time and I end up in a ridiculous crawl crouch, stumbling behind him. I can see that he's going to beat me to the elevators, but unless there's one waiting for him, I should catch up to him there. I see a little flash of chrome in his right hand. He has the gun. He picked my pocket while I was asleep and he has his little .22 back. The sight of the gun slows me. I'm not sure I want to catch him if he has the gun. As I consider this, he suddenly and for no apparent reason turns to the left and plows straight into the wall.

He rebounds off the wall and pauses a moment to shake his head. I take two giant steps, throw myself at him and grab his right leg as he steps forward. He goes down full length, no time to use his arms to break his fall. The gun is bounced out of his hand and slides a few feet down the hall. I scramble up onto his back, pin his arms with my knees and grab him by the neck with my left hand. With my right, I reach out and scoop up the gun. I stick the barrel up against his cheek. His mouth is muffled by the carpet, but I hear him.

—Like, chill, man! Chill!

I dig the barrel in deeper.

—Yes, I get it, Hank! Chill, man!

I disentangle myself from him, keeping the gun in place. We stand up together.

—The room, Russ.

—Yeah, man, like, the room. No problem.

We walk the few yards back to our room and no doors open, no one looks out to see what the ruckus is about. I love this hotel. I close the door behind us and relock it, including the little chain. Russ is looking at his face in the mirror over the dresser, inspecting the carpet burn on his chin. I can't help it; as I go past him, I give him a little shove in the back. He falls right into the mirror, banging his forehead hard enough to cause a small crack in the glass. He straightens and then slides down to the floor along the dresser drawers, which make little clunking noises as he goes. He sits there, holding his head.

—For chrissake, Hank. Will you quit, like, hitting me on the fucking head!

I squat down and look at his eyes. Again, the left pupil is a little bigger than the right. No wonder he can't walk a straight line. I check the clock: 7:49 P.M. The fucker switched off the alarm. I climb up on the bed, grab the remote, switch to Channel 11 for the Mets game, and turn up the sound. Bottom of the first: zip, zip. I wait for them to flash a score from the Giants game. At the end of the inning, they tell me what I want to know: Giants 1, Dodgers 0, top of the third.

Russ gets himself up off the floor. He looks for something but can't find it.

—Hey?

I watch TV.

—Hey, what happened to my last beer?

—I drank it.

—Fuck.

He digs in one of the grocery bags until he comes up with a six-pack of Coke, a bag of chips and a can of peanuts. He comes over to the bed and stands there, waiting. I look up at him, then scoot over to make room. He climbs onto the bed, hands me a soda, and puts the chips and nuts between us.

—So, what's the score?

8:45 P.M. I'm sitting on the bottom edge of the bed, two feet from the TV screen. Top of the fifth, still no score. The Mets and the Braves are locked in a pitchers' duel. The starters have combined for fifteen strike-outs already and show no sign of slowing down. Out west in Dodger Stadium, they're jammed in the bottom of the fourth, picking away at each other, the hitters going high into the counts and knocking foul balls all over the fucking place. The Giants are still up 1–0, but L.A. has the bases loaded and S.F.'s starter is already wearing out. The an-nouncer for the Mets game keeps giving updates on what's happening out in Los Angeles, but the fact that I can't actually see the game is driving me up the fucking wall. And now it's time to go, and I can't bring myself to shut off the TV.

I'm going to wait until the end of the Dodgers' fourth. I can't do it, I just can't go without knowing if the Dodgers take the lead. The Mets knock down the Braves in order, chalking up two more strikeouts and the coverage goes to a commercial.

—Fuck, fuck, fuck, fuck.

Russ is still reclined at the other end of the bed. He's a Mets fan. Every time they notch another out, he pumps his fist and gives a little whoop. I'm trying to remember that it could be worse, he could be a Dodgers fan. It's 8:56 P.M. The game comes back on and we're in-formed that the Giants are in the middle of a pitching change. Mean-while, the Braves go to work on the Mets. I look again at the clock. Fuck! Fuck me! I turn off the TV. Russ jumps off the bed.

—Whoa! Like, what the fuck?

I collect the first-aid kit and cell phone and put on the Yankees jacket, sunglasses and headphones.

—Time to go, Russ.

—Oh, man. Oh, man!

—I know. Come on.

At the door, I turn and take a look at the room. Cans and crumbs and leftover food all over the place. I take a twenty from my pocket and toss it on the bed for the maid. We walk down the hall and push the button for the elevator. Russ is antsy.

—Where do we go?

—We need a car.

—A car?

—Yeah.

He looks at me, the elevator goes ding and the doors open. We step inside and wait for the doors to close.

—Hank?

—Yeah?

—Why do we. Mmmm. Why do we, like, need a car?

The doors are still open. I realize that neither of us has pushed a button and I lean over and press my finger against the one labeled L.

—We need a car because I don't want to risk any more cabs or subways and so we can listen to the game while we wait.

The elevator is very slow.

—I thought we were, like, going to the. Mmmm. Going to the cops. I thought you were turning me in.

I look at him as the elevator eases its way down to the lobby.

—I'm giving you to Roman.

—What?

—I'm giving you and the money to Roman. Roman will take you in.

—What the fuck?

—I can't just take you to the police.

—Are you fucking. Mmmm. Are you, like, fucking nuts? You're fucking crazy. Fucking Roman? ZOMBIE MOTHER FUCKING ROMAN?

—Russ!

—Fuck that!

The doors open on the lobby and a group of ultrahip European teenagers are standing there, waiting to go up. Russ spins away from me and takes a quick step out of the elevator and trips over nothing, tumbling into the crowd of tattoos, piercings and bleached hair. They catch him and keep him on his feet while I wrap an arm around his shoulders and take a firm grip on his right biceps.

—Thank you. Thank you very much. He's OK.

They cram into the elevator, making cracks in French about drunk Americans. Fucking French classes. I wish I'd taken Spanish in high school. I start walking Russ toward the door.

—Take it easy, Russ. Just take it easy. It's, it's gonna be OK. You're gonna take the fall, but you're gonna get out of it alive. And. It's gonna, you know, be fine.

He's still shaking a bit, not because of his balance, but because of how hard he's crying.

I would rather have rented a car, but I don't want to go someplace where I'm gonna have to stand around and let people look at me for twenty minutes, and I don't trust Russ to go in alone. It takes me a while to talk Russ into the backup plan, but eventually he gives in. Even woozy as he is, it takes him less than a minute to break into a locked car and hot-wire it. We sit there with the engine idling. I put a hand on his shoulder.

—OK, let's go.

He kind of shrugs my hand from his shoulder.

—No.

—Why?

—Mmmm. Apart from, like, not wanting to drive myself to my own fucking execution, I'm not sure I should, like, be behind the wheel, feeling like this. I can barely, like, walk a fucking straight line thanks to you going all, like, Babe Ruth on my head.

—You have to drive, Russ.

—Mmmm. Why? Why the fuck do I have to drive?

—Because I don't.

He looks at me.

—Are you. Mmmm. Are you, like, kidding, man? You're from Cali, man. All you guys know how to drive.

—I know how to, I just don't. So let's get the fuck out of here before the owner of this fucking thing shows the fuck up.

—Let him! Let him. Mmmm. Let him show up and call the fucking cops. That would be, like, great, man. Save my fucking life.

I make a fist and lunge at him. He flinches back and I pull the punch before it makes contact. He keeps himself pressed against the driver's-side door and I take deep breaths.

—Why me, Russ? Huh? Why the fuck did you pick me to give your goddamn cat?

He looks out the window at Ninth Avenue.

—I figured, you know, that you'd, like, take good care of him. I mean, Bud's a great cat. I didn't want to leave him with just anyone.

—Yeah.

We sit for another half minute.

—Just drive the car, Russ. Take it real easy and if you start to black out or feel funny, just say something.

—OK.

He takes the wheel and puts the Celica in first.

—Like, where to, man?

—Just get us out of here. I'll tell you where to go once we're moving.

He pulls away from the curb nice and slow and eases us into the downtown traffic. I turn on the radio and try to find the game.

We circle the block and take Broadway back downtown to Canal Street, then take East Broadway to Montgomery. We scoot across the FDR into the Pier 8 driveway right at the bottom of Manhattan. I point the way and Russ drives us slowly down the access road past the NO UNAUTHORIZED VEHICLES BEYOND THIS POINT sign. I jog out here a few times a week and I've never seen a single cop, just the occasional parks department truck. We cruise along nice and easy until we reach the Houston Street footbridge where it crosses over the FDR to the baseball diamonds of the East River Park.

We park on the access road next to a baseball diamond. Nearby, I can hear the traffic whizzing past on the FDR, but it's not nearly loud enough to cover the sound of my cursing. Dodgers 3, Giants 1. New York and Atlanta are still scoreless and the starters are closing in on a new record for combined strikeouts in a single game. Russ has lost interest in the games. He stares out at the East River beyond the playing fields and smokes Camel Lights, one after another. The dash clock in the Celica is broken, but it's 9:47 P.M. by Russ's watch. Roman should be here just about anytime.

Roman wanted to meet someplace secluded in Red Hook. I told him to fuck off and we settled on the East River Park. It doesn't close until midnight, but at this hour and this time of year, there's just a few joggers and dog walkers. A ways away, some kids in jackets are playing three-flys-up under the night-lights of another diamond. Russ takes a last hard drag on his cig and flicks the butt out the window. The Braves close out the bottom of the sixth and the broadcast goes to commercial. S.F. and L.A. raced through the fifth and are wading into the sixth themselves.

Russ keeps touching his bandage where it covers the stitches I put in. There's a tiny pink stain there and every time he pokes it, he winces a little.

—Just stop fucking with it.

He touches it again.

—Really, Russ, you don't want to fuck around with that until a real doctor checks it out.

He looks at me out of the corner of his eye, then digs in his pocket for another smoke and lights it.

—I'm never gonna see a fucking doctor.

The game comes back on.

—The cops will take you to a doctor.

—I'm, like, never gonna see the fucking cops.

I'm trying to listen to the game with one ear and Russ with the other.

—He can't kill you, man, you're his fall guy. He needs you.

—You just. Mmmm. You just, like, don't know what the fuck you're talking about.

Something's going on. Atlanta got their lead-off hitter on first and the number two guy sacrificed him to second. Runner on second, one out, heart of the order coming up. No word from the announcer about the Giants.

—You're gonna take the fall, Russ, because you fucked up. You're gonna go to jail and you may fucking die there, but Roman's not gonna kill you.

The Braves' number three hitter smacks one straight back to the pitcher for the second out. The pitcher spins and fires the ball to second, just missing the double play. The cleanup hitter steps in. Still nothing from L.A.

—You fucking idiot. You're, like, such a fucking. Mmmm.

—Cool it.

—Such a fucking idiot.

—Don't fucking push me.

—Fuck you, you fucking idiot.

Two quick strikes followed by three straight balls and the catcher is going out to the mound to settle his pitcher. The announcer has mercy on me and gives an update from the West Coast: Top of the sixth and the Giants have the bases loaded with one out. The Dodgers pull their starter.

—Russ, this would be a good time for you to can it.

—Fucking idiot! Fucking idiot! Fucking idiot!

—Russ!

The Mets' catcher settles in back behind the plate, the hitter is in the box and the pitcher steps up on the rubber.

On the other coast, the Giants counter the pitching change by bringing in a lefty to pinch-hit.

—Hey, by the way, fucking idiot, how is it you're planning to get out of here after you send me to be killed, seeing as you don't, like, drive or whatever?

Atlanta's man makes loud contact. The announcer is describing the ball's arc toward deep left field. The color commentator goes bananas, screaming that the Giants' hitter has just smashed a monster to deep center. On opposite coasts the balls soar toward the outfield walls.

Russ turns the radio off.

—Huh, fucking idiot, how ya gonna get out?

—Fuck!

I grab his right hand with my left and try to pull it off the volume knob; he grabs my wrist with his left and I can't pull free.

—Fucking idiot! Fucking. Mmmm. Idiot!

—Fuck, Russ! Fuck, Russ! Fuck!

Now I grab his left with my right and we tug-o'-war, grunting. The knob snaps off.

—Russ! Fuck! Russ!

I grab his throat with both hands and squeeze as hard as I can. He has a grip on my fingers, keeping them from closing completely, keeping him alive.

—Fucking murderer! Fucking all my friends! You fucking murderer!

Tears are boiling up around my eyes. I press my weight into him and force his body back against the door. I squeeze harder.

—Hank.

—Shut up!

—Hank.

—Shut the fuck up.

—Hank, he's gonna—

—Shut up! Shut up! Shut up!

This bastard. This selfish fucking bastard.

—He's gonna kill us both. He's gonna fucking kill us both.

Somewhere beyond my crying and Russ's gasping breath I register the sound of a car. Headlights flash three times, illuminating the interior of our stolen car. Russ's face is purple, his eyes bugging out of his head.

—Kill. Kill us both.

Twenty yards away, Roman pulls up and parks his car. I look at my hands and what they're doing, and I let go of Russ's neck. He gasps and chokes and heaves up a little of his lunch onto the seat.

—Kill us both. Mmmm. Kill us both and put us both in the frame. Mmmm. And the cops will, like, seal it up tight cuz they, like, love a closed case.

The headlights flash again and Roman steps out of his car. He stands there, waiting for me.

Russ massages his neck.

—Jesus, Hank, it's not like you couldn't listen to the rest of the game on the Walkman.

We meet in the middle. He's wearing a different black suit and there's a nice collection of scratches on his neck and chin where he was raked by some of Edwin's birdshot, but otherwise the guy still looks great. A fucking pro.

—Hank.

—Fuck you, Roman. Where's the cat?

—Miner in the car?

—Yeah. Where's the cat?

—The key?

—I have it here. The cat, Roman.

My hands are shoved deep in the pockets of my jeans, which I figure is a good idea since it keeps Roman from seeing how much they're shaking. He watches me, flicks his eyes toward Russ in the Celica, then makes a little waving gesture back at his own car. Bolo gets out of the front passenger seat. He's carrying my bag. It's unzipped and as he walks toward us I can see that Bud is inside, nestled back in his little bed of towels. Bolo cradles the bag from underneath with one massive hand and with the other he scratches Bud behind the ears.

—Hey, man, this is a great cat.

I stare at him.

—I mean, me? I'm really a dog person, but a cat like this? *This* is a great cat.

Roman looks over his shoulder at his car and waves again. Whitey gets out of the backseat and stumbles just slightly. He shambles toward us. In his right hand he's holding one of the machine pistols they used to kill my friends, in his left he has a half-empty liter bottle of Smirnoff. He stops when he gets to our little group and sizes me up. His eyes are red and puffy from crying and drinking. He takes a huge mouthful of the vodka, swallows most of it and spits the rest on my shoes. Roman reaches out and rests a comforting hand on his shoulder.

—He's just a bit worked up. That was his boyfriend got killed back there at the bar. They were planning a ring ceremony for the spring.

—That's a real fucking tragedy.

Whitey goes for me, but Roman clamps down on the shoulder and pulls him back before he can get across the five feet that separate us. Me, I just keep my shaking hands in my pockets.

Roman gives Whitey a gentle shove toward my car.

—Go get Miner.

Whitey looks me over one more time and heads for the Celica. Roman gives a little grimace and sighs through his nose.

—You're getting hard, Hank.

—You want the key?

—Yes, please.

Slowly I take my hands from my pockets, keeping them balled in fists to try to hide the shaking. But as soon as I open them, the keys start jingling. Roman looks at my hands and back up at my face. I can't look away.

—Hank.

I find the right key by touch, never looking away from his eyes, and start twisting it loose from the ring. I breathe deep, in and out, trying to settle my hands.

—Hank.

I have the key off the ring and I squeeze it in my palm, the jagged edges digging into the skin.

—You don't have to be frightened any longer, Hank. You are safe now, I promise you.

I nod.

—Hand me the key.

I open my hand and hold the key out to him and he reaches for it slowly.

—So what does it open, Hank?

The key jumps from my shaking palm and falls on the ground, its bright pink base easily visible in the dim light. Roman gives me an understanding little half-smile. I smile back.

—Sorry.

—It's all right.

Behind me I hear a car door open.

—So, what does it open?

The pink key stays there on the ground between us.

—A unit at Manhattan Mini Storage. The number's on the key.

He nods. I look at Bolo and Roman looks at him as well.

—Give him his cat, Bolo.

Behind me, I hear Whitey.

—Fuck-face, out of fucking car. Fuck-face, out.

Roman starts to bend to pick up the key and Bolo reaches over him from behind to pass me the bag with Bud inside.

—Makes me feel like shit about what I did. He's such a great cat.

Behind me:

—Fucking car is for getting out of, fuck-face.

Bolo's hand is hooked in the bag's strap and we juggle the bag a little over Roman's back as he starts to rise with the key. Bud gets pinched and lashes out with the claws of his right paw, catching Bolo on the thumb.

—Fuck!

I take hold of the bag as he jerks back his arm to stick the thumb in his mouth and his elbow clips Roman hard on the back of the neck.

—Fucking cat!

—Fuck-face, out!

Roman is knocked down, almost doubled over. He pulls himself quickly upright and something is jarred from his coat pocket and drops to the ground with a sound somewhere between a clank and a thump. We both stand there, staring down at the brass knuckles as if they were the ace of spades fallen from the sleeve of a gambler just as he was pushing away from the table with his winnings.

Those bruises on her neck.

Behind me, a balloon pops.

* * *

We all watch as Whitey walks back toward us still holding the bottle, but no longer carrying the gun. With his right hand, he points at a dark splotch on the collar of his shiny white Nike jacket. We are frozen. He reaches us, and we see that the finger is not pointing but is jammed up to the second knuckle in the hole Russ shot in his neck with the .22 I left for him on the cracked foam rubber front seat of the Celica.

Nobody moves except Whitey, who walks slowly to Roman's car and climbs in the backseat. He sits there, plugging the hole in his neck with his finger, takes a long slug of vodka, and weeps silently.

Roman reaches inside his jacket for his gun. Bolo does the same with his free hand, keeping his injured thumb in his mouth. I turn back toward the Celica as Russ rises from the driver's seat with the little chrome pistol in his right hand and Whitey's machine pistol in his left. I am ten yards from the car. I start running, Bud clutched to my chest.

Russ pulls the trigger on the machine gun. He's unprepared for the force of the blow-back and the gun leaps upward, dragging his hand in a high arc and spraying the sky with bullets. Behind me, I hear two scrambling thumps as Roman and Bolo hit the dirt. I've gone two yards.

Something explodes behind me and a mini shock wave hums past my right hip. A hole appears in the Celica's left fender. I zig hard to the right, trying to clear Russ's firing line as he brings the machine gun back to shoulder level. He pulls the trigger again. He's ready this time and bullets rip up the tarmac just behind me. He fires a short burst and re-aims. I'm accelerating. Six yards covered.

I'm approaching the car from the driver's side and Russ is blocking the door. Russ fires again and I can't keep from looking back. Roman and Bolo are frozen, facedown on the road. A patch of chewed-up tarmac appears a few feet from them and stretches toward them and stops just short of their heads as the gun's clip goes empty. Russ drops the machine pistol and takes aim with the .22. Ten yards.

I try to stop, and instead I skid on the gravel scattered over the road.

I plow into Russ just as he squeezes off all five rounds left in the .22. He's thrown sideways by my impact and the bullets fly into some bushes by the side of the road. There's no time to circle the car. I start shoving him in through the driver's-side door, pushing him all the way over to the passenger's seat. I'm piling in behind him, trying to get Bud's bag into his lap as I settle into the driver's seat, reach to turn the key, and grab a handful of loose wires.

—FUCK, RUSS!

—What?

—THE CAR, HOW DO I START THE FUCKING CAR?

Out on the road, Roman and Bolo are peeking out from behind their hands, which are covering their faces. Russ reaches over to the steering column, grabs the two wires he exposed before and starts scraping them together. Roman and Bolo get to their feet. The Celica is making sounds like it wants to start, but it won't turn over.

Roman looks around at his feet, bends over and picks up his gun from where he dropped it when Russ started shooting. Bolo walks slowly toward us, his left thumb in his mouth and a 9 mm dangling casually from his right hand. Behind him Roman is trying to aim at us, but Bolo is in his way.

The Celica goes WAH-WAH-WAH!

Bolo walks up to the front of the car and starts to raise his pistol. Roman is moving a few steps to his right, looking for a clean shot. The engine catches, but the clutch is out.

The Celica leaps forward in little hops and slams Bolo in the knees, folding him over the hood. I stomp on the floor, trying to find the clutch. Russ holds Bud, pressed tightly against his neck. Roman gets off a shot, but our motion spoils it and he takes out the side window behind me. I get my foot on the clutch pedal. The engine coughs and recatches. Bolo is on the hood.

I let the clutch out and hammer down on the gas. Gravel spits out behind us and the rear end fishtails and Bolo slides off the hood. The tires catch traction and we jet forward. I cram it into second and aim for Roman, ten yards away. He doesn't bother with another shot but dives out of the way as I crash through the bushes and around his car. I jump us back onto the access road and put it in third as we race down the road toward the pier and the FDR on-ramp.

I spare a glance to check Russ. He's sideways in the seat and getting himself straightened out, all the while holding Bud close. I look back at the road.

—Russ.

—Yeah?

—Put on your seat belt.

—Sure.

In the rearview, I see Roman getting his car turned around to come after us.

Driving, it seems, is like riding a bike: you never forget. The wheel feels good in my hands, my feet find the pedals with ease and I flip the shift knob from gear to gear until it's in fourth. I cannot deny my true nature. I am a Californian. And just like every true Californian, I like to drive. Christ, I love to drive.

The Celica is a beige hatchback about fifteen or twenty years old. It has some problems. The wheel has an inch of play in either direction, the alignment pulls slightly to the right, it has no power or acceleration, the tires are bald and the brakes are mushy. Still, it should be much quicker in the corners than Roman's big-block cop sedan. That would help if there were any corners here. The access road is just one long straightaway back to the gate and Roman is already right behind me, trying to stick his car's nose up my ass and nudge me off the road.

The kids on the diamond are lining up at the chain link to watch as we blow past. Most of the pedestrians are along the water side of the park, but a few are scattered on the road. I shift my right hand toward the center of the wheel, jam my thumb down on the horn. My high beams are on and ahead of me it looks like clear sailing. The car lurches as Roman slams into the rear bumper.

The wheel jumps a bit in my hand and we swerve to the left. We glance off a park bench and bounce back to the center of the road. I get control and slam the gas pedal back to the floor. Roman drops back for a second to see what will happen, then he's right back on us. Next to me, Russ has his legs jacked out straight in from of him like he's trying to hit an imaginary brake pedal. His right hand is frozen around the "Oh, my God!" strap and he's holding Bud with his left.

—Hank?

I keep my eyes on the road.

—Yeah?

—I don't want to be a backseat driver, but ya know this thing does, like, have a fifth gear.

Shit!

I hit fifth and we pull away smoothly. It won't last. Just ahead the Williamsburg Bridge cuts the sky above us. Below it, running parallel to the big bridge, the Delancey Street footbridge crosses the FDR and drops its ramp smack into the middle of the access road. There's space to go around on either side, but it looks a lot smaller going out at seventy than it did coming in at fifteen.

Roman taps us again and I veer slightly left. He guns it and pushes up alongside us on the right. I edge farther to the left, trying to line up with the thin space between the foot ramp and the row of lampposts along the road there. I'd like to spare a look for Roman, but the play in the wheel is giving me fits. Never fear. He reminds me of his presence by giving us another shove before peeling off right to line up with the gap on that side of the ramp. The shove takes us over too far and the driver's-side rearview snaps off against a lamppost. It ricochets into my window. The window shatters instantly, and hundreds of little pebbles of glass collapse into my lap while the rearview flies past my left ear and into the backseat.

I flinch and blink. When I open my eyes, we're at the gap. I have to jerk the wheel to get us back on line. We swerve through the narrow space and I think I feel the bumper clip something as the rear end gives a slight tug. We're through but come out veering to the right. I try to put us straight on the road. It's too late. We broadside Roman's car as he comes through on the other side of the ramp. His car is much bigger than ours and we rebound back to the center of the road.

He loses the wheel for a moment and scrapes the side of his car down the iron fence on that side of the road. A fountain of sparks roostertails into the sky and we pull away again.

The road takes a nice easy arc to the right, passing Corlears Hook Park on our left. Just ahead it narrows down to one car's width as it passes the pier's storage yard. Roman is just about on us as I gear down and brace myself.

—Russ, hold on to Bud.

I catch his rapid nodding out of the corner of my eye as we hit the eighteen-inch speed bumps at just over forty miles per hour. The front end springs up and, as it starts to drop, the rear hits the bump and pops up, driving the front down at an even steeper angle. I pump the brakes and try to keep the wheels pointed straight ahead. We bounce and skitter to the next one and hit it hard. We come down skidding to the left. I try to steer into the skid and goose the gas. We get traction and I straighten us out for the last bump and ease over it at twenty. Just behind us, Roman hits the first bump at top speed.

He just about flips but hangs on. The second one pops him off the road and into the chain link of the storage yard. His car plows to a sudden stop against the fence and we're in the parking lot. I cut the wheel hard right, heading for the exit, jump the light at the intersection there and hairpin us straight up the FDR on-ramp, picking up speed. We pass Roman's car, still pointed the opposite direction on the access road. He's already moving, headed for the FDR.

I try to get lost in the traffic. I mix in and slow down to match the flow. We pass under the Williamsburg Bridge again, going north this time. Russ is nuzzling the back of Bud's neck and whispering to him and Roman drives right up on us.

We're in the far right lane and he pulls up on our left. I look out the window. Bolo is there, just a few feet away, sucking his scratched thumb. Roman doesn't spare me a look, just keeps his eyes on the traffic. I can see Whitey still in the backseat, but I can't tell if he's alive or dead. I'll never lose them as long as this is a race about speed. I need to slow the chase down. I pull onto the Houston Street exit ramp. Roman brakes fast and veers over to follow us. At the top of the ramp, I ignore the stop sign and blaring horns of the other cars and take us halfway around the traffic circle and onto Houston headed west. Roman trails.

Traffic is heavy and Roman stays right with us. From the middle lane, I take a right off Houston onto Avenue A. I cut in front of several cars and the drivers all lean on their horns. Roman gets tangled in the mess and I take a lead down the avenue.

The weekend traffic has us slowed way down by the time we get to 9th Street, Roman is back with us. But that's OK, because I can already see the lights up ahead.

It looks like a movie set up on my block: cop cars, news vans, barricades and rubberneckers galore. Roman has caught on and he's dropping back. It might be worth it to *me* to drive through and chance being recognized, but not even Roman can get through all those cops with a dying Russian gangster in his backseat. He turns off at 12th Street, heading east. He'll have to detour a few blocks. Otherwise he'll no doubt end up at a similar mess a block away outside Paul's. Russ takes his face out of Bud's neck, looks up and registers the scene.

—Hey, Hank, like, what the fuck? Mmmm.

—Just take it easy, man.

—Mmmm.

—Easy.

He rubs his nose against Bud's face.

—Hear that, Buddy? Take it easy. Mmmm. Easy. Mmmm.

I look at him. He keeps his face close to Bud's.

The cops wave cars through the intersection at A and 13th one at a time and they creep past my apartment building. We get to the front of the line and the cop holds us there for a second with an upraised palm as crosstown traffic passes by. I spot a few people I know from the block mixed in with the reporters and sightseers. I pull up the collar on my jacket and hunch down a little in the seat.

The cop waves us through and never once looks in the car. The cops have been forced to use barricades to create room for a narrow lane in the middle of the street. We edge along and I picture a similar scene in front of my parents' house. Reporters on the front lawn, strangers driving by to gawk and neighbors on porches pointing their fingers and shaking their heads. Russ never looks up from Bud's neck. We're held up at 14th by another traffic cop and I look east down the street, trying to see if Roman has circled around. I can't see him, but now this car has become a target and I want out of it. The cop gives us the OK and I turn left just as the Celica starts to cough and shiver.

We wobble across the intersection and I pull us over to the curb just past the bus stop on the right-hand side of the street. I look out the window and the traffic cop is pointing from himself to us, signing, asking if we need any help. I smile and wave "no thanks" back to him. He nods and turns back to his job.

—Russ.

—Mmmm.

—Russ!

—Mmmm. What?

—The car died.

—Mmmm.

—Russ?

—Yeah?

—Are you OK?

He takes his face from Bud and looks at me. His left pupil has swollen, almost eclipsing the entire iris.

—Like, I don't know, Hank. I don't feel too good.

We have to get out of this car.

—It's good to see you, Buddy. Mmmm.

We have to get out of this car.

—Good to see you. Mmmm. Sorry, I'm sorry I, like, left you for so long, Buddy.

We have to get out of this fucking car. The cop back at the intersection keeps glancing over at us. A few blocks away, Roman and Bolo are dumping Whitey or stuffing him in the trunk and coming after us. The left side of Russ's face is sagging and frozen and he keeps rubbing it against Bud and whispering to him. We have to get out of this car before that cop comes walking over here to see what's up, but I don't know where to go next.

The cell phone rings.

—Buddy, Buddy, Buddy. I missed you, Buddy. Mmmm.

It rings again.

—Buuuuddy.

I take it out of my pocket and stare at it as it rings a third time.

—I'm sorry you, like, got hurt, Buddy. Mmmm. That was, that was really my fault.

It starts to ring again and I flip it open.

—Hello?

—Hello?

—Hello?

—Is this Russ Miner?

Fuck!

—Uh, yes.

—Mr. Miner, this is Detective Craig Williams of the New York City Police Department.

Oh, fuck.

—Yes?

—Mr. Miner, are you alone? Are you free to speak?

—Yes.

The cop is looking over at us again.

—Mr. Miner, we've been tracking your credit card transactions and found you had opened this account in the last twenty-four hours.

—Uh-huh.

—That's how we got this number.

—Uh-huh.

—Mr. Miner, we believe that you are in great danger.

—Uh, why?

—Mr. Miner, do you know Henry Thompson? His parents were called from this number earlier today.

Oh, oh, fuck.

—Uh.

—Are you with Henry Thompson? Is he holding you against your will?

Are you fucking kidding me?

—Uh.

—If you're not free to speak, just answer yes or no. Do you understand?

—Uh.

The cop is now openly staring at us. I keep my face well inside the shadowed interior of the car.

—Mr. Miner? Russ? Russ, this is a very dangerous man. Mr. Thompson is a very dangerous man. We know you're in trouble, but if you're with Henry Thompson, you are in worse danger than you know. We can help. Do you understand?

—Uh.

—Russ, we want to help you. Russ, are you still there?

I turn the phone off and toss it in the backseat. Russ takes his face away from Bud again and looks at me with his crooked stare.

—Who was that? Anybody I know?

I get out of the car, walk around to Russ's side and start to help him out. The cop waves one of his buddies over to take control of the traffic and strolls toward us.

I have Russ out of the car and we're moving away. I'm counting seconds. I'm counting seconds until I get to thirty so I can look back and see if the cop has stuck his head in the car to gander at all the broken glass and the hot-wired ignition. I make it to twenty before I turn.

He's not looking in the car, he's got his back to the car. He's got his back to the car so he can talk to Roman, who has just pulled up in his now Russian gangster–free sedan and who is, no doubt, asking about the two guys in the beige Celica. I hustle Russ down the steps of the L train station at the end of the block.

* * *

Getting the fucking tokens takes for-fucking-ever. Russ leans against me while I dig out one of the twenties. The guy in the booth wants to know how many we need and I blank out for a second, trying to figure if I should get more than one token each, just in case. Then I get a grip on where I am and how close Roman and Bolo are and I tell him to just give me a couple and please hurry. He slides the tokens through the slot and starts counting out my seventeen dollars in change, all in singles. Then I feel the breeze from the tunnel that means the train is coming. The token guy stuffs the bills at me and I grab them and drag Russ to the turnstiles. It's another project just to get the two of us through and then down the next set of steps. The train is pulling in, but it's on the opposite track, heading into Brooklyn. I start moving Russ down the platform toward the far end, away from the entrance and the turnstiles.

—What do you say, Russ?

—Mmmm. I don't know, Hank.

We're moving along OK now. I'm on his left side, helping him, but he does seem to have some control over the left leg and all I really have to do is keep him balanced.

—You feelin' any better?

—Hank?

—Yeah?

—What the hell are you doin', man?

—Well, Russ, I'm trying to get us out of here.

—But, like, all those cops back there, man. Let's just. Mmmm. Let's just, man, just hand me over, cuz, like, I think I'm pretty fucked up.

We're getting close to the end of the platform and I can see the tunnel brightening ahead of us as a train approaches the station. I look back up the platform in the opposite direction. Still no Roman. We get to the end and I lean Russ against the wall. He has Bud's bag hanging from his neck and Bud is trying to squirm out. I push him back in and zip the bag all the way shut as the train comes rocketing into the station.

—The thing is, Russ, I thought we might go pick up the money. Then

I thought we might go see a doctor and get you fixed up. Then I thought we might take off someplace and hide out. What do ya say, man, sound good?

—Yeah, that's, like, cool and all, but you, like, gave fucking Roman the key. Mmmm. You gave him the key, man.

I pull Russ to the edge of the platform as the train comes to a stop. The doors slide open with a little sound. *Ding-dong!* We stand aside while a load of young artist poseurs from Williamsburg pile off to go drinking in the East Village.

—I gave him the wrong key.

—Huh?

—I gave him the key to *my* storage unit, Russ. We still have the money.

As we step into the last car of the train, I catch some action at the other end of the platform: Roman and Bolo plunging down the stairs and through the crowd, trying to make it into the first car.

—We, like, still have the money?

—That's right, man, we still have it. So just relax and everything's gonna be OK.

Ding-dong! The doors slide halfway shut, stop, and slide back open the way they do when someone is blocking a door somewhere on the train. *Ding-dong!* They slide shut all the way. Me? I'd say Roman made it onto the train.

The train will make three stops before it reaches the end of the line at Eighth Avenue. I'm trying to figure how long it will take Roman and Bolo to work their way back through the whole train to us. The trains are eight cars long. Every other car has a locked door; they'll have to jump cars at each station to get around the locked doors. I'm thinking about the layout of the stations between here and the end of the line, thinking about where to make our break. We pull into the Third Avenue station.

Ding-dong! The doors open and a few people get on and off. I've got Russ parked in a seat. I go to the door and stick my head out. At the far end of the train, in the second car, Bolo is doing the same thing. He sees me. I duck back into the car. *Ding-dong!* And we're off again. Next stop: Union Square. When the train pulls in we'll be near the stairs at the back of the platform. We can make a run for it, hope they don't see us get off, and catch another train or hit the street.

I grab Russ's arm and start to lift him off the seat, but he's just deadweight. I look around the car. No one is paying the slightest attention to us. New Yorkers: God forbid you should look up, you might see something. I sit next to him and feel his wrist. There's a pulse. Hopefully he's just blacked out and not in a coma. We're hitting Union Square.

—Russ, come on, man. Time to go. Let's go.

No response. The train is stopping. I can leave him here. There is no reason not to leave him here. Except, of course, that Roman and Bolo will kill him if they find him.

—Russ.

I slap his cheek lightly. Nothing. In his lap, the bag shifts slightly as Bud moves around. *Ding-dong!* People are pouring off the train, on the train. I step to the door and look out. Bolo is there, still in the second car. He waves. I wave back and step off the train. He says something to someone inside the train and he and Roman both step off. I step back on. They step on. I step back off. Roman stays on the train. Bolo jumps onto the platform and starts heading toward me. *Ding-dong!* I dive back on as the doors slide shut. The doors stop and slide back open. *Ding-dong!* They close all the way. He made it back on. But it was worth it to watch him dance. Next stop: Sixth Avenue.

Russ won't come around. We pull into the Sixth Avenue station. *Ding-dong!* I look out the door again. Bolo and Roman duck out of the second car and into the first door of the third car. They're gone from view for a moment. I pray for the doors to close before they can get any closer. No luck. They pop out the doors at the near end of the fourth car and jump into the fifth car. *Ding-dong!* They'll hit another locked door between the six and seven cars. That's as close as they can get until we pull into Eighth Avenue. The end of the line. I sit on the seat next to Russ and take his hand as we start to move.

—Wow.

I look at Russ.

—Wow, man, I just, like, went out there.

He shakes his head and looks around.

—So yeah, man, let's, like, get that money.

We pull in at Eighth Avenue, standing in front of the door, waiting for it to open. It takes forever. *Ding-dong!* The stairs are right in front of us. Russ holds on to me and we rush ahead of the other passengers and up the stairs into the station proper. Two cars behind us, Roman and Bolo get pinned in the thick of the crowd trying to cram up the one stairway.

We hit the top of the ramp that leads into the heart of the station and I pause to look back. Roman and Bolo are at the bottom of the ramp. They're moving quickly through the crowd, Bolo cutting a path for them. I look at the turnstiles, but Russ is just moving too slow for us to make a break for it on the street. I turn right, deeper into the station, heading for the A train platform.

We pass two down staircases, both closed for repairs. Russ has his left arm draped over my shoulder and is doing a little hop-skip to keep up. I hear a train pulling into the station on the A-C-E tracks, but I can't tell if it's on the uptown or downtown platform. I make a guess and drag Russ to the left and down the stairs to the downtown platform, with Roman and Bolo breathing down our necks. If there's no train we'll be pinned down here.

There's a C local right there, doors open, and an A express that's just pulling to a stop on the other side of the same platform. At the bottom of the stairs, I look back. They're at the top, looking right at us and coming down fast. The A stops. *Ding-dong!* People dash back and forth across the platform, transferring from train to train. I take us to the right toward the A train, making sure Roman and Bolo see us heading that way before we disappear from their line of sight. The crowd is thick and I use my elbow to make some room for us as we loop around the backside of the staircase Roman and Bolo are on. Around and toward the C train.

We circle the stairs and, as we come around the other side, I see the back of Bolo's head towering above the crowd. He and Roman stand at the foot of the stairs for a second, looking for us on the A. *Ding-dong!* The doors of the C train are closing just ahead of us. I kick out with my right foot and the doors smash against it. *Ding-dong!* They pop back open and we jump inside onto the C. And so do Roman and Bolo, ducking in through the next door in the car, about ten yards away. Bolo holds up his scratched thumb and gives a little grin like he's the fucking Fonz.

We pull out of the station. Russ is spent and leans against me, resting his head on my chest while I lean on one of the floor-to-ceiling poles. Behind me, I hear the voices of bridge and tunnel teens whispering, calling us faggots. Roman and Bolo just stand there at the other end of the car, watching us, close enough to have a conversation if we raised our voices a bit. They seem happy to be close to us and to stay close until we get away from the crowds. The Jersey boys behind us are getting brave, talking louder.

—Fucking faggots.

—Yeah, fucking ass-fucking faggots.

—Look at them. They have AIDS and they *still* act like faggots.

Their voices are loud enough to be heard by most of the people in the car and I can feel tension building. Bolo is trying not to laugh and Roman is shooting little laser beams out of his eyes into mine.

—Ass-fucking, disease-spreading, sick, fucking faggots.

I take Russ's arm from my shoulder, lean him against the pole and turn toward the voices. People observe this out of the deliberate corners of their eyes and the tension in the car jumps. Everyone is watching and listening now, but pretending not to. I stare down at the five boys on the bench seat.

—Hey, faggot's a toughguy.

The train is slowing as it approaches the station.

—Got a problem, butt stuffer?

They all look the same. They all have the same too short hair, too big muscles, too small eyes, the same pin-fucking-heads. This will be easy. This will almost be fun. The biggest one gets up as we pull into the station.

—What about it, shit-dick, you got something to say?

The train is coming to a stop. I look over at Roman, smile at him, then turn back to the boy. He's still talking.

—Come on, you fucking child molester. Say what's on your fucking mind.

The train stops and I pucker up and make a little kissy face at the boy. We're two feet from each other. He grabs at me and I kick him hard in the shin. He yelps and I swing my right elbow up and into the hollow just below his chin. He falls back gasping as his friends jump up off the bench and come at me. And all the queers on this train in the heart of the West Village just a few blocks from the Stonewall Inn, where the gay rights movement was born in a transvestite riot, go bat-shit. *Ding-dong!*

The doors open. I grab Russ as we are pulled with the tide of the brawl pouring out of the train. The A express we saw at Eighth Avenue is on the other side of the platform. *Ding-dong!* We plow through the small riot and safely into the A train. The doors don't close. I watch as Roman and Bolo brutally force their way through the melee toward our train. The doors don't close. They step aboard at the far end of the car again. Across the platform, the C train still hasn't moved. I hold Russ tight against me and duck out the door and right back onto the A train. Roman and Bolo don't bite. I do it again. They don't bite. The C is still there, across the platform. The fight is still there, going strong as the city works out a little of its sexual tension. We dodge out the door again and keep going this time. They don't bite. *Ding-dong!* And I drag us through the closing doors of the C train.

Roman and Bolo jump off the A. *Ding-dong!* And back onto the A as the doors slide shut and their train pulls out. Right behind ours.

* * *

The trains run on parallel tracks. For a while our C local has a bit of a lead. But then the A express carrying Roman and Bolo picks up speed and soon it's running right alongside us. I watch through the scratched Plexiglas window while, just a few feet away on the other train Bolo mouths curses at us and Roman shakes his head. Then they are speeding away, ahead of us on the express track, racing toward Canal Street, as we slow to make our first local stop at Spring Street. I ease Russ down into a seat and try to remember how to breathe.

Russ sits there slumped against me. Bud rustles around in the bag and I unzip it a bit to see how he is. He sticks his head out through the hole and forces it open so he can stretch up and rub his head against Russ's chin. The train is entering the station.

—Let's go, guys.

I take Russ's arm and it's deadweight. He's blacked out again. I sit back down. The car is quiet, almost empty, just the few people who didn't get off to join or watch the fight. There's a little drool at the corner of Russ's mouth and Bud is licking at it. I feel his wrist, then alongside his throat and then I put my ear against his chest.

His eyes are open. I slide them closed. He looks asleep. I have to force Bud back into the bag. The train pulls to a stop. I take the bag from around Russ's shoulder and drape it around my own. I stand up. The doors open, I step out. And all my bridges are burned, because now I really am a murderer.

Ding-dong!

PART FOUR

SEPTEMBER 30, 2000

Final Day of the Regular Season

—Hello?

—I love you, Mom.

—Henry.

—Tell Dad I love him, too.

—Oh, Henry.

—I got to go, Mom. Bye.

I stand there on the corner of Prince and Mercer, holding the pay phone receiver. It's about 10:30, half an hour since we met Roman in the park. I can't stop shaking and it's making it hard to get change in the slot to make my next call. All around me, kids from NYU and weekenders from Jersey are walking the streets of SoHo, asking for directions to Balthazar. I bite down hard on my tongue until I taste blood and the shaking eases up.

The card is in my back pocket where I put it when I changed clothes at my apartment. It's folded inside the police photo of Yvonne's bruises. I fold the picture back up, put it away and dial the number. It rings once.

—Yes?

—It's me.

—'Bout time.

—Yeah.

—That's some fucking mess you got over there, boy.

—Yeah.

—Shoulda called me like I said.

—Yeah.

—Got anything to say 'bout that?

—Sorry.

—Yeah, well. So you ready to work together now?

—Yeah.

—Good, glad to hear it.

Ed can't come for me right away. He tells me I'll have to wait and lie low until tomorrow evening. He tells me where and when to be, then hangs up.

Every time I get a chance to stand still, I realize how much everything hurts and how tired I am. The wound in my side burns, my face throbs, all my bruises ache and my feet are cramped beyond belief. I stand here on the corner and look around at the normal people who aren't being hunted by psychotics and the police, and I hate them.

I stink of sweat and my clothes are a mess. I'm a wreck and I look it and I need a place to lie low and to not be noticed until morning. I eat two Vics and try to sleep on a sheet of cardboard spread out on the sidewalk under a construction scaffold outside the Angelika movie theater and no one bothers me at all. I'm now homeless in New York and, just like all the other homeless, I have become conveniently invisible.

It's not good sleep. I'm cold, the ground is hard and when I do manage to drift off, some pain or other fights through the chemicals and wakes me soon after. Mostly I lie on my right side with my back pressed up against the building and watch people's feet walk past. I have Bud's bag half-open and I keep one hand tucked in there, feeling him breathe and purr. I think about Russ, dead and alone on a downtown local. I think about my aluminum bat, the murder weapon, splotched with blood and covered with my fingerprints. I can't remember if I left it in my apartment or his. No matter. The cops will have it soon, if not already. I wonder if Roman and Bolo grabbed an uptown train back to Spring Street or if they got off at Canal to wait for our train. What will they do if they find Russ? My head is clogged with mud. I wish I had a beer. I can't tell if I'm falling asleep or just blacking out.

Yes, I have the nightmare. Yes, it's changed. Yes, Russ is in there now. I don't want to think about it.

At some point, while I sleep, Bud crawls out of his bag and curls up under my chin. When I wake he's still there, trying to keep me warm.

It's light out, but Ed and Paris won't pick me up for many hours. Bud is making a pained sound and I dig in the bag until I find his little bottle of pills. I hold him tight and force his jaws open and push one of the pills to the back of his throat. I hold his mouth shut until I feel him swallow. I look at the label. He's supposed to take them with food. Fuck. Food. When was the last time he ate? I tuck him back in the bag, trying not to hurt his leg, and zip him in. Getting myself off the ground takes a couple of minutes. I can't catalog the pains; everything hurts. I take a look around. It's early Sunday morning. Little traffic, no people. I love Sunday in New York. The city exhales at the end of the weekend. It's nice.

I walk up the block to the grocery at the corner of Mercer and Bleecker. I keep my Yankees jacket zipped way up and I have on my sunglasses and headphones. I try to get some news on the radio, but the batteries are dead.

The store is empty except for the kid at the cash register looking at a martial arts magazine. He gives me a once-over, but I think it's just because I look broke. I grab a couple cans of 9Lives, some AA batteries and a bagel with cream cheese wrapped in cellophane. I look at the beer; the coolers are locked until noon on Sundays. I get a bottle of water. The kid rings it up and I pay with the singles I got in change when I bought the tokens. On my way out of the store, I see the papers and remember the games. I want to check the scores, but I look at the headlines instead.

The *Daily News*: MANHUNT!

The *Post*: MANHUNT!!!

The New York Times: Suspect Sought in Barroom Slayings

All feature large reproductions of my booking photo. I glance at the kid. He reads his magazine, not bothering with me now that I've paid. I flip the *Daily News* over and look at the sports headline: THE SHOTS HEARD ROUND THE WORLD! I think about simultaneous home runs being hit last night while Russ and I fought in the car. I can't bear to read the details of "one of the most bizarre and serendipitous events in the history of America's favorite pastime." Atlanta 2, New York 0. San Francisco 5, Los Angeles 3. And I missed it. And now the Mets and the Giants are all tied up for the wild card with one game each left. Tonight. And I'm gonna miss those, too. Because I'm gonna be at a fucking showdown.

The clock next to the register says 8:22 A.M. I have almost nine hours to kill and I need to stay out of sight until then. I shuffle my way over to Broadway and Prince, just another stinky bum with a bad haircut and a cat in a bag.

The token booth in the station for the N and R trains has a photocopy of a Wanted poster taped to the window. Guess who? I give the girl one of my twenties and ask for a fifteen-dollar MetroCard. It's a great deal: they give you one extra ride free. She slides me the card and the five bucks change and never once looks at me. I walk down the stairs to the platform and wait about fifteen minutes for the N and take it out to Coney Island. Where else am I gonna kill the day?

SPANG!

There was no one on the train, so I opened a can of 9Lives, unzipped the bag and let Bud out. He went right through that first can. When it was empty I filled it with water from my bottle so he could have a drink, then opened the second can and watched him eat all of it.

SPANG!

I unwrapped my bagel and had my own breakfast. It didn't taste like anything at all, but I ate it in about thirty seconds and wished I'd had another. I drained my water bottle and put all the garbage back in the grocery sack and stared at the advertisements in the train. Dr. Z: dermatologist extraordinaire. Learn English! Jews for Jesus. Get your high school diploma now! It took about forty minutes to get to Coney Island, so I read them all a few times.

SPANG!

I got off the train at the end of the line, crossed over Surf Avenue and walked along the edge of the midway. The season is over and most of the stuff is closed for the rest of the year.

SPANG!

I stood by a fence and looked at the original Cyclone, half-collapsed and overgrown with weeds and ivy. On the other side of the midway the "new" Cyclone teeters, looking like it might fall to pieces any second itself.

SPANG!

I climbed the stairs up to the boardwalk. A few of the snack shacks were open and I thought about grabbing a dog. Maybe later. I crossed the wood planks to the sand and walked over the beach to the edge of the water and sat down.

SPANG!

I sat there for a good long while, trying to clear my head, to think. No luck. I got up and headed back to the boardwalk for that dog. And that's when I saw the guy tinkering around with one of the pitching machines.

SPANG!

He wasn't planning to open, so I had to talk him into it. Finally I gave him a twenty and he showed me a cage I could use. A softball cage. I gave him another twenty and he said I could use the fastball cage. I bought some tokens, grabbed a bat and stepped into the cage.

SPANG!

I put Bud down out of the line of fire, slipped off my headphones and sunglasses and dropped a token in the slot.

SPANG!

The machines pitch Spaldings. A light flashes on the front of the pitching machine to let you know when the next one is coming.

SPANG!

I let the first couple whiz past to get the timing and placement, then I stepped into the box. The balls came in just a little high and outside. I let another one by, then got myself hunkered down. I balanced myself just back of center, so I could lift my lead foot before throwing my weight forward. I kept my elbows in and circled my bat. The light flashed. The ball came to the top of the machine and shot toward me. I stepped into it, rotating my hips and shoulders, extending my arms and pulling the bat through the strike zone, letting my whole body do the work, not just my arms. The ball was huge, brilliant white and moving about eighty miles per hour. I haven't swung at a ball since the day I broke my leg.

The bat makes contact. The impact makes a noise. It echoes around inside the hollow aluminum cylinder and sounds like this:

SPANG!

If it weren't for the fucking net, the ball would have gone over the Cyclone. And so would the next couple dozen I hit.

Now the torque I'm putting on my wound is starting to hurt like hell.

SPANG!

Jimmy crack corn.

SPANG!

'Cause I don't care.

SPANG!

The balls jump off the bat like they're scared and I groove homer after homer. My body relaxes. My mind clears.

SPANG!

I do the one thing I have ever been truly great at.

SPANG!

And for the first time I can remember, I look back at the road that led me here.

SPANG!

The long slide of my life from teenage superstar to alcoholic bartender.

SPANG!

The break in my leg that ended my baseball career before it started.

SPANG!

The calf that wandered out on the road and sent me and Rich crashing into a tree.

SPANG!

That sent Rich crashing into a tree.

SPANG!

The girl who dumped me and left me alone in New York.

SPANG!

The booze I poured down my throat.

SPANG!

The nowhere job that ruined my feet.

SPANG!

The cat Russ left me.

SPANG!

The bad guys chasing me around.

SPANG!

Mom and Dad scared and confused.

SPANG!

The friends who have died.

SPANG!

Been murdered.

SPANG!

The friend I have murdered.

SPANG!

All because I've spent my time waiting for things to work out for the best.

SPANG!

Like I fucking deserve it or something.

SPANG!

SPANG!

SPANG!

SPANG!

SPANG!

And something is certain.

The past is over. My life will never be what it was. And considering what I've made of my life so far, that may not be such a bad thing after all. It's time to stop hoping things are going to work out and start giving myself a chance to get out of this alive. Because I'm tired of being everybody's stupid fucking patsy. It's 11:00 A.M. and I have a friend to see back in town.

SPANG!

I get off the N train at 8th and Broadway. The streets are filling now with shoppers and brunchers. I duck my head down, walk along the edge of the sidewalk and mutter to myself. People stay out of my way and make a point of avoiding eye contact in case I might ask for change or help of any kind.

On 9th Street I stop in front of an old tenement building, just around the corner from Sixth Avenue. I could buzz his apartment, but he might freak and call the cops. So I'm gonna have to try something else. I walk up the steps to the intercom box. There are four apartments on the top floor. I push the button for the first one, wait, get no answer. I push the second one.

—*¿Hola?*

—Uh . . .

—*¿Hola? ¿Qué pasa?*

—Uh, *nada*. Wrong, uh.

—*¿Cómo?*

—*Numero no bueno.* Sorry. *Gracias.*

—*De nada.*

Fucking French classes. I push the third button.

—Yes?

—UPS.

—UPS?

—Yeah.

—You guys deliver on Sunday?

   Shit.

—Sure, seven days a week.

—Wow, never knew that.

—Twenty-four, seven.

—Wow.

—So you want to buzz me in?

—What is it?

   Uh.

—It's a box, how do I know what it is?

—Well, who's it.

—Look, you got a package. You want it, buzz me in.

   BUZZZZ.

I run up the stairs to the second floor and the apartment at the end of the hall. I knock loudly on the door. I hear a door open up on the top floor. I knock again and I hear someone moving around inside the apartment. Upstairs, the guy is waiting for his package.

—Hey, UPS? You down there?

—Comin' up.

I knock again. A sleepy voice from inside.

—Yeah. Hang on.

Tim opens the door a crack and looks out. When he sees me his face goes pale and he tries to slam the door shut, but I've already got my foot jammed in the opening.

—Let me in, Tim.

—Oh, fuck. Fuck.

—Let me in. Please let me in.

The guy from the top floor is coming down the stairs.

—UPS?

Timmy is trying to hold the door closed against me, his skinny arms shaking.

—Help. Help.

He wants it to be a scream, but he's so scared that it just wheezes out with no force at all.

—Please, Tim. I need help.

—Help. Help.

The guy from the intercom is getting close.

—Hey! U! P! S!

Tim's face is red with strain. I put my weight into it and shove him back into his apartment. I'm through the door and closing it behind me and he's trying to run away, but it's a studio and there's no fucking place to go. I lock the door and look out the peephole and see the back of a guy in boxers and a T-shirt standing on the landing and looking down the stairwell. I turn back to the room. Tim is scrambling up the ladder to his loft bed. I can see the wire to the phone leading up there. I grab the wire and give it a yank and the phone flies off the loft to the floor and lands on a bunch of dirty clothes. Tim makes a scared sound, looks at me and climbs the rest of the way up onto the bed. I can see him up there, huddled in the corner, rocking back and forth and making a quiet keening sound.

I take Bud's bag from my shoulder and put it on the floor. I walk across the room to the ladder and climb it until my head sticks up over the edge. Tim pushes himself farther back against the wall and grabs a pillow and points it at me as if it were a weapon.

—Don't you hurt me. Don't hurt me. Don't hurt me.

I want to leave. I want to leave him alone and out of all this, but I can't.

—Tim.

—No.

—Tim!

—Oh, God.

—Tim! I didn't. I swear I didn't. I. I. I.

Slowly I climb the rest of the way onto the bed and crawl over to him. I take the pillow out of his shaking hands and put it in his lap and put my head on it and wrap my arms around his waist.

—Oh, Jesus, Tim. I. I. I.

After a while he climbs down, gets a pint bottle of Tullamore Dew from a shelf and drinks it.

The truth is, Tim's connections to the underworld aren't much more extensive than mine. But he knows a guy and makes a call. We're gonna have to go out to Brooklyn, to Williamsburg and that's got me a little nervous. I've been burning up a lot of luck walking the streets. Tim tells me not to worry, makes a call to another guy he knows.

We sit in his apartment waiting and Tim alternates sips of his Dew with huge bong rips. He offers me both. I pass. As it is, I'm getting pretty baked just sitting here breathing the secondhand smoke. His phone rings once. He puts the bong aside and drags a Levi's jacket from the laundry pile. I collect Bud, get him in the bag and head for the door. Tim stops me before I can open it.

—So check it out. Both these guys I called are supercool, but they expect to be paid.

—No problem.

—Sure, but just check it out. The guy out front? Getting him up on a Sunday, that costs extra, so he's gonna want a couple hundred.

—No problem.

—Yeah, but check it out. The other guy? His stuff usually runs a couple grand. Now, with the rush job and the hazardous nature of the duty, that could go up to five or six.

—No problem.

—Cuz I have a relationship with these guys.

I reach inside my jacket and pull out the bundle of hundreds I took from the big bag. I peel off ten and hand them to Tim.

—I'll get you more.

Tim looks at the cash in his hand and the cash in my hand and nods.

—No problem.

Outside, a Lincoln Town Car with tinted windows is parked at the curb. We climb in the back. The driver is Puerto Rican, not too tall, big square shoulders, perfectly groomed hair, wearing a nice suit. He's got Barry White on the CD player: "I'm Gonna Love You Just a Little

More, Baby." Tim pulls the door closed and the guy turns in the seat and puts out his hand. Tim gives him some skin and points a thumb at me.

—Mario, this is Billy. He's learning the trade.

Mario offers his hand and I give him skin. He smiles.

—Good to know you, Billy. You guys got a joint?

Timmy smiles and whips out a bone and passes it to Mario, who twirls it under his nose and sniffs it like a cigar. He nods and smiles.

—Sweet. Where to, guys?

Timmy leans back in his seat.

—Williamsburg. Metropolitan, off Graham.

—You got it.

Mario puts the Lincoln in drive and pulls away. He pushes in the dashboard lighter and slips on a pair of huge blue-tinted sunglasses. The lighter pops out. He uses it to spark the joint and takes a massive hit. He grins and exhales the smoke between his clenched teeth.

—Sweet. Super sweet.

He offers the joint to us and Tim shakes his head.

—No, man, enjoy. But can we get some privacy back here?

—You got it.

Mario touches a button on the dash and a polarized glass screen rolls up between us.

Tim tells me more about the guy we're going to see and I watch the streets reel past as Mario drives us to the bridge, over the river, into Brooklyn and to a small yellow duplex in the heart of Williamsburg. Tim points at the front door.

—Check it out. There's two doors and neither one is marked. Push the bell for the one on the right and he'll let you into the hall. There's an intercom in the hall and when he asks you who you are, tell him you're Billy. Right?

—Sure.

—So, you sure I can't wait or come get you later?

—No, but you can do me a favor.

—Sure.

—Stay away from home for the next twenty-four or so.

Tim scratches his nose and rubs his eyes.

—Sure. Why?

—Check it out, Timmy. The cops got to be looking up all the regulars from the bar, so they'll be calling sooner or later.

—No problem. I know how to talk to cops.

—Sure, but some other guys might call, too.

—Oh.

—Yeah. So just go hang out somewhere. Don't go home at all today.

—What about tomorrow?

I drape the strap of Bud's bag over my shoulder and put my hand on the door latch.

—Tomorrow they won't be around.

—Cool.

—Yeah. Cool.

I open the door and climb out. The driver's window zips down, weed smoke and Barry waft out. Mario smiles at me from behind his glasses. I take three hundreds from my pocket and hand them to him. He nods his head.

—Sweet.

He reaches inside his jacket, takes out a card and hands it to me. It's glossy black and has *Mario* etched across its face in gold Gothic script. Beneath his name it says *sweet* and then a phone number. I tuck the card in my pocket and he puts out his hand. I give him some skin.

—You need a lift, call me.

I nod. His window zips back up and the Lincoln pulls away smoothly and disappears around a corner.

There's a White Castle just up the street and my mouth actually waters at the thought of steam-grilled miniburgers, but it's just another public place where I could be spotted. The duplex in front of me is a two-story wood job, exactly the kind of building they don't have in

Manhattan. In fact, the tallest buildings around here are no more than six stories. The sky seems huge and open and I can see storm clouds moving in from the south.

I walk up to the right-hand door and push the little black button set into the door frame. I hear a chime and then a loud buzz and a click as the door unlatches for me. I step quickly inside and the buzz stops. I close the door and I'm standing in a small entryway with a linoleum floor and Sheetrock walls and an old steel factory door in front of me. There's an intercom unit set into the wall next to the door with the Plexiglas-shielded lens of a videocamera above it. I push the talk button.

—I'm Billy.

A moment's pause, then another buzz and click and I push the steel door open and step through.

It's not really a duplex. The interior of the ground floor has been gutted to make a single large space. It looks like a living area. I can see a couch and a TV and, off in a corner, a bed. But I can't see much more because of the guy standing in front of me, holding the big gun.

The gun is a Desert Eagle .45. I know because I have seen it waved around by so many bad guys on TV. The dude on the other side of the gun is in his twenties, has black hair with bleached tips, is wearing a vintage *Star Wars* T-shirt over very groovy green corduroys and has the prettiest blue eyes I have ever seen. He blinks them and shakes his head tightly from side to side.

—Get the fuck out, Maddog.

Clearly there has been a misunderstanding.

—I'm Billy.

The gun is pointed at my face.

—You're a fucking mad dog killer. Get the fuck out.

Oh.

—No, I'm.

—Get the fuck out so I don't have to figure out a way to get rid of your fucking corpse.

—Tim sent me.

—No shit. If you see him before the cops gun you down, you can tell him I'm pissed. Get. The. Fuck. Out.

—Can I show you something?

I start to move my hand toward my jacket pocket.

—Don't put your hand in that pocket.

My fingertips are inside my jacket. He jabs the barrel of the gun an inch closer to my face.

—Don't put your hand in that pocket.

My fingers are all the way inside. The gun moves closer still and the end of the barrel now looks big enough for me to stick my head inside. My hand is in the pocket.

—Leave it there. Leave your hand in that fucking pocket.

I start to take my hand out.

—Don't! Don't!

He has the barrel of the gun stuck up against my right eyebrow. He's got his arm stretched out to the limit. Trying to keep as far from me as possible so he won't be splashed by too much of my blood when he shoots me, I suppose. My hand is out of my pocket. His pretty eyes are locked on mine.

—Drop it. Fucking drop it.

I drop it and it hits the floor with a soft flap. We stand there. Then he takes three quick steps straight back away from me and looks down at the bundle of hundreds on the floor.

—It's about nine grand. I have a bit more on me, but I might need it. I can get more to you later. I didn't kill any of those people they say I did.

He looks from the cash to me and back again.

—How much more?

—A lot, but it may take a while.

He looks down again, the gun still on me, and then backs up.

—Fuck it. Nine's good for now.

He stuffs the gun in his waistband.

—*I'm* Billy. Let's go up to the shop and get started. Bring the money.

He turns and heads for a spiral steel staircase over by the bed. I pick up the cash and follow.

* * *

Billy has an awesome stereo. Most of the components are exotic German stuff I've never heard of, the speakers wired throughout his workshop to provide virtually flawless surround sound no matter where you stand. We're listening to the Psychedelic Furs' *Mirror Moves*. I haven't heard this stuff since high school. It's really kind of cool. Billy moves around the shop, switching on various pieces of computer equipment and gathering tools and materials.

—These guys really never got their due, ya know? There was so much crap being ground out in the early eighties that they just kind of fell through the gap, except for "Pretty in Pink." And that was more a hit because of the movie, which I do love, don't get me wrong. But listen.

I listen.

—This stuff holds up. Try listening to fucking ABC or Flock of Seagulls now, or even Duran Duran and it just sounds dated. Totally dated.

The second floor has been gutted just like the first, but up here it's all shop space. Billy sets stuff out on a bench next to his drafting table and a custom desktop computer, that looks to be based around a couple Power Mac G4s. He waves me a bit closer and switches on a set of lamps and shines them in my face.

—Come here. Let me get a good look at you, Maddog.

I step closer and he takes hold of my chin and tilts my face this way and that in the light.

—I'm not a mad dog.

He lets go of my face and takes a step back to look me over.

—I didn't kill those people. I'm not a mad dog.

He sits down in front of his computer.

—At this point, man, I don't really give a fuck.

—I do.

He looks at me over his shoulder.

—Fair enough, Maddog. As long as you're paying, you didn't kill anybody. But like I said, I really don't give a fuck. So can it and I'll try and get some work done.

I sit on a folding metal chair, unzip Bud and take him out. He's awake, but a little dopey I think. Those pills kind of knock him out. I put him on the floor and he curls up under my chair. Billy starts doing things with the computer and pieces of paper and plastic and pens and razor blades and ink. I stay out of the way.

—I'm gonna give you some hair.

Hours have passed. Billy sent out to the White Castle and had a sack of burgers and fries delivered. It was really good. Bud is walking around, checking stuff out. I've been watching Billy, doing what he tells me to.

—It will be better if the passport and the driver's license show you with some hair, especially if it's two different styles. That way everything doesn't look like it was done at the same time. Thing is, I don't want to give you your natural color, cuz then you'll just look like the Wanted posters. So you're gonna be blond, OK?

—Sure.

—OK.

He took a few photos of me earlier and scanned them into the computer. He's already digitally removed the bruises and cuts from my face and now he starts laying in various styles and shades of blond hair. I've moved my chair close so I can peek over his shoulder. He is good. He's really fucking good.

—So, for the passport, I'm giving you a little buzz thing and how about this moppy thing for the license?

I just watch while he moves things around with his mouse and occasionally pushes a button. He gets up and goes over to a set of large printers. He feeds a small sheet of plasticized cardboard into one.

—Those will burn for a while. So, let's do some work on you.

He leads me to a corner of the shop concealed behind a heavy rubber drape on ceiling tracks, like in a hospital. He pulls back the drape to reveal a bathroom. He switches on more lights and looks at me again.

—You're stuck with the bruises. I could put some makeup on them, but it wouldn't last very long. Leave them alone and if anyone asks,

tell them you were in a car accident. Tell them you got rear-ended and
smacked the steering wheel with your face. The hair I want to change.
That fuzz is too dark for the blond I gave you in the photos. We can't
match the color exactly, but we can bleach it so it looks like you're trying to be hip or something. You ever bleach your hair before?

—No.

—It hurts, gonna burn your scalp like hell.

It does hurt. Quite a bit.

My name is John. John Peter Carlyle. Billy made me write it out a
couple hundred times before he'd let me sign it on the documents. He
said I needed to work at it to make it look natural. And it does, it looks
great, it all looks great. Billy has everything laid out on a table and he
explains it all to me while he takes sips of Dr Pepper from a two-liter
bottle.

—The passport and the license should get you through any kind of airport thing and past any border. I put stamps for Mexico, Canada and
France in the passport to give you a little travel history, backdated
everything and distressed it all so it looks like you've had it for a while.
The problem is, there's no backup identity in any of the official com-
puters. If a cop or someone actually runs your name through a computer or tries to zip that driver's license, it's gonna come up blank and
the jig will be up, so don't let it happen. Got that?

Bud is back in my lap. I scratch his ears and nod.

—OK. Now, the credit cards? Those are different. I do most of my
business in high-end plastic. Carlyle is a fake identity, but he has an
actual credit history. You could use those cards and as long as you paid
the bills, you could just hang on to them. Don't. Use them for plane
tickets cuz they look for people booking last-minute trips in cash. Use
them for the tickets, then get rid of them. You got a wallet?

—No.

He digs in a crate under the table and pulls out two cardboard
boxes. One is filled with used wallets, the other with photos.

—Take a wallet. Bend it around, twist it up a bit. Also take a couple pictures. Don't go crazy, cuz if someone asks you who's in the picture, you need to be able to answer. Carlyle is single according to his credit applications, so take a girlfriend and maybe a nice middle-aged couple to be your folks, but no kids.

I sift through the photos in the box. I find one of a pretty brunette leaning against a tree. I find another of a couple in their early sixties standing in a kitchen somewhere, looking happy.

—And give me all your old ID. Carry that shit around and you'll end up giving it to some teller, she asks for a second piece of ID to cash a check.

I hand him all my ID, everything that says Henry Thompson.

—Don't talk to people, but don't be rude. If they ask you where you're from, say New York. Keep the details to a minimum and don't improvise. You get on a plane, tell some hag in the next seat you live on West Eighty-second, next thing you know, she lives there, too. Give her a bogus address, turns out it's hers. Then you got to kill the bitch or something. Best bet, wear that Walkman and don't play it too loud and no one will fuck with you. And don't try to fly in those clothes; they reek.

I tell him thank you and collect the papers and plastic: passport, driver's license, Social Security, gym membership, bank card, library card, Blockbuster membership. I put Bud in the bag and head for the door, followed by Billy. He stands aside to let me into the little exit hall.

—You should get rid of the cat.

I stare at him.

—You're carrying around a cat, man. I can give you papers and bleach the hair, but you're still a dude walking around with a cat and that's a pretty big fucking identifying feature. "Did you notice anything unusual about the man?" "Weeelll . . . He was carrying a cat, if that's any help, Officer." Get what I mean? Leave the cat here. I'll take care of it, I know a chick who digs cats.

—I can't.

He looks me over like I'm just about the stupidest sack of shit he's ever seen.

—Some mad dog. OK, look: It's dark out and it's supposed to rain some. Plus, with the big game, there shouldn't be a lot of people out tonight. You try to stay away from bright public places and, uh, keep the cat in the bag.

—Great.

I open the outer door. Sure enough, it smells like rain and I can feel the muscles in my damaged calf starting to cramp. I scratch at my head; it itches and burns from the bleach job.

—I'll send you more cash when the dust clears.

—Whatever. Look, don't scratch like that or it'll scab up, look like shit and feel even worse.

I stop scratching.

—Thanks.

—No problem. Well, you go get 'em, Maddog.

I let the door fall closed behind me. John Peter Carlyle and I head for the L train back to Manhattan. Me, myself and my cat.

The asshole in the seat across from mine won't stop looking at me. He's got a goddamn magazine. Why doesn't he just fucking read it? He'll look at it for a couple seconds, then glance up and check me out again. Fuck! I've got my Walkman and my sunglasses and my new blond hair and my reeky clothes and this guy just can't take his eyes off of me. He looks at me again and I stare right back at him. He puts his eyes in his magazine, then glances back up to find me still staring at him. He looks back down.

—Hey.

He keeps his face in the magazine, I think it's *Film Comment* or some shit.

—Hey!

Man, he can really read that magazine when he wants to.

—Hey, you. Scorsese.

He looks up a little.

—Yeah, you. You got a problem?

He looks back at his magazine.

—Hey. I said, "Do you have a problem?"

He doesn't look up, but he mumbles something.

—What was that? I didn't hear that.

—I don't have a problem.

—So then mind your own business and don't stare at people. It's rude.

He gives a tiny nod and keeps his eyes locked on the page in front of him. I stare at him for a few more seconds, then take a quick look around the car. Passengers with something to look at are doing so and the ones without are either staring off into space or have their eyes closed. No one will look at me or that other guy for the rest of the trip. My heart goes BANG-BANG-BANG!

The train passes under the East River and stops at First Avenue in the heart of my neighborhood. The guy with the magazine and several other passengers get off, but I see him and a few of the others board the next car down. Trying to get away from the smelly freak. I watch the people getting on the train, fearing a familiar face, but I don't recognize anyone. Most of the new passengers are wet. The rain must have started up.

The train moves on. I think about the chase last night, on this train, through these same stops. I still don't know what happened to Russ. He must have been found by now. I looked at a little news on the TV back at Billy's, but they didn't say anything about Russ. It was all about the murders and the search for me. I turned it off before I could get too freaked out.

At Union Square, some yahoos wearing head-to-toe Mets gear get on. They're mouthing off to one another and talking real fucking big for a bunch of fans whose team is skidding hard. I want to say something and put them in their places, but I keep my head down and my mouth shut. If I ever had any good karma, it's been cashed in and then some.

The train stops at Eighth Avenue, end of the line. The Mets fans pile out in a herd, jostling their way to their favorite sports bar. I trace the path I took with Russ last night, up the stairs and the ramp. This time I take the turnstiles out of the station and go up to the street.

There's a nice soft shower falling. I left Billy's around 6:30, so it must be just about 7:00. The Mets game starts at 7:30 if this rain doesn't cause a delay and fuck things up. I walk west on 14th into the meat-packing district.

Past the actual meat markets and the underground sex clubs and the new chichi restaurants, 14th Street runs into Tenth Avenue. The street is half cobbles and half ripped-up tarmac here, crosshatched by old train tracks and shadowed by an industrial skyway that links two warehouses. I wait in a patch of darkness, leaning against a billboard's support pillar. Up the way is a gas station for cabs and the street is dotted with Yellows waiting to be retrieved by drivers on coffee and piss breaks. The Metro buses do driver swaps here as well, so there's a short line of buses parked along the block. But the real trade is still the hookers. The area is essentially devoid of residential housing or re-tail, so no one has bothered to clear out the whores, which is good news for all the businessmen who stop here in their SUVs on week-days to get a quick hum job before they split back to their families in Connecticut. Most of the trade is pretty bent, not the little-boy hus-tlers you find on Christopher Street so much as transvestites and transsexuals. I wave off a couple offers. All and all, things are pretty slow, what with it being a Sunday and the rain and the big game. Come by here after the game if the Mets win and the place will be hopping.

I think about these things and they mostly keep me from thinking about Yvonne's apartment being a short walk away and that helps me not to think about Yvonne and that helps me not to think about Paul's and that helps me not to think about Russ and how I really did fuck-ing kill him. Shit, oh, shit.

The Caddie glides to a stop at the curb several feet away and the rear passenger door swings open.

I walk over and stick my head inside. Paris is behind the wheel, not looking at me, Ed reclines at the far side of the backseat. It's dark in-side the car and looks even darker because of the sunglasses I'm wear-

ing. The sunglasses, I now realize, that are just like the ones Ed and
Paris sport. Ed is looking at me from over his glasses and below the
brim of his cowboy hat. He pats the seat next to him. I look at the
street around me and let a few more drops of rain fall on the back of
my neck, then climb in and close the door. Paris puts the Caddie in
drive and Ed shakes his head.

—Christ, you stink.

I crack the window to let some of the smell out and take off my headphones.

—Look at you. Man, Paris, take a look at the boy.

Paris turns his head to take a look at me.

—Looks like crap.

He turns back to the road.

—No, nah, man. He looks tough. You lookin' tough, Hank.

—Thanks.

—Sure, sure. So, not to be rude, but where the fuck's our money?

I take off the sunglasses.

—Drive over to Twelfth and Twenty-eighth. Chelsea Mini Storage.

—No shit?

—No shit.

Paris makes a turn at 23rd and takes us to Twelfth, then heads
north. Ed is watching me and smiling.

—Really, man, I can't get over it. Couple days ago, you were just some
cat with the shit beat out of him, but now you got something. You look
like a player now, son. Focused, determined. Look at me.

I look at him.

—No, man, look me in the eyes.

He takes off his sunglasses.

—That's it, stare right in there.

I stare into his sleepy, bent eyes for a couple seconds, then fear
crawls all over me and I look away. He slips his glasses back on.

—That's all right, man. That is all right. You definitely got a little East-
wood going on in there. Without a doubt. Way to go.

I unzip the bag. Bud sticks his head up and forces the zipper the rest of the way open so he can slide out. He stretches and starts to groom. Ed frowns.

—A cat, huh?

—Yeah.

—That's cool, I guess. Just don't let it fuck up the upholstery.

The Caddie pulls to a stop and Paris turns off the engine.

—We're here. It's closed.

I look out the window and see the sign posted on the office door, which very clearly sets out the weekly hours for Chelsea Mini Storage. I take special note of the fact that they are open until 8:00 P.M. every night of the week except for Sunday, when they close at 7:00 P.M. I freak.

—Fuck! Shit! Piss! Tits! Motherfucker! Shit!

I pound my head against the back of the front seat and Bud hops from my lap down to the floor.

—Un-fucking-believable! One, just one fucking fucked-up fucking thing can't fucking work. FUCK! Fuck me! Fucking God! I. I. I.

I wrap my arms around myself and rock back and forth.

—Why doesn't anything work?

Ed puts a hand on my shoulder.

—Take it easy, man. No sweat. We got it covered.

I look up and he gives my shoulder a little squeeze. Paris reaches under the front seat and pulls out a double-barreled shotgun, sawed off to about twelve inches.

—Yeah, man, we got it covered.

The drizzle is starting to turn to real rain. I stand outside the office door with my headphones and sunglasses on and knock on the glass. It's 7:37 P.M. There's one guy inside, trying to get things settled for the night so he can go home and watch the game. I knock again. The guy looks over at me and I wave. He shakes his head and goes back to work. I take out the key to Russ's unit and tap on the glass with it. He looks up again and I wave the key at him. He points at the sign with the posted hours and then at the clock on the office wall, shakes his head and goes back to work. I start rapping on the glass with the key. The guy tries not to look up, then finally does and I wave for him to come over. He points at the clock, flips me off and goes back to work. I start knocking as hard as I can without breaking the glass. He looks at me, then turns and walks out of the office through a door at the back. I keep knocking. He comes back into the office followed by a big guy in a security guard uniform. The boss guy sits back at his desk and the security guard walks over to the door. I stop knocking and he yells through the locked door.

—We're closed.

—Yeah, I know, but I have to get some stuff from my unit.

—We're closed.

—Yeah, but I really need my stuff.

—We're closed.

He turns his back to walk away and I start banging on the glass again. He turns back.

—Knock it off.

I bang harder.

—You best knock it off or you gonna get it.

Bang, bang, bang.

—OK. You want it, you got it.

He takes the keys from the clip on his belt, unlocks the door and pushes it open. As I move back, Paris steps from the shadows next to the door. He presses the barrels of the shotgun against the guard's face and marches him right back into the office, followed by me and Ed. The boss guy sees us come in and stands up and puts his hands on his head. Ed locks the door and I take the bandanna he gave me back in the car out of my pocket and tie it around my face. It's black, just like the ones worn by the brothers DuRanté.

I'm an outlaw.

Every now and then, if you're lucky, you get to see someone capable of true excellence do what it is they are best at. As a boy I got to see

Willie Mays play baseball. He never got credit for half of what he did because he made it look so easy. I don't know how hard armed robbery is, but Ed and Paris make it look easy.

They work fast and I try to keep up. They force the guard and the boss out of the office and into the loading area, near the elevators. Paris keeps the shotgun where they can see it, while Ed does all the talking and occasionally points at them with a Colt that looks identical to the one Paris used to shoot rats at the dump.

—Who else is in the building?

The boss shakes his head.

—No one.

—Bullshit! Who else?

—No one.

Ed steps over and slaps him lightly on the cheek, like he's a stubborn child.

—No one?

—They all split fast so they could watch the Mets game.

—Are the elevators still on?

—Yes.

—Are the alarms armed for the upper floors?

—No.

Ed reaches out and gives him that little loving slap again.

—I will kill you. I will kill you.

—Off, they're all off.

Ed turns to me.

—Where to?

—Fourth floor.

Paris stays behind in case of trouble and the rest of us get on the elevator. Ed makes the guard and the boss stand at the far end of the elevator so he can cover them, while I operate the controls and take us to the fourth floor. I pull the doors open and Ed and I step out, followed by the others. I tell them the unit number and they lead the way.

At the door, Ed covers them and I open the lock and pull the door open. Ed takes a quick look inside.

—Clean that shit up and bring the bag out.

I go inside and stuff the cash Russ and I left scattered on the floor back into the hockey bag, then I zip it up and drag it into the hall. It's heavy. Really heavy. Ed steps away from the door and waves the guys into the unit. He steps inside the unit, close to the boss.

—Where's the alarm pad?

The boss nods.

—Right next to the office door in a locked case.

—Where's the key?

—On the ring in my pocket. It's the small silver round one.

Ed slips his hand in the boss's pocket and pulls out the keys.

—How do we activate the alarm?

—Eight-four-five-one. Then press "cycle." You have thirty seconds to leave and lock the door with the biggest key on the ring before the alarm goes off.

Ed walks very close to him.

—Tell me again.

—Eight-four-five-one. Cycle. Thirty seconds.

The boss tries to cower away from Ed, but Ed slips an arm around his shoulders and pulls him close.

—I'll kill you both. I'll come back from the dead and kill you both.

—Eight-four-five-one cycle thirty.

Ed backs out of the room and I close the door and lock it. He helps me carry the money to the elevator. We go down, get Paris, activate the alarm, lock the door behind us, throw the money in the trunk, get in the Caddie and drive away. Ed pulls the bandanna from his face and looks at me.

—See, we got it covered.

We're in the apartment they grew up in.

—Roman got the Chink, and your boss got Bert, and Russ got Ernie. So who got Russ?

Their mother died some years back, never having reconciled with her hoodlum sons. A cousin got the lease and the brothers arranged for the apartment to be maintained as a hideout. Ed told me about it as we drove out here to Queens. Paris listened and added nothing of his own. I watch Bud lap milk from a little blue bowl on the linoleum kitchen floor.

Paris is sitting at the Formica-topped kitchen table, surrounded by the cash, tapping out numbers on a calculator and scribbling them down in a yellow legal pad. Ed and I sit on a beat-up couch with plastic covers. He's drinking a Heineken. I'm drinking ginger ale.

—I got Russ.

Paris looks up from his figures and Ed nods his head.

—No shit?

—No shit.

—What'd you get 'im with?

—A baseball bat.

—Fuck.

I'm squeezing little dents into my soda can, then popping them out. Pop, pop, pop, pop.

—Well, Russ was a OK cat, but I guess he kind of screwed us all. Damn, a baseball bat?

—Uh-huh.

—I'm tellin' you, Hank, watchin' you, it's like watchin' a egg get all hard-boiled. No shit.

Paris clears his throat and Ed looks over at him.

—Well?

—Four million five hundred twenty-eight thousand.

—No shit?

—Yep.

—How 'bout that? Only twenty-two K short. Let's hear it for Russ keeping his fingers out of the till.

I take a swig of my soda.

—Except for trying to rob it all.

—Well, yeah, but the man wasn't exactly made of steel, ya know?

—I know.

—Great thief, though. Great fucking thief.

He and Paris raise their beers and drink a toast. My stomach churns as I think about the pulpy dent I put in the side of Russ's head. I sip more ginger ale and look out the tiny slit window, which lets no light into the basement apartment. I get up off the couch.

—I need to use the can.

Ed has gone over to the fridge for another beer.

—Down the hall on the right. Hold the lever down for a second or it won't flush all the way.

I put my soda can on the coffee table, grab my bag and walk down the shag-carpeted hallway.

—Don't take forever. I want to make that call.

The walls of the hallway are lined with photographs, each one marking the passage of another year. The first is of a handsome young couple with their newborn, a chubby little Paris. The next one is the same: the couple is on the plastic-covered couch, Paris between them getting bigger. Ed arrives in the third photo and sits in his big brother's little lap. They grow, Paris a shy beanpole and Ed, small and intense, always wearing the outfit his brother wore a few photos back. At the tenth picture, the father disappears. There are six more. In each the boys edge toward one end of the couch and their mother toward the other, until in the final picture they sit at opposite ends, staring into the camera, unsmiling. Soon after this point, these small, beautiful boys will whip another child to death. I look at the eyes in the photos: Paris looks afraid, Ed looks hurt. I go into the bathroom.

The toilet has one of those fuzzy covers and a cushy seat. I sit to pee just because it looks so comfy, and it is. I hold the handle down and keep it there while the toilet flushes. I take off my jacket and grimy sweatshirt and crusty T-shirt and unwind my bandage. I dig the first-aid stuff out of my bag and clean my wound again and rewrap it. Then I find an extra T-shirt and a heavy flannel in the bag and put them on. There's a wicker laundry hamper in the corner and I toss my dirty stuff inside. When I packed the bag, I didn't bother with pants. Way to think ahead, asshole. I look in the mirror and John Carlyle looks out. He looks like he'd like to kick my ass. I open the door and go back down the hall so I can use Ed's phone to set up Roman and Bolo to be murdered. I feel pretty good about it. Does that make me a bad person?

Ed tells me what to say.

—You're a shit eater, Roman.

Great lines.

—And you aren't too fucking smart, either.

Fucking Shakespeare.

—Isn't that right, Roman; you're a shit eater and you aren't too fucking smart?

He's not talking yet, so I improvise a little.

—Use that key yet, Roman? Go and open that storage unit yet? By the way, you can have any of my old stuff. I'm gonna buy new stuff with my four and a half million fucking dollars. Just don't take the beanbag chair. I love that fucking chair.

It speaks.

—You're making a mistake.

—The only mistake I'm making is not calling the papers and telling them about you. The only mistake I'm making is not spending a few grand of my money on making you dead.

Ed is twirling a finger at me, telling me to get on with it.

—Instead, I'm gonna give you four million. Do you want to know why I'm gonna give you four million and keep only a half million for myself?

—Yes.

—I'm gonna give you four million to help me get out of town and to help keep the Russian fucking Mafia from coming after me. I'm gonna give you that money to get you out of my fucking life forever. And then I want to go away. Sound reasonable?

—Yes.

—Good.

Paris is out front getting something from the car. Ed sits right across the little kitchen table from me. I try not to look at him too much while I'm talking because he has his sunglasses off and those fucking eyes are creeping me out.

—At ten, I want you and Bolo to walk over to Astor Place and stand out on the traffic island, the one with the big cube.

—And?

—And just stand there, stand there and stand there with cars passing by until I feel safe and then I'll walk over from wherever the fuck I am and I'll give you a very big bag full of money.

—And?

—And then I will go away and I will trust that you won't shoot me in front of a city full of witnesses. I will trust that you understand it is in your best interest that the police do not catch me, because I will tell them all about you. I will trust you understand that if the Russians find me, I will tell them it was you that killed their boys. Which may be a fucking lie, but who's counting?

I hear the front door open and close as Paris comes back in. Ed is gesturing for me to wrap it up.

—Are we all together on this, Roman?

—Sure.

—See you at ten.

—Too bad about Russ.

—Yeah, too bad.

—I mean, his dying at your hands. That pretty much screwed you and your chances of being Mr. Innocent In Over My Head. That was your point of no return, Hank. No going back now. No normal life for you.

—Yeah, pretty much. Your point?

—Don't fuck with me too much, Hank. I've got a temper. I'm known for it. And you're a murderer now. No one will miss you when you're gone.

—Good point, Roman, I am a murderer. Don't forget that. OK?

I push the power stud on the phone and break the connection. Ed is nodding his head and smiling.

—Now that's the shit, right there, that's the shit. Very slick. "I am a murderer. Don't forget that." And just, click. Just hang up. Very slick. What do you think, Paris? Pretty slick, huh?

Paris is standing in the doorway of the kitchen, holding a large black alloy attaché case. A little grin slides along his lips.

—Yeah, slick.

He hefts the case and points at the table.

—Why don't you clean that off and I'll show you something real slick, Mr. Bad-Ass.

The town I grew up in was a gun town. We never had them in my family, but most of the kids I knew grew up shooting and hunting. I'd go up in the hills with them or out to the Rod and Gun Club and plug away for a few hours. I'd flip through their back issues of *Gun* magazine and *Soldier of Fortune* and look at the guns and read about stopping power and firing rates and blow-back and concealment profiles. It was like knowing about cars or my favorite ball players. I fired rounds from an M1 Carbine, a .357 Magnum, a .38 Police Special, a 9 mm Chinese Mauser knockoff, a Ruger .32, a couple of .30-06 hunting rifles, several shotguns and any number of .22 rifles and handguns. Russ's .22 was the first gun I've picked up in over ten years. I haven't fired one since I was eighteen.

Paris sets the case on the table, works the little combination locks, flips the catches and opens it up. The interior of the case is lined with black foam rubber. Nestled in this lining are eight very beautiful tools designed for the single purpose of ending human life. Ed reaches into the case and runs his fingertips over all the steel.

—So how 'bout it, Hank? You wanna carry a piece on this or what?

When I was a kid, my mom would let me go to R-rated films as long as they were rated R because of sex and cursing, not violence. I got to see *Saturday Night Fever*, but not *Friday the 13th*. I wasn't allowed to watch *Hogan's Heroes* because it treated war like a game and a joke. I wasn't allowed even a toy gun. When the kids in the neighborhood played cops and robbers, I used a stick. And when I went shooting with my friends, I never ever let her know. I look at the guns in the case: some vintage pieces, like the set of Colt Peacemakers; others so modern and efficient, they look more like computer components than weapons.

Ed takes a small gun from the case and holds it out to me.

—This is perfect for you, a real classic.

I know this gun. It's a .32 Colt Detective Special. It's a narrow snub-nose revolver with the hammer filed down to a nubbin so it won't snag on anything as you whip it out of your shoulder holster. It has no safety, minimum recoil, is designed for concealment and very short range combat. I take the gun from Ed.

—Careful, it's loaded.

I keep my finger off the trigger and keep the barrel of the weapon pointed at the floor. I thumb the catch and flip the cylinder open: full load, five rounds. I empty the bullets into the palm of my left hand, flip the cylinder closed, place my finger on the trigger, raise the weapon, point it at the wall, inhale and, in the pause just before I exhale, I squeeze the trigger in a single smooth motion. The action is just a bit tight, so that it gives you a real sense of control at the firing point. The hammer pulls back as the cylinder rotates and then snaps down hard with the sound unique to an empty gun.

—Hey, Paris, looks like our boy knows what he's doing here.

Paris nods.

—Just full of hidden talents, ain't he?

I hand the gun and the bullets back to Ed.

—I'll pass. My mom wouldn't like it.

I nod in the direction of a little black-and-white TV, with rabbit ears on top of it, that sits on the kitchen counter underneath a picture of a black Jesus.

—Any chance we might get a look at the game on that thing?

The brothers DuRanté look at each other and you'd think those boys might never stop laughing.

* * *

Mets vs. Braves: top of the third, no score, rain delay. The Giants game won't start for a couple hours yet.

We flip on the news. They've found Russ. Some do-gooder got concerned when Russ's body tumbled to the floor of the C train and lay there without moving for about five minutes. She waited until she got out at the JFK stop and told the station manager that there was a guy on the train who looked pretty sick. The train had pulled out of the station by then, but he radioed ahead. A couple stops down the line, some cops checked it out and things moved pretty quickly after that. They're calling him one of my "known associates" and have added his murder to the list of crimes for which I am being sought.

Paris has been taking the guns and the money to the Caddie, along with a few odds and ends from the house, while Ed and I flip through the few channels that come in clearly on this relic TV.

—How's it feel, Hank?

—What's that?

—Being wanted?

I think about that. I think about it for a while.

—OK, I guess. I haven't really been wanted for a long time.

—Infamous.

—Yeah.

—Kinda cool, isn't it?

—Kinda.

—Got no past, nowhere to go back to.

—Yeah.

—Just today and maybe tomorrow.

—Yeah.

—'Cept, course, you got people out there still. Right?

—Yeah.

—That's tough, man, very tough. Me and Paris, we only got each other, so we just roll. Be tough to have folks out there worrying after you.

—Yeah.

—Best way to deal with that? Know what it is?

—What?

—Just don't think about them. Just don't fucking think about them at all.

Paris comes back in, walks over to the TV and switches it off.

—Fuckin' thing will rot your brain. Let's go.

Once again, Paris drives while Ed and I ride in the back. Bud sits in my lap, being mellow. The Caddie is vintage prime, so there's no tape deck, but Paris grabbed an old boombox back at the apartment and he has it up in the front seat with him. He drives with one hand and, with the other, he sorts through a shoebox full of old cassettes, some store-bought, some homemade, none with cases. He pulls them out one after another, checks them out and tosses them back in the box. He pulls one out, reads the hand-lettered label on its front and sticks it in the player.

—Check it out.

He hits play. It's Curtis Mayfield, "Keep on Keeping On." Ed leans forward.

—Oh yeah, baby, oh yeah. You know this, Hank?

—Sure.

—Curtis. Wow.

He reaches into the front seat and turns it up. He and Paris sing along a little.

—*Many think that we have*
  blown it.
But they, too, will soon admit
That there's still a lot of
  love among us
And there's still a lot of
  faith, warmth, and
  trust
When we keep on
  keeping on.

They start laughing and Ed squeezes his brother's shoulder and leans back next to me.

—That was our mom's shit, all the classic soul, all the funky stuff. Talkin' all the time about the music of our people and a "positive black self-image."

Up front, Paris is still singing along under his breath. Ed leans his head close to mine and whispers.

—That's kinda why she washed her hands of us. Far as she was concerned, we turned out just another couple a nigger hoodlums and she raised us for better. I wrote her off years before, but Paris took it pretty hard, bein' cast out and never talkin' to her before she died. He's my big brother, but *damn*, he's sensitive.

We're on the Queensboro Bridge, heading back into Manhattan. Ed points straight ahead.

—Take the scenic route. All goes well, none of us will see this place again, 'least not for a long-ass time.

Paris takes us west on 59th, along Central Park South, past the Plaza and the Ritz, to Columbus Circle and down Broadway. Someone visited me from California once and said he thought of Times Square as the pumping heart of New York. I told him it was more like the running asshole. But it is something to see, at night, in the rain.

By the time we reach Broadway and Astor, "The Underground" is playing. It's all fucked up, distorted guitar and Curtis growling "the underground" over and over. Paris stops at the curb. I open the door and step out into pouring rain. I want to bring Bud, but Ed is afraid he'll get in my way, so he's making me leave him behind.

Ed sticks his head out the door. Rainwater streams off the brim of his hat. He's holding Bud, keeping him from leaping out of the car after me.

—Now just do as you're told this time, no fucking improvisation. We took you in this once. Fuck up again, I'm gonna take off the leashes an' put the fucking dogs on your ass. Got it?

—Got it.

—Be cool, Hank. In an hour, you're gonna be on your way to a new an' better life.

He ducks back into the car with Bud. The door slams shut, the Caddie rolls off. They gave me an old ball cap with an eight ball inexplicably embroidered on the front. I pull the cap down tighter on my head and walk around the block to my post.

I sit in the window at Starbucks, the one on Astor Place as opposed to the one a block away on Third Avenue. New Yorkers like to complain about the proliferation of Starbucks and Barnes & Noble shops in their great city. They bitch about the "malling" of Manhattan. But me? I'm all in favor of anyplace in this city that has a public bathroom.

The rain is keeping people at home. A few of the tables in here are occupied by NYU students or street people with enough change for a cup of joe. Based on appearances, I could belong to either group. Outside, the streets are wet and empty. Rainy Sunday night, plus folks are probably waiting at home for play to restart out at Shea. I look up at the sky. There's a good wind blowing and the clouds are moving along pretty damn fast. They should get it in.

The pain from my wound is growing, spreading. I could take a pill. Shit, I could take a dozen pills. I need to stay sharp. The pain will help me to stay sharp.

I sip my decaf herbal tea and look out the window at the cube. Astor Place, St. Mark's, Fourth Avenue, Bowery and Lafayette all collide in an impossible knot of an intersection out there, and in the middle is a sliver of a traffic island. And in the middle of the island is the cube. Black steel, maybe eight feet to a side, it sits there balanced on one of its corners. It's mounted on some kind of pivot so that if you give it just a little shove, it rotates. It is a prime example of ugly fucking municipal art.

The tea doesn't really taste like tea and it tastes nothing at all like beer, but it has no caffeine or alcohol, so it's good for my surviving kidney. I also got a croissant, but I don't have an appetite just now because it's a few minutes to ten and I really want to see Roman and Bolo walk out onto that traffic island and stand there in the rain.

Then I will get up and go to the pay phone by the bathroom (which I already checked to be sure it works) and I will call Ed and Paris and they will drive over from where they are parked nearby and, while I watch, they will shoot down Roman and Bolo in the street. After that, I will step outside, Ed and Paris will pick me up and we will speed away. I don't see much point in trying to imagine what might happen after that.

Out in the rain, Roman and Bolo cross over to the traffic island from the direction of St. Mark's.

They're both carrying the kind of cheap umbrellas that vendors hawk for five bucks a pop when the rain starts up. Roman is wearing a long raincoat over his suit. Bolo is out there in just his leather pants and motorcycle jacket. He has his left hand pressed down on his head, trying to keep the wind from blowing his long hair around. I watch them getting wet for a moment.

A gust of wind comes along and blows the cheap umbrellas inside out. Roman turns his to face the wind and it flops back into shape. Bolo takes his hand from his head to fix his own and all that black hair flies off in the wind and lands in the gutter a few feet away.

I turn to run for the phone and bounce off the real Bolo, who is standing right behind me with a Band-Aid on his thumb where Bud clawed him. He points out the window.

—Fucking Russians got nothing but shit for brains.

—I can understand you thinking *I* might be stupid. I mean, I'm big and strong and I have dark skin, so people see me and figure I must be the dumb one in the group. But Roman? What? You think *he* suddenly grew a brain tumor or something?

We're sitting at my table. Bolo picks at my croissant, keeps one eye on me and another out the window on the decoys.

—Asshole. You had Ed's fucking card on you when the cops picked you up. We knew you'd been talking to him. "Meet me at ten and just wait." Come on. You get away with the money and then you call us to give it back? That had fucking bushwhack written all over it.

I nod toward the fake Bolo, adjusting his wig in the rain.

—New friends?

—Shut the fuck up. I will tell you when to talk. Fuckin' shithead Russians. I told him to pin that fuckin' thing down, but he wanted to use fucking spirit gum. In the rain. Idiot. Now talk about pissed? I'm pretty flamed. And Roman, well, imagine. But the Russians? Shit. We tell them you kacked two of their top ex–Red Army special forces guys, and not only that, but you also took all the loot. They started talking about black market nuclear weapons and shit. Roman tells them we need two more guys, we're lucky they didn't send some fucking Cossack militia riding through the streets on horseback. Roman talked them down, though, explained the whole deal was too loud as it is. Once you get them settled, those guys understand terms like *covert operation*. All fuckin' ex-KGB and shit. So when are the coons supposed to show?

—When I call them.

He throws a piece of croissant on the table.

—And when were you gonna fuckin' tell me that?

—When you told me I could talk. Man, you really are kind of the stupid one.

—Watch it.

—Seriously. I mean, I thought Ed and Paris had mastered the whole *Of Mice and Men* thing, but Roman is so George and you are so fucking Lenny.

He holds up a giant finger and presses it against my lips and keeps it there for a second.

—OK? Enough. Where are you supposed to call them?

He takes the finger away.

—They're nearby. I don't know where. I'm supposed to call Ed's cell from the pay phone.

He looks over at the pay phone and the few customers scattered through the café and takes out his own cell phone.

—Does Ed have caller ID?

—Don't know.

He puts the cell away.

—OK. Let's walk over there and make that call. You go first and go easy.

—Where's Roman?

He just looks at me, gestures for me to get up. I stand. He stands. I turn and start toward the phone. He follows.

Halfway to the phone I stumble and break my fall by grabbing one of the little café tables. I freeze like that, getting my balance and taking a good grip on the edges of the table, then I speak loudly and clearly.

—I AM HENRY THOMPSON. I AM WANTED FOR MULTIPLE HOMICIDE.

It works great.

There isn't a beat or a moment of frozen silence. I say my name and people just freak and scatter. I lean back, lifting the table high off the floor, swinging it to my left. I spin around, the table building velocity. Bolo revolves into my line of sight, standing motionless, more stunned by my announcement than anyone else in the place. Frozen, he does nothing to dodge the table.

The impact jolts the table from my hands. It flips and a corner clips me on the chin. I flinch back and the table drops and lands on my toes. I stumble back, crashing through several chairs until I hit the wall ten feet away.

Bolo is standing perfectly still in the middle of the room. A little hole has been punched into his left temple by the triangular base of the table. Blood wells up and gushes out of the gap and floods down the side of his face like it's running from an open faucet. He puts his hands out as if trying to find his balance, his eyes locked on mine. He wobbles, rights himself and picks up his left foot to step forward. Immediately he's out of true and his arms windmill and after that, it's all about the bigger they are and the harder they fall. He goes down face first, sending chairs and tables skittering and crashing across the floor. Then he lies there and quickly bleeds to death while I feel at the cut on my chin and massage my throbbing toes.

The decoys must have seen people scrambling from the Starbucks.

I run out the door on one side of the place and the decoy dressed like Bolo goes in on the other side. I spare a glance through the windows that line the street and see one Bolo standing over the corpse of the other Bolo, then I'm crossing the street toward the cube sculpture and the fake Roman standing there. I'm worrying about where the fuck the real Roman is, and thinking maybe that's really him, when he lifts his arm and points it at me and it goes BANG and the bullet buzzes past me and that's not Roman. He wouldn't shoot me without knowing where the money is.

The Russian Roman is to the right of the cube. I run to the left and put it between us before he can take another shot. He dodges to his left and I go to my right, listening to his skipping feet as he tries to juke me into the open for a clear shot. I back away from the cube until I can see his shoes. He's edging around to his right now, letting the sound of the rain cover his creeping steps. I move in close to the cube, put my shoulder against it, and push it counterclockwise. It's big and doesn't move very fast, but has tremendous mass. I feel the softest of thuds vibrate through its bulk and step back to get a look. He's laid out on the pavement with a gash on the back of his head, his gun on the ground a few feet from his grasping hand.

I dive down on the slick cement under the edges of the balanced cube and my cap bounces from my head. I put my hand on top of his just as he grabs the gun with his right hand. I look at him. He could be Blackie or Whitey, whatever their fucking names were. I use both my hands to keep his right pinned on the gun and the gun pinned to the ground. He's trying to pry my fingers loose with his free hand. I drag myself forward on my elbows, open my mouth wide and bite down hard on his fingers. There's blood and rainwater in my mouth. He screams. I get the gun and hit him in the head with it. A bullet strikes the pavement next to us, skips once, peppering me with little cement chips and hits him in the face.

I hear Russian behind me. I let go of the gun and flip over onto my back. The Russian Bolo, minus his wig, stands on the edge of the traffic island, pointing his gun at me.

—Freeze and give us our money!

—I don't have it.

—Freeze and give us the fucking money!

Sirens somewhere. I lie there next to the dead fake Roman and shake my head.

—Get up! Get the fuck up!

I stand up and behind him I see Roman come up the steps of the 4-5-6 subway station just outside the Starbucks. Guns blazing. One in each hand. Just like in a John Woo movie.

He shoots the Russian Bolo in the back. He shoots him and shoots him and shoots him as he walks over. Then he stands over the dead body and shoots it some more until his guns are empty.

—I told them not to hurt you till we had the money.

I point at the corpse at his feet.

—Well, I guess he learned his lesson.

—I told you, Hank. I told you I have a fucking temper.

He starts to reload. I start to run. I take two steps, see the gun at my feet, stop, pick it up and turn to do I don't know what the fuck. He's finished reloading. I go back to running. Running is something I know how to do. The sirens are very loud and, down Bowery, I can see flashing lights heading for the intersection.

I run east on St. Mark's, cut north on Third Avenue and east again onto Stuyvesant. I shout as I run.

—I know where the money is! Don't shoot me, Roman! I know where the money is! DON'T SHOOT ME!

He doesn't shoot me. Behind me, I hear sirens and screeching tires and bullhorn voices and Roman yelling. I run through the rain and the shadows and into the little square outside St. Mark's Church at Stuyvesant and Second Avenue. I look back up the street to the intersection at Third Avenue. Roman is showing his badge to a bunch of cops and pointing in various directions. I see flashing lights coming up Second Avenue. I hop over the cast-iron fence and into the small churchyard and hide in the bushes.

The cop cars drive past. I can hear sirens and megaphones at Astor Place. And the chop of helicopter blades from above. I peek out from the bushes but can't see much beyond the square. I scuttle to my left, hop another fence and dodge behind the pillars that support the church portico.

St. Mark's Church is the oldest place of Christian worship on the island of Manhattan. It says so on a plaque next to the door. Lots of important people are buried in its small graveyard. The plaque says that as well. I read these facts over and over while I hunch behind the pillar, holding a gun and waiting to be found. I get tired of waiting.

I shift around until I'm squatting with my left shoulder pressed against the base of the pillar. I flick the safety off the gun, but I keep my finger away from the trigger because I can't keep it from clenching over and over again. I take a few breaths. I can't hear anything nearby. I peek out and see Roman's knee right in front of me and bump my head into the barrel of his gun.

The rain is still pouring and little beads of it run down the barrel of his gun onto my forehead and drip right into my eye. I try not to blink because he told me not to move and I think he really means it. No one else is on the street, the civilians are hiding inside and Roman has the uniforms he ran into working the other streets. He presses the gun a little harder against my head and I know it must be making a little white circle there.

—Do you have the money, Hank?

—No.

He's standing right over me.

—Do Ed and Paris have the money?

—Yes.

The rain is starting to taste salty, but that's just because I'm crying. It's difficult to cry so hard and not move.

—Do you have any way of getting the money at this point?

—No.

Standing over me, looking down at my crouched and curled body.

—The mistake you made, Hank, was in thinking of it as simply money.

Four and a half million dollars in cash is not the same as four and a half million in the bank. In fact, you would be hard-pressed to find a bank with resources like those on hand. Four and a half million in cash is more a symbol than actual money. For Ed and Paris, it represents their life's work. For the Russians, it is an investment, which they can use to expand into markets that only accept cash payment. And for myself, it represents freedom, a chance to regain a life I gave up long ago. Bolo and the rest just saw the money. Like you. And they're all dead. Do you see the connection I'm making?

Looking down at me. Looking down at me from an angle that keeps him from seeing the gun pointed at his knee.

I pull the trigger. He falls back. His gun goes off. The world explodes and starts ringing. The bullet vibrates my skull as it passes by and I feel the muzzle flash sear and blister my scalp. I lurch upright as Roman tumbles down onto the steps of the church, his gun flying out of his hand.

He sprawls there, the lower half of his right leg semidetached and pumping blood into the rain. He's reaching inside his coat and, as he pulls out his other gun, I step forward and bring my foot down on his wrist, pinning it to the ground. I point my gun at him.

He opens his mouth and spits out a little rain.

—You . . . you really are making a mistake. You don't know what it is, but . . . Christ, that hurts. But this is a mistake. Trust me.

I nod.

—I trust you, Roman.

—Well. OK, then.

I shoot him in the chest. He convulses when the round hits the bulletproof vest. He spits out more rain.

—Oh, for chrissake, Hank.

—Sorry, I forgot.

I point the gun at his face and pull the trigger again. He dies this time.

When I was about eleven or twelve, I was over at a friend's house and we were messing around with his BB gun. We plunked away at cans and little green army men for a while and then we started shooting leaves off trees and stuff and then a bird came along. My friend took a shot at the bird and missed and gave me the gun to take my turn. I aimed very carefully and tried my damnedest to hit that bird, believing deep in my heart that I could never hit it. Bull's-eye. Knocked it right off the branch. But didn't kill it. It sat on the ground and kind of flopped around in pain and we watched it, not really knowing what to do, and my friend said we should kill it and put it out of its misery. I couldn't do it, so he took the gun, pumped it up, put the barrel right next to the bird's head and killed it for me. Shooting that bird felt pretty fucking bad.

I tuck the gun into the front of my pants and walk around the corner. With all the ruckus they're making, the cops may or may not have heard my shots. I walk as far as 10th Street, sort of heading home maybe, and some headlights switch on and I stand there as the Caddie pulls up from where the brothers had it parked, waiting for my call. Ed opens the rear door and steps out.

—What the fuck, man? I told you, no fucking improvisation.

I walk past him and collapse into the car. He climbs in behind me and closes the door.

—Like I said, what the fuck, man? Where are the bad guys?

I scoop up Bud from the seat and put him on my lap.

—I'm the bad guy here. I'm the fucking bad guy. Get me the fuck out of here.

—I'll give it to you, Hank, that is one cool cat. An' you? Well, shit.

I'm down on the floorboards in the back, Bud curled up on my stomach. Ed is up on the seat. He talks to me without looking at me. He doesn't want the cops at the roadblock to know there's anyone besides two black guys in the car. Both he and Paris have removed their sunglasses and cowboy hats. In this car, they look like a record producer and his driver/bodyguard. Paris has switched tapes and we're listening to *One Nation Under a Groove*, Funkadelic's finest.

—Hey, Ed?

—Yeah?

—Aren't you guys kind of wanted yourselves?

—Sure.

—So?

—See, Hank, all these cats are thinking about is you. I mean, your ass was just in a gunfight a few blocks from here. So they're on the look-out for a skinny white dude, not a couple of black hard-asses wanted for robbin' banks in the Midwest. Follow?

—Sure. But this car is kind of distinct.

—You think we robbed in this baby? No way, man. This thing has been in storage in Jersey awaiting our return. We used a whole shit-load a cars to do our jobs. This honey is clean.

—Yeah, but.

—Shut the fuck up. It's our turn.

They've got the traffic blocked up at Union Square. Anything heading south is being diverted. Anything going north, west or east that might have come from the vicinity of Astor is being checked out. Paris pulls us forward and stops. The beam from a flashlight dances over the interior. Ed turns his head and nods. We pull forward. Ed glances down at me and winks.

—First time bein' black kept me from gettin' hassled by the cops.

We drive west. From the footwell I look up through the windows and the buildings swerve by overhead as Paris turns left on Seventh Avenue, taking us downtown toward the Holland Tunnel. We drive. Ed reaches forward and taps his brother on the shoulder.

—Here.

From my angle, I can just see the back of Paris's head as he nods. He pulls the car over and stops. Through the window behind Ed I can see part of a tenement and an old warehouse. I think we're somewhere below Houston, in Tribeca. I start to pull myself up onto the seat, but Ed puts his hand on my chest and gently pushes me back.

—Just stay there for now.

I settle back into my spot. My wound is throbbing. Throbbing. It feels like someone is stabbing me in the side. My feet hurt.

Funkadelic swings into "Maggot Brain," their endless guitar solo from hell. Ed picks his hat up from the seat and holds it in his lap, fiddling with the shape of the brim.

—I'll tell you, Hank. Me and Paris are torn.

—How's that?

Paris swivels around in his seat so he can look down and see me. It's the first time I've seen his eyes. They look anxious.

—Well, what you did back there, that's some pretty wicked shit. Very impressive.

—But?

Ed rubs the top of his head.

—Truth is, the smart play for us would be to just bump you and dump you.

Bud purrs, sleeping on my stomach, rising and falling with my breath. I scratch him behind the ears with my left hand.

—See, the heat on you is gonna be pretty fucking intense. Combine that with the heat on us and things could get sultry.

—Yeah?

—So, another option, we could just drop you off and let you do for yourself. Give you some scratch and shake hands.

—Fair enough.

—Sure, that's fair enough, but is it the right play? The smart play? Follow?

—Sure, I follow.

I scratch Bud with my left hand. My right hand is tucked under his belly.

Ed looks at his brother and Paris nods.

—Thing is, people out of the life, they always talk about "honor among thieves." But it ain't really like that. See, honor ain't much of an issue, but trust is. Trust is definitely an issue. Now, all this that just happened, this whole mess, it went down because of misplaced trust. Now, we never trusted Roman or his cronies, an' least of all the fucking Russians. But Russ? Known him since we were kids. You bet we trusted him. When he went south on us? Well, color us shocked. But more than that, color us hurt. Deeply. Something like that happens an' a man is likely to question things, things he thinks he can believe in. Question his own judgment. That's bad. Lose trust in yourself, that's the final blow. You follow?

—Sure.

I scratch Bud some more. I want to keep him mellow. I want to keep him mellow because I don't want him to jump up. Because then Ed and Paris would see the gun tucked in my waistband. The gun my right hand is resting on.

—What I told you before, about having no past, no connections. No family. That's all well and good, as far as it goes. But the truth is that it only goes so far. Me an' Paris, we beat the odds more than our fair share. Know why?

—No.

—Because we are greater than the sum of our parts. That greatness comes out of three things: faith, love and trust.

He offers his hand to Paris.

—I love you, brother.

Paris takes the hand.

—I love you, Ed.

They unclasp hands and look at me.

—Roman, Bolo, Russ? Truth is, you didn't kill those guys. They killed themselves. Them, the Russians, the Chink? They'd be alive an' have the money, if only they could have trusted each other. Trust is a feeling, Hank. It's something you feel for another person, like love or hate. It comes about because you see what a man does, who he is. A man does what he says he's gonna do, values his friends, his family, an' tries to do right by them? You can't help but trust a man like that. You can't help but feel trust for that man. A man like you.

He quits playing with his hat and puts it on.

—So your call. We can dump you here with a couple hundred grand for a job well done, you can make a run, try to start over someplace. Take your chances with the Russians that way, cuz they'll be lookin' for all of us. Maybe you can go to the cops, try to spell it all out, take your chances with the truth. Get to see your mom an' dad again that way. Or, come with us. Have a new life. A new family. Be trusted. An' I think that maybe, that's what might be best for you. Cuz the truth is, Hank, whoever you were a week ago, you're not him anymore.

Really, it's not as hard a choice to make as you might think. Because after all, he's right, I'm not the man I was a week ago. I'm not half that man. I stop scratching Bud and uncurl the fingers of my right hand from around the pistol.

—I'm in.

They smile. Beautiful smiles, just beautiful. Ed reaches down and pats me on the knee.

—Cool, very cool. Paris?

—Cool.

—All right. Hank, stay down on the floor in case they got something set up at the tunnel entrance. Once we get into Jersey it should be cool. We'll head south, got something set up at a county airport down by A.C. Gonna take a trip. Sound good?

—Yeah. Yeah, that all sounds great.

—All right, let's roll.

Paris starts the Caddie. Ed leans back in his seat.

—You know, Hank, we're pretty fuckin' sorry about the way we did your girl like that. Truth is, we went a little hard. Roman did such a good job messin' you up and gettin' you scared, we felt we had to send a strong message so you wouldn't miss the point. Fact is, when you didn't call us right away, I thought we might not have gone hard enough. Anyway, we'll make it up. An' we appreciate you takin' it like a pro. It's always best not to let a twist get in the way of friendship. *Cherchez la femme.* Women always fuckin' up a good thing.

I take Bud by the scruff of his neck and pull him off to the side. This is a fucked angle to be shooting from and the first bullet takes Ed high in his right shoulder, instead of his ear like I wanted. It throws him into the corner of the seat and I work on Paris before he can get the car moving. I can only see a sliver of his head, so I throw four rounds through the back of the seat where his body should be. His head flies forward, the car lurches twice, and the volume on the music goes through the roof. Ed starts stomping his cowboy boots down on my thighs, trying to stick his heel in my balls, but I get my knees up in the way. The bullet in his shoulder has killed his right arm and he's trying to get at the gun in his shoulder holster with his left. I shoot him in the right thigh and he stops kicking at me. I raise the gun and shoot him in the stomach. Raise it again. And in the chest. Again. And the last bullet takes off his hat. I scramble and pull myself up and look into the front seat. Paris is sprawled, half on the seat and half in the footwell. It looks like all four bullets hit, but it's hard to be sure because his chest is so ripped up. He's opening and closing his mouth.

—Ed? I'm hurt. Ed?

He dies. Without me having to shoot him again.

I drop the gun on the seat, reach forward, grab the keys from the ignition and hit the stop button on the boombox. Bud has crawled into his bag to hide. I zip him up and pull on the door handle. It's the one that doesn't open from the inside. I don't think I can get past Ed's body, so I crawl into the front seat and out the passenger's-side door.

The Caddie is at an angle, half in the street. The rain has stopped. The street is empty for now. Down the block, a car alarm is sounding. I walk around the car and open the trunk. I'm thinking about the suitcases Ed and Paris put in the car back at the apartment. I'm thinking about clothes without blood on them. But there it is, right on top. A big fucking bag, full of money.

I open a suitcase and grab a few things and stuff them in with Bud. He tries to jump out, but I push him back in and zip up. I close the trunk and walk away.

I get about five feet before I go back and take all the money. Then I run as fast as the four and a half mil will let me.

*   *   *

I'm walking up Seventh Avenue, out in the open. I hide behind a Dumpster and strip off the bloody Yankees jacket and pull on a black sweatshirt that hangs on me like a sheet. Must have been Paris's.

I have no idea where to go next and this bag is fucking heavy. At James J. Walker Park, I see a homeless guy with a shopping cart loaded with garbage bags full of bottles and cans, along with the rest of his life and belongings. He's sitting on a wet bench, trying to light a wet cigarette butt with a wet match. I sit at the opposite end of the bench. He glances at me, then goes back to the smoke. I dig around in my pockets. I gave all my hundreds to Billy, but I've still got a bunch of twenties. I pull out five and hold them out to the guy. He looks at them, then he looks at me.

—Want to sell your home?

He haggles me up to one forty and I let him keep most of the stuff. I pile some crap around the duffel bag and pull on his old overcoat and head back up the avenue. Behind me, the bum finally gets his cig lit and sits there smoking it like he's Nelson fucking Rockefeller. What was I thinking giving him twenties? I've got four and a half mil in this bag. Oh well, next time, old-timer.

I'm heading right into Greenwich Village. There are more people out now that the rain has stopped, but there is definitely a mood on the street. The city is afraid of me. I push my cart. Past Sheridan Square, I see the Riviera Sports Bar. It's packed. I push my cart past and, on the 10th Street side, I see a little window level with the sidewalk. It's set right on top of a heating grate and through it I can see clearly into the basement bar and all the TVs in there with baseball on them. It looks like the game has restarted at Shea, and the Giants game is on as well.

I pull the cart over to the wall. I dig out a blanket, spread it on the grate and sit down with Bud's bag on my lap. When I unzip the bag, he pushes away from me. I put my hand inside and tickle him between the eyes. He likes that. It takes a while, but he's settling down. I reach under him for the bottle of Vics and swallow a couple. I don't need to be sharp anymore.

Bud has some blood drying in his fur. I spit on the edge of Paris's huge sweatshirt and work at the blood. Through the window I watch both games.

The Braves and the Dodgers are taking it easy, resting their best players for the postseason, trying not to let anyone get injured. The Giants and Mets go all out, pitching their aces and fielding all their starters, even if they have to play hurt. I watch both games through the window right up to the last outs, long past the point where it is clear that both the Mets and Giants are being creamed and will be forced into a one-game playoff tomorrow to decide the wild card. They'll play here in New York. My Giants in town. God, I'd like to see that game.

I stay on the grate with Bud. It's pretty warm. When the bar closes, some of the guys toss me their spare quarters as they pass by on the way home. That's pretty cool because I need to make some calls and I don't have any small change. The bum had fragments of the Sunday *Times* in the cart and I've been thumbing through the travel section. Truth is, I've never been much of anywhere. It all looks good. I make my decision. There's a pay phone right outside the bar. It works. I make the call and set it up. There's another call I need to make, but I can't now, I just can't. I sit back on the grate.

Fucking Giants. Fucking Giants. Fucking Giants.

I don't think I sleep, not really, but the sun comes up quickly. Time flies when you're thinking about all the people you've killed. I get myself up and moving. I have things to do.

More headlines at the newsstands.

Daily News: SHOOTOUT!

The *Post:* WILD, WILD, WEST!

The New York Times: Four Dead in Late Night Gunfight

* * *

I end up back on 14th Street, the axis of my life. Krazy Fashions is right there off of Sixth Avenue. I slip a pack of fifties into my pocket, leave the cart on the street and go into the store, hauling the big money bag and the little cat bag.

Do they think I'm a criminal? I walk in off the street, stinking and beaten and start passing out fifties. Of course I'm a criminal. But they just don't care and they sure as shit don't think I'm *the* criminal. I keep Bud zipped up in his bag and I get outstanding service. I buy a nice, light olive three-button two-piece Italian suit, a cream Yves Saint Laurent shirt, oxblood wing tips and a selection of underwear and socks. The staff tosses my old shit, gives me a robe to wear and does the alterations while I wait. I keep Bud in the bag and he keeps quiet. I borrow the phone and, about the time the suit is ready, my car pulls up outside. The Pakistani guy that owns the store carries my bag out for me and puts it in the trunk. I slip him a couple extra fifties and he tells me to come back soon.

I slide into the back of the Town Car. Mario holds out his hand and I give him skin. He's listening to the *Saturday Night Fever* sound track: "If I Can't Have You."
—Newark International.
—Sweet.
   He put us on the road and turns his head to look back at me.
—Got a joint on you, man?
—Sorry.
—No sweat.
   He reaches into his breast pocket, whips out a bone and sparks it. He tokes and holds it up for me.
—Bro?
—Thanks.
   I take the joint and rip off a lungful. It burns like shit and, as I pass the number back, I start hacking. Mario takes the joint and hands me a bottle of water. I take a couple swallows between coughs.

—Thanks.

—No sweat. Take another?

He offers the joint again. I pass. The one hit is mellowing me out, mellowing me and helping me not to think too much.

The cops are in evidence at the airport. Heavily. Mario drives us to the dropoff curb for American departures. He hops out, opens my door and fetches my bag from the trunk. I put the bag on the ground and kneel next to it. I open it about six inches, reach in, pull out three packs of hundreds and wave Mario down to my level. I give him the cash.

—One for you. Give two to Tim and tell him one is for Billy. OK?

—Very.

—You know who I am?

—Undoubtedly.

—Stay cool, Mario.

—Very.

He takes the cash and gives me skin. I let a skycap carry my bag to the counter and tip him twenty.

—Aisle or window?

—Aisle, please. And if you can get me next to an empty seat, that would be great.

—No problem.

My reservation is all in order. I pass the ticket girl John Carlyle's Visa card and passport. She looks from me to the picture, twice, then slides it back. Her eyes flick to my face a few times as she does the paperwork.

—Got rear-ended.

—Oh, my God. Was anybody hurt?

—Not badly. Just me.

I have a thought.

—Uh, is there any room in first class?

—Sure.

—Would you mind, I think I need the, uh, I'd like to upgrade.

—No problem.

It costs a lot.

—Bags?

—One to check, one carry-on.

I fill out the tag, she attaches it to the big black bag and I watch all that money slide away on the conveyor. Nothing ventured . . .

—You're all set, Mr. Carlyle. You might want to hurry a bit, that flight is getting ready to board. Have a nice trip.

I take my ticket and head toward my gate. I pass about five or six cops standing in a circle, talking about the Mets. My picture is still on the front page of all the papers, and I am unseen. I feel powerful. Then I get to the X-ray machines and remember I have a cat in my bag and no papers to take him on board.

The bathrooms are off to the left. I go in and take the first stall. I put the bag on my lap and unzip. Bud pokes his head out and I give him a little rub. I should have left him with Billy. He would have given him to the chick who digs cats. Now?

I dig around in the bag until I find his pill bottle. I read the label very carefully. I'm supposed to give him two a day, one in the morning and one at night. I chuck Bud under the chin and shake three of the pills into my hand. I feed them to him one after another, then hold him until he's still. I stand and set Bud down on the floor. I take off my jacket and shirt and pull up my T-shirt. I sit back on the toilet, unwind the Ace bandage from my middle and pick Bud back up. It's hard, but I manage to hold him against me and wrap the bandage around him at the same time, making a kind of sling for his body. I look in the bag and find the spare bandage and use it as well. I stand up and he stays put, bound to my stomach by the double bandage. I tuck the T-shirt back in, button and tuck in my Yves, put the jacket back on and do up all three buttons. I open the stall door and step out. In the mirror it doesn't look bad, a beer belly.

* * *

I get to the checkpoint. I set the bag on the conveyor and watch it slide through. I walk through the metal detector and set off no alarms. I don't sweat, I don't tremor, my eyes are not shifty. I am a criminal mastermind. I am cold as ice. The cops and the airport security are barely looking. I have already become a myth to them. No one so wanted could ever make it this far, so they sip their coffee and bitch about their jobs and I stroll past.

I stop at the pay phones. When she picks up, I hear a series of clicks and voices in the background.

—It's me, Mom.

—Are you all right, Henry? Are you all right?

—I'm OK, Mom. I'm going away.

—Where?

—I can't say.

—Oh. They're here, Henry. They want to talk to you.

—I love you, Mom.

—Oh, Henry.

—Tell Dad I love him.

—Henry.

—I love you.

—I love you, Henry.

First class is nice. They give me a hot towel and I put it over my face to hide all the tears.

When the seat belt light goes off, I go to the can with my bag and unwrap Bud. His breathing is shallow. I hope he's OK. I pad myself with some towels from the bag so I still look fat and put Bud back in. I leave it a tiny bit unzipped so he can breathe easier. The whole flight, they offer me cocktails. I take a couple Vics instead.

We land in Cancún. I've never been to Mexico before, but I've heard customs is very easy here. When I go to claim my luggage, the money bag is already there, revolving on the carousel.

The customs agent looks at my face and at my passport. He grimaces a little and looks inquisitive. I smile ruefully.

—Car accident.

—*¿Si?* Ouch.

—*Mucho* ouch.

He laughs and stamps my papers.

—Have a nice visit, sir.

—Thank you.

I'm walking toward the exit. Up ahead there is a small traffic light. As passengers arrive at the light, they push a little button. If the light flashes green, they exit the airport. Red, and they and their bags are subjected to a random search. I push the button.

It's a very Christmassy kind of green.

EPILOGUE

Single-Game Playoff

The town is about an hour south of Cancún. It's small, nice. I'm in a bar. The bar is on the beach; it has no walls and is covered by a roof of logs and thatched palm leaves. Instead of a stool, I sit on a rope swing suspended from the timbers of the roof. I sway in a warm breeze and, if I dangle my legs right, my toes drag back and forth in the sand. It is early evening and a thunderstorm is swinging in from offshore. Lightning is crackling over the perfect sea and bathwater-warm rain will soon fall. There are pretty girls everywhere and the stereo behind the bar is playing Stevie Ray Vaughn's "Pride and Joy." Bud is sprawled on the bar next to me, woozy but awake. The bartenders think it's very funny I brought my cat, but they like him. Everybody likes Bud. The pretty girls especially like Bud. I have a room up the beach a little. It has a balcony and a hammock. I stopped by the gift shop long enough to buy some shorts and sandals, took a shower in my room and left the money bag in the closet. Then I took a walk and found this place.

On the bar I have spread out various relics I found in Bud's bag. The plane ticket I would have used to get home at Christmas. Mario's card. Ed's card. Roman's card. The police photo of Yvonne's neck. I think about how mad she used to get at me for always living in the past. I close my eyes and feel the sun and the breeze and see the pile of bodies behind the bar at Paul's. Russ holding Bud. Ed and Paris holding hands. Bolo putting out his arms for balance just before he went down. Roman just wanting me to get it over with.

On the bar they have set out bowls full of Spanish peanuts dusted with chili powder. I take a handful and eat them one by one. They're good. I hold one out to Bud and he licks the powder off.

I'm drinking Jarritos orange soda. Soon, at 6:00, it will be happy hour. For every drink I order, they will bring me three. At 6:30, they will turn on the TV above the bar and show the satellite broadcast of the Mets vs. Giants, live from New York. I curl my toes and crunch the cool, damp sand. My feet don't hurt at all. Someone rings a bell. It's 6:00. I signal the bartender and order a beer.

Please turn the page for an
exciting preview of

CHARLIE HUSTON'S

SIX BAD THINGS

I'm sitting on the porch of a bungalow on the Yucatán Peninsula with lit cigarettes sticking out of both my ears.

I like to go swimming in the mornings. When I first came to Mexico I liked to go drinking in the mornings, but after I got over that I took up swimming and I discovered something. I have unusually narrow ear canals. Go figure. I discovered this while I was trying to sober up while paddling around in the lukewarm morning waters, and found that my ears were clogged. I tilted my head from side to side and banged on my skull, trying to dislodge the water, but no luck. I plugged my nose, clamped my mouth shut, and blew until it felt like my brain might pop out of my ass. No good. I crammed Q-tips up my ears, prodding at the blockage. That's when things got really bad. For a few days I walked around half deaf, feeling like my entire head was packed with water logged cotton. Then I went to a doctor. I have a habit of saving doctors for a last resort.

Dr. Sanchez looked in my ears and informed me of the tragic news: unusually narrow ear canals. The water was trapped deep inside, and my irresponsible Q-tip use had sealed it in with earwax. He loaded a beer-can-size syringe with warm mineral water and injected it into my ears until the pressure dislodged the massive clogs of wax and washed them into the small plastic basins I held just below my ears. He gave me drops. He told me never to stick anything in my ear other than my elbow and laughed at his own joke. He nodded sagely and told me the solution to my problem was quite simple: when my ears became clogged, I must stick a cigarette into either one and light them. The cigarettes, that is. Then he handed me a pack of Benson & Hedges and told me they were his preferred brand for the task and charged me a thousand pesos.

So. I am sitting on the porch of a bungalow on the Yucatán Peninsula with lit cigarettes sticking out of both my ears. The cigarettes burn and create a vacuum in my ears, sucking the moisture into the filters. I have a towel draped over each shoulder to catch the hot ash as it falls. I've been doing this a couple days a week for years and it always works. Of course I do now smoke two packs of Benson & Hedges a day, but there's a downside to everything in life.

The sun has dipped far in the sky behind my back, and the reds of the sunset are reflected in the perfect blue sea before me. I adjust my sarong so that the soft breeze will waft higher on my legs. The heat of the cigarettes has become intense. I reach up and pinch them out of my ears, careful not to squeeze so hard that the waxy fluid trapped in the filters leaks out. I dump them into an ashtray resting on the porch near my feet, slip the towels off my shoulders, stand up and start walking toward the water. The beach is pretty much abandoned. A ways off to my right, I can see a small group of local boys covered head to toe in sand, kicking a soccer ball around on their homemade field. In the opposite direction, the silhouette of a pair of lovers kissing. When my feet hit the wet strip of sand near the water's edge I give my sarong a tug, it falls to the ground leaving me naked, and I walk down into the gently lapping waves. The beach slopes away so shallowly from the shore that I can walk upright in the water for almost fifty yards before it will cover my head. I walk in the water with the sun sinking behind me, hearing the soft slap of the tiny waves quite clearly in my unclogged ears. I'll probably have to do it all over again when I get out, twisting the cigarettes into my ears, lighting them, and waiting patiently while they burn down, but it will be worth it. I want to take one last swim today. I'm going home tomorrow and I don't know if I'll ever be able to come back here.

Machine guns wake me up in the morning, but they're just in my head. I have my backpack ready by the door, the waterproof money belt draped over it. I go to the bathroom and stand under the showerhead. The water is a gentle warm sprinkle, not the thing to snap you out of a nightmare. Still sleepy, I close my eyes. Pedro explodes past me backwards, his torso stitched open by a cloud of bullets. My eyes snap open. I walk out of the shower and drip water across the bungalow floor to the boombox. I search the CDs for something loud. Led Zeppelin? Something *fast* and loud. The Replacements. I put in *Pleased to Meet Me,* the opening chords of "I.O.U." flare out, and Paul Westerburg starts screaming. I turn it up.

I finish my shower, pull on a pair of cotton fatigue-style pants, grab keys, sunglasses, my papers and a hefty wad of pesos. I check the money belt, make sure the extra passport and ID are where I can get to them easily, and strap it on. A tank top, short-sleeve linen shirt, a pair of trail sneakers, and I'm dressed. I grab the backpack and sling one strap over my shoulder.

—Come on, cat.

Bud leaps from the comfy chair, walks over to the kitchenette cabinet and meows.

—Sorry, Buddy, no time. You can eat at Pedro's.

He meows again. I walk over, grab him by the nape of his neck and put him on top of the pack.

—Fresh fish at Pedro's. Trust me, it'll be worth the wait.

I turn off the box, take a last look around. Did I forget anything? I mean, other than not to fuck up my life again? Nope, all taken care of. Back door bolted, storm shutters padlocked. Good enough. I walk onto the porch and set Bud and the pack down next to the door.

I'm pulling the tarp off the Willys when I see a white Bronco turn off the trail a quarter mile down the beach and come bouncing across the sand towards me. Could be they just have a few more questions, but I don't think cops roll up on you at dawn to ask questions.

I drop the tarp, wave, and point to the bungalow with a big smile on my face. One of the Federales in the Bronco waves back. I walk to the bungalow, grab Bud and the pack, step inside, lock the front door, go out the back, and dash across the sand into the jungle that is my backyard. All I have to do is get to Pedro's and I'll be OK. Unless the cops are there too.

The Bucket is right on the beach. It's a small place, a thatched palm roof over a bar, no walls. Stools don't work on the beach, so eight rope swings hang from the beams, and sets of white plastic tables and chairs are on the sand. There's no electricity. Pedro hauls bags of ice down here every morning on his tricycle and dumps them into corrugated tubs full of bottles of Sol and Negro Modelo. If you order a cocktail, you get the same ice the beer sits in. If you want to eat, Pedro has a barbecue he made by sawing a fifty-five-gallon drum in half.

I'm at The Bucket around nine every day after my morning swim. Pedro gets the coffee pot off the barbecue grill, pours me a cup, and drops yesterday's *Miami Herald* in front of me. His wife gets the paper every day when she goes in town for the shopping or to pick up the kids from school. Pedro brings it to me here the next day. I glance at the sports page. Dolphins this, Dolphins that.

Pedro has *chorizo* on the grill and a frying pan heating up. He cracks a couple eggs into the pan, gets a plastic container of salsa from the cooler bag on his tricycle and stirs some in, scrambling the eggs. He takes a key from his belt, unlocks the enameled steel cabinet beneath the bar, grabs the bottles of booze and starts to set them out. I walk around to the grill, give the eggs a few more stirs and dump them onto a plastic plate. The *chorizos* are blackened, fat spitting from the cracks in their skin. I spear them, stick them on the plate next to the eggs and sit back down on my swing at the bar. Pedro brings me a folded towel and sets it next to the plate. I open it up and peel off one of the still warm tortillas his wife made at home this morning. I stuff a *chorizo* into the tortilla, pack some of the eggs around it, fold the thing up, take a bite and sear the inside of my mouth just like I do every morning. It's worth it.

Pedro is about my age, thirty-five. He looks a little older because he's spent his whole life on the Yucatán; his face is a dark, sun-wrinkled plate. He's short and round, has a little pencil moustache, and wears heavy black plastic glasses like the ones American soldiers get for free.

He tops off my coffee.

—Go fish today?

I look out at the flat, crystal-blue water. Up in town, the tourists will be loading into the boats, heading for the reef to go diving, or to the deep water to fish. The local fishermen here have already gone out and Pedro's boat is the only one still in, anchored to the shore by long yellow ropes tied to eight-foot lengths of rebar driven into the sand. I could fish, take the boat out by myself or wait for Pedro's brother to show up and go out with him for an evening fish. If he doesn't have a job tonight.

—Not today.

—Nice day for fishing.

—Too nice. I might catch a fish. And then what? Have to bring it in, clean it, cook it. No, no fishing today.

—Game on later?

—Every Sunday, Pedro, there's a game every Sunday except for the bye week.

—Who today?

—The Patriots.

—New England.

—Right.

—Fucking Pats.

—You're learning.

I met Pedro up in town a few years back when I first came to Mexico. I came to Mexico hot. Running. I walked out of the Cancun airport, got into a cab and told the guy I wanted to get out of Cancun, down the coast somewhere. Someplace smaller. He took me about an hour down the road to a little vacation town. Small hotels along a nice strip of beach. It was OK for awhile. The tourists were mostly mainland

Mexicans, South Americans or Europeans. Not many North Americans at all. Then they started building this giant resort community on the south end of town and that was it for me.

I found this spot: driving distance to town, a handful of locals with vacation *palapas,* some expatriates living in bungalows, some backpackers and day-trippers looking for a secluded beach. But no bar. Pedro was working in the place I spent most of my time in. I knew he wanted his own business and he knew I wanted a place to hang out in. We made a deal.

I'm a silent partner, I pay my tab like any customer and nobody knows I backed Pedro to open the place. I gave him half the bar for moving here to run it; he's working off the other half. Shit, I could have given him the whole thing outright. I got the money. God knows I got the fucking money.

The day-trippers are starting to drift onto the beach. They hear about it in town or read about it in Lonely Planet and come looking for unspoiled Mexico, but they're usually pretty damn happy they can get a cold beer and a cheeseburger. The expats will come around in the evening when they get back from fishing trips or working in town. The locals mostly show up on Friday and Saturday evening to drink the way only a hard-working Mexican can drink. Me, I drink soda water all day. Haven't had a real drink in over two years. I take another sip of coffee, light the first cigarette of the day, and get back to the sports page. It's the healthy life for me now.

The Dolphins have a problem. Their problem is a head coach who happens to be an idiot. I have a problem. My problem is the Miami fucking Dolphins of the National fucking Football League. When I got down here, I found out I couldn't give up sports. I tried to get into *futbol,* but it just didn't click. A basketball season is like a basketball game, only the last two minutes count. And unless I was ready to watch bullfights that left football. Baseball? Yeah, I like baseball. I would have liked to have spent the last three years watching, listening to, and reading about baseball just like I did the thirty-two years before them, but that's one of the things I had to give up. I got into football because I always hated football and nobody looking for me is gonna look for a guy who likes football. It makes it harder for people with Russian accents to find me and kill me.

Why Russian accents? Because that's the way the Russian gangsters who want me dead talk.

At noon Pedro takes the radio from beneath the bar, clicks it on and twirls the dial 'til the fuzzy sounds of WQAM Miami come through. He extends the antenna, alligator clips one end of a wire to it, and clips the other end to the sheet of chicken wire that covers the palm roof. Suddenly the signal jumps in loud and clear.

I sit at the bar, sip seltzer, and smoke and listen. The game drones on predictably. The Fins jump out early with three unanswered touchdowns, stand around while the Pats cut into their lead just before the half, and then come out flat for the third quarter. By the start of the fourth quarter, they're hanging onto a three-point lead, and the coach is calling plays as if they were still up by twenty-one.

A shaggy backpacker wanders up the beach and over to the bar. He shrugs out of his pack and takes a seat on the swing next to mine. Pedro is poking at some ribs on the grill. The guy is sitting backwards on the swing with his elbows on the bar, looking at the ocean. He looks over his shoulder at the radio. The Pats have just pinned the Fins on their own two-yard line. He looks at me and nods his head.
—Football.

Nothing odd about that, a perfectly reasonable observation. Except that he says it in a Russian accent, which is not something we get a lot of around here. Me, I take it in stride, just spit-take my seltzer all over the bar. I'm smooth like that. The guy slaps me on the back while I choke.

—OK?

I nod and wave my hand.

—Fine. Choke. Fine.

I point at the radio.

—Fucking Dolphins.

He shrugs.

—American football. Too slow.

The Fins try to run up the gut three times, get one yard and punt miserably to their own thirty-five. Pedro comes over and the guy orders a shot of tequila and a Modelo.

—Hockey, very fast, good sport to watch. You like hockey?

—Not really.

—European football, soccer?

—Not really.

—But to play, yes? Americans like to play soccer, but not to watch.

—I guess.

The backpacker guy nods his head and smiles like he approves, takes a sip of his beer.

—What about baseball? You like baseball?

Just after sunset I walk back up to the north end of the beach. My bungalow really isn't much, but it's bonito in its way. Wood walls up to about waist level topped by screen windows that circle the one room building, with heavy storm shutters that I mostly keep open. I step up on the porch, past the canvas-back chair, small wooden table and hammock, and dig the key from the Velcro side pocket of my shorts. In the normal course of things, if I was just a guy down here living on the beach, I wouldn't really need to lock my door. But I'm not that guy and I do need to lock my door. I have secrets to hide. I open the door and secret number one says hello.

—Meow.

I got into some trouble when I lived up in New York. I did a guy a favor and I got into some trouble for doing it. The favor he asked me to do that led to all the trouble—to me being on the run in Mexico—was he asked me to watch his cat. I said yes. And here I am three years later, still watching his cat.

Bud jumps down from the bed and limps over to say hi. One of his front legs was pretty badly broken in all that trouble, so he has that limp, and some of the fur on his face grows in a weird little tuft because he has a scar from the same encounter that broke his leg. The guys that did the leg-breaking and the scarring are dead. Someone felt bad about that, not Bud. He rubs his face against my calf and I bend down, scoop him off the floor, and drape him over my shoulders.

—Jesus, cat, you're getting fat. You are a fat fucking cat, and no two ways about it.

I open one of the kitchenette cupboards, grab a can of Bud's food, scoop it into his bowl, and he leaps off my shoulders and digs in.

—Enjoy it while it lasts, cat. You're going on a diet.

I leave the music on and walk down to the water. The water is perfect. It's always perfect. I wade out, lean back, let my legs drift up and my arms float out until I am bobbing on the surface of the Caribbean, looking up at the stars. And for half a second I almost forget the Russian backpacker who set up his tent at the opposite end of the beach. The one who might be here looking for me and the four and a half million dollars that the Russian mafia thinks is theirs.

I have that money.

But it's not theirs. It's mine.

I killed for it. And I'm gonna keep it.

ABOUT THE AUTHOR

Charlie Huston is the author of *Six Bad Things*. He currently lives in Manhattan with his wife, the actress Virginia Louise Smith.

ABOUT THE TYPE

This book was set in Fairfield, the first typeface from the hand of the distinguished American artist and engraver Rudolph Ruzicka (1883–1978). Ruzicka was born in Bohemia and came to America in 1894. He set up his own shop, devoted to wood engraving and printing, in New York in 1913 after a varied career working as a wood engraver, in photoengraving and banknote printing plants, and as an art director and freelance artist. He designed and illustrated many books, and was the creator of a considerable list of individual prints—wood engravings, line engravings on copper, and aquatints.